We Were Never Here

WE WERE NEVER HERE

Jennifer Gilmore

An Imprint of HarperCollinsPublishers

HarperTeen is an imprint of HarperCollins Publishers.

Library of Congress Control Number: 2015038962
ISBN 978-0-06-239361-6

Typography by Sarah Creech
18 19 20 21 22   PC/LSCH   10 9 8 7 6 5 4 3 2 1
❖
First paperback edition, 2018

For my mother

We Were Never Here

Part 1

Day 1: It Happens at Camp

It's a single moment: It's on the archery field on the third-to-last day of my first year as a CIT—counselor in training. I watch the campers all pull back on their bows, and they're all in a line, ready to shoot.

I'm thinking about the most random things. How camp is ending and all these girls still look so young. When I was a camper here, we'd toilet-paper other girls' cabins. We used to sneak into the boys' side of camp. We'd run out in the night and sprint through the woods, snapping tree branches. We'd shine flashlights in the boys' faces and watch them wake up screaming.

But now it's different, though sometimes we slip away from the bonfires, the sound of singing behind us as we couple off, fan out, stray, lie out all night long.

And I'm thinking about two nights before, when Nora and her friend Raymond and David B and I went down to the lake. Dave and I sat on the dock and dragged our feet through the water and kissed until our mouths were numb.

I'm thinking about the feel of the water when, as suddenly as a heart attack, a pain tears into my side. I double over and the head counselor yells, "Put down your bows!" just like we'd practiced on that first day in the safety part of class, the part everyone barely listens to because who thinks something will actually *happen*?

The campers all set down their bows, and there's that creepy sound of the arrows not shooting, then the short, sad sound of the wood of the arrows hitting the wood of the bows.

That's the sound of my whole life changing.

Just like that. Right there. That kiss on the dock, my bare feet in soft water, that was the last time I was myself.

I had no idea then that something so small—that single stab of pain—could do that, just change absolutely everything.

Day 1: But Still Before Any of It Really

This is how it starts. Like this: The head counselor takes me off the field and I go to the camp infirmary, a place that's kind of like a regular camp cabin and kind of how I imagine an old-fashioned country doctor's office would be: jars on metal counters filled with tongue depressors and cotton balls, all this dust shifting in the light, like no one has moved in here for a week. It's time for afternoon swim, so I imagine the lake. I can picture the girls in our cabin walking down the path, towels folded over their arms as they stick their gum on the gum tree, which is really an evergreen whose trunk is stuck with everyone's chewed gum. Then I think of the kids all lining up after swimming, tilting their heads so Frank and Rhonda, the lake counselors, can squeeze alcohol into everyone's ears so they don't get ear infections from the moldy lake water. When I was a camper, we'd make paper boats and put candles inside and push them, lighted, out onto the water. *I wish I wish I wish,* I'd think. I wished to be skinnier, to be prettier, for green eyes. I think I also wanted to be more like my sister, Zoe, who is a year older and does everything first, including having a boyfriend, this super-nice guy named Tim, who she's been with for over six months. Every day after school the two of them go up to Zoe's room and close the door.

I think for a moment of David B and me. How we could hear the sound of Raymond and Nora giggling, Ray trying for Nora like everyone else had. Guys never like me that way. Only Dave, who uses the word "wicked" all the time because he's from Bangor, Maine, near our camp, and I guess they say that a ton there. Dave is a tennis instructor, and while he has really nice legs, tan and smooth, strangely hairless, he also makes birdhouses and God's eyes. Like constantly. I never thought of him at all until the Fourth of July when he bought illegal fireworks and set them off, howling. There was something so reckless about that. It made me rethink David B.

Now I lie down on the dusty cot—the pillowcase smells like a combination of insects and wildflowers—and I hold my hands across my stomach. I throw up until I'm empty. I can't even drink water, because that will make me throw up again. The nurse calls my mother, and I tell her: I have no idea what's happening to me. No, I say, it's not like the flu at all. I have had the flu before, and when I did, after it was over, my mother set a flat Coke by my bed and there was this feeling of, I don't know, finishedness. But now it just goes on and on and on, and, to add to that misery, I go to the bathroom all night long. All night. And my mother isn't anywhere near here.

Whatever an infirmary feels like in the day, at night it is the setting for a horror movie; everywhere there is blackness except for the gleaming bits of glass and metal that glimmer in the dark.

I hate horror movies. Sometimes I think they are the only things that truly scare the hell out of me. I like roller coasters and running hard and I like being in the woods at night, but I don't understand anyone seeking the fear inspired by the kind of horror in a movie.

But now? What if every day of my life is like this? That is different fear.

Nora sneaks in through the window that night, while everyone's asleep, and she climbs into my little cot and we turn on our backs and look up to the wooden beams crossing the ceiling, the cobwebs threading the corners like the Jacob's ladders the campers make with string.

"I kissed Angelo," Nora tells me. I can see her eyes are wide-open, like two black holes, staring in the dark.

I wonder why she didn't choose Raymond. Did he kiss so terribly she had to unhook him and throw him back like a bad fish? I know the real reason. Nora isn't into anyone who wants her. She's barely into wanting to be my friend, because I do what she says. I guess that registers as me wanting her more in some crazy way.

"No. Way!" I hit her on the shoulder. Angelo is the oldest boys' counselor, and he's been here since we were little and he is wickedly handsome, long-haired and tanned, always barefoot, kind of dangerous. Last week he snuck out of camp, got drunk in the town, and shaved off his eyebrows.

Nora is silent. I don't say anything either. I'm thinking about how no one wants David B. No one sits in a circle and says, I wish that guy would make me a God's eye, in purple. It's always the freaks who like me, never the normal, beautiful ones who tie sailor's knots and swim the butterfly. Truthfully, though, I always like the freaks back. And truthfully, I have a soft spot for David, so eager to please. I think I'm just the opposite. I seem so normal. I play field hockey, for God's sake. I spend a lot of time trying to get my brown hair to turn blond in the sun. I'm pretty tall. I think too much—I can see other people watching me, judging. Let's just say I could never dance, not outside of my room anyway. I don't hold hands with my mother. In hockey I'm the kamikaze. I'm the one between the goalie and the world. I come out screaming for the free hits.

In that silence with Nora, the pain bites into me, like it takes out a huge chunk, and then I have to throw up, and also go to the bathroom, and so at the same time as I'm going to the bathroom, I'm throwing up in a metal bowl. Why are those bowls you throw up in shaped like lima beans? Or sad smiles? I have no idea.

"You should go," I tell Nora. I don't want her to see me like this. I don't even want to see myself like this. "I don't know what's wrong." I'm crying for a lot of reasons, all at once.

Nora is crying too.

"Why are *you* crying?" I say.

"Angelo scares the piss out of me without his eyebrows," is what Nora says. I know it's a friendship that, as Nana says, *You need to turn the light out on and close the door*, but I can't.

I run to the bathroom again—this time I make it—and when I come back, Nora is sliding out the same window she came in from. She gives me a salute and then she's gone.

Anchors aweigh, I think, because at camp, this is how we talk.

Also because the final regatta is on my mind. And the camp

talent show. And that hockey tryouts at school are in two days. And that soon all the campers and counselors will be hugging one another good-bye.

The next day and night I'm in that infirmary and nothing changes, only I am more in a daze now and I have that feeling inside that is just like watching some crazy person come out of the woods with an ax, ready to kill the couple in the lighted house. It's that kind of awful fluttery panic. I can hear the nurse on the phone with my mother again. Now I can only nod my head when she places the phone at my ear, but of course my mother can't hear that.

Outside, though, I know there is all the bustle and thrill and sadness we wait all summer for during those last two days of camp. It's the whole summer wrapped up, the most important days.

The last night event I had been to was a hypnotist—Rhonda from the lake got hypnotized, and she walked across the stage and sang a little of the song "Yellow," and when the hypnotist snapped his fingers and she came to, she said she didn't know the lyrics to that song. I wasn't sure if I totally believed it, but I kind of did, and even if you believe it just a little, that's all it takes really. Just the littlest part, then it can be true.

I wish I could be hypnotized to not feel this but no, I'm in and out of this crazy haze of pain and sleep and throwing up. There is also the feel of the camp nurse and her cold and hot compresses on my forehead, like she can't decide which one is the right one.

Then, camp's over. And I'm gone.

Day 3 Begins

I'm in a haze, but I know my mother comes for me. I feel her before she walks through the door, and I'm thinking how I've never been so happy to see my mother. She's in jeans and one of the long linen shirts that she refers to as a tunic, not the suits she usually wears to work, downtown on Capitol Hill. She works for a nonprofit. My mother does all this good for the environment. Also, she doesn't have any lipstick on.

From there we take a plane back to Washington, DC, where I'm from. Well, I'm from Virginia, but it's close enough. In any case, we have to take an ambulance to the airport. I think of all those hospital shows, and I know that the sixteen-year-old girl who gets flown in a special plane to a hospital in another state has something terribly wrong with her. Someone hovers over me and asks me if I'm comfortable and then it's nighttime on the plane, and I look out the dollhouse windows and there's the Washington Monument, the Reflecting Pool, the Lincoln Memorial. They are all so close it's like the plane is flying in between the monuments, and then up into the sky, and then back in again.

"Mom!" I say. "Look how close we are to the buildings!"

"That," my mother says, smiling at me, "is the pain medicine talking. I'm glad it's working." She brushes my hair behind my ears with her fingers in a way that says, *I'm so glad you are letting me do this.* Her fingers make my neck tingle.

Outside it looks indigo blue, deep, and there are stars, and the lights from the city are everywhere. I can see a dangling crescent moon.

I am in a whole other world. Camp is as far away as a circling planet. I'm in all this pain and then there's what's happening outside the window: Everything is horrible and beautiful, both at the exact same time.

Day 3: World Building

We go straight to the hospital, where I am still. Now. When my mother and I get here, my father and my older sister, Zoe, are waiting for me. The only one missing here is who I want to see most: our dog, Mabel. My father stands up when I arrive, as if I am someone very important.

"My baby," he says. He has a stuffed animal with him.

"Lizzie," Zoe says, breathing.

Seeing Zoe like this—tentative, scared, waiting for me, and also without Tim—again makes me realize something is really wrong. Maybe I am dying. And there is something about seeing my dad there with this big teddy bear that makes me really sad. I'm also sad I might be dying. I mean that truly. I have seen the movies; I have read the books. A teenager dying is a terribly sad thing. It just doesn't feel like it's happening to me. How could it be? Hockey tryouts are tomorrow. I'm supposed to be there. David B and I never said good-bye.

I'm not just sad, I'm also terrified about all the things that will never happen to me now, or all the things that I will never make happen, but it's still in me to be a little annoyed about the teddy bear, so I stick with that. I am not seven, I want to tell him. How will this stuffed animal help me?

But then my father sits the teddy bear down on the bed, and I bring it to my chest. It's impossibly soft, as soft as his gray cashmere robe that I like to wear when he's at work. It's comforting to hold, like it *fits* me. I think of wearing my father's wool sweaters. And his overcoat. I used to find all these random things in his pockets: scraps of paper, dried-out pens, old nickels. I look over and see Zoe looking at me, which she never does, and I hold the bear tightly, feel its silky hairs along the tip of my nose. If I were alone, I know I would take this opportunity to out-and-out cry. But with everyone here, my eyes sort of leak, a faucet that you just can't turn tight enough.

"We're going to find out what's going on," my father says. "Right away."

"We are," my mom says. "It's the colon, we know that. But for now we're on the cancer ward, Lizzie."

"Colon," I say. "Cancer," I say. My heart does that panic fluttery thing that makes me realize should I make it out of here, ever, a slasher movie will be nothing for me. I will never again be the girl waiting at Glitter or Dippin' Dots until *You're Next* and *Evil Dead* are over.

My mom nods. "Yeah, not the ideal thing, but the best gastroenterologists around are in this hospital. We want you here, and sadly, this ward is the safest place for you. We're going to get to the bottom of all this." She kisses the top of my head. I feel her words on my scalp.

I'm definitely dying, I think. I think, I will never get to Spain, which is surprising because I never knew going to Spain was important to me. Also, the language I take in school is French. I look at my family again. Who are these delightful people I once thought were so boring? I think of them missing me, and I won't deny that initially I get a pang of pleasure imagining their mourning me. They will leave my room as is, even though I never cleaned it up before camp like I'd promised my mother, and I think of what they'll find. My notebook filled with Birdy lyrics, an embarrassment to be sure. The Converse shoe box filled with all the random things I've saved: an origami bird, a ticket stub to the Glen Echo carousel where I went with my friends Dee-Dee and Lydia, notes from Mark Segura when I sat in front of him in algebra. I can't believe I saved those. English papers I got A's on. Feathers. Pom-poms. Gold stars. Little-girl stuff all crammed in; I can barely close it anymore.

Everything is different now, here. Here everything fits into this teeny-tiny, lonely world.

I can't think of the real things. Like if I go, will I miss my family? Do the people who die, especially the young people, do they go through everything alone now? Are they all alone?

I look at my family again. Differently, just for a moment. I don't want them to let me go.

But a nurse comes in and says they have to. It's way past visiting hours, she tells them. My mother clutches me before going, and my father swishes the hair out of my face. And then I am alone.

Here is what it is now: there is a bed and a tray that moves over the bed or swings parallel to it, and an old bulky television, which hangs from an ugly white(ish) wall. I have a roommate;

a thick, ugly, blue movable curtain divides our two sides. I'm hooked up to a bunch of IVs. They come right out of me; the plastic tubing is taped down along the inside of my arm. I'm not allowed to eat anymore. One of the IVs is this milky white liquid that feeds me through my veins. A plastic bracelet with my name and birth date scrawled on it scratches at my wrist.

My roommate still hasn't moved; I half wonder if she's even alive. No, I full-on wonder this.

"I'm Lizzie," I say to the curtain, when my family has been forced away. The room is dark now. *Dark* dark. I'm telling you: it's way worse than the infirmary in here.

"Mm-hmm," she says.

"Well, what's your name?" I ask the curtain.

"Thelma, honey," she says. "I'm Thelma."

I wait for her to continue, but that seems to be it.

"Lizzie?" Like it's a question now. "Nice to meet you," I say, though I do wonder if those kinds of rules for meeting people actually translate to this type of a setting. I mean, it really wasn't that nice to meet Thelma.

She turns up the television, and the local weather screams at me. Apparently, outside of here, tomorrow is going to be a nice day. Of course.

Thelma has the window, but when I get up to go to the bathroom (I know that makes it sound so very easy, but it is complicated and hard as I can barely swing my legs over the side of the bed here, let alone push myself off this bed and totter alongside my metal IV tree, and as often as I have to go, it is never without drama), I can look out through the slivers of the open parts of the curtain and see the sun go down against the building across the way.

Why is the sun going down so sad?

After my scintillating conversation with Thelma, I drift off to sleep thinking: this is not happening to me. This cannot be happening to me.

I really want to go home.

I wake up when a nurse comes to take my vital signs. She comes at me with needles and thermometers. The machine that takes my blood pressure squeezes my arm so tightly I forget I have fingers. I feel the now-familiar shot of pain in my stomach, and when she leaves I'm all alone. I picture all the campers with their huge bags of laundry boarding the buses for home. I try not to think of hockey tryouts. Mr. Crayton setting up the orange cones, yelling at everyone to run faster, legs higher.

I really, really want to go home.

Day 4: A Lot of Information

At like 5:30 a.m. the medical students show up, flipping through their charts and whispering to one another. Someone adjusts my IV like he's dimming a light.

Don't I even get a good morning?

Then they all go in for my stomach, which makes me scream in pain, and then they get so scared they're doing something wrong—they are just *students*, after all—they run out of the room, and then the real doctors come.

The pain doctors.

"On a scale of one to ten," they ask, "ten being childbirth, what's your pain?"

"I'm sixteen," I say. It is not the first or second or third time I have felt the urge to cry this morning.

"Childbirth is the worst pain on earth," one of the women says, tilting her head to the side.

The man nods.

And how would he know this?

"Okay," I say. I want to say ten, my pain is a ten, but if I do, that will seem like it is in fact a lot less but I am being a baby. "Nine?" I say, but the pain is ten.

Anyway, the way Nana tells it, this can't be as painful as child-birth.

They both nod and write stuff down, flip their folders shut.

"We need to deal with your pain first, before anything," one of them says, and they all trot away.

It's not even five forty-five.

At six fifteen there's another knock at the door. Why do they even bother knocking? No matter what, they just walk in, announcing: Time for blood! Adjusting your saline! and truck over to my bed.

"What," I say. It's more like a growl.

The door opens a crack, and I can see the tip of a head topped with dirty-blondish-red hair, I guess you'd call it strawberry blond, but that sounds more like it's a girl. This is a boy. He's got freckles splashed across his cheeks, and even from the bed I can see his long lashes blinking at me. His eyes are pale blue. It's a sweet face.

"Hey," he says. "Are you up?"

I look around as if to see if he's talking to someone else. "Seri-ously?" I say. I am in a paper-thin hospital gown and I am under the covers. I haven't showered since camp, and believe me, it's not like I haven't needed one.

This boy opens the door another inch or so, and now I see he's wearing a blue oxford shirt, untucked, wrinkled, and his jeans are loose and faded. Also, there's a red woven leash wrapped around his hand. It's like he just stepped off a sailboat or could be the lead in a rom-com, or a counselor at the boys' side of camp, *not* a weird one. If I were the kind of girl to throw off my clothes and dive off the dock I made out with David B on, this is the boy I would want to do that with, the guy I hope sits next to me as we roast marshmallows and sing stupid camp songs. But this is also the boy who would never like me back. Instead of comfy on a surfboard or on the bow of a boat, I've got Dave. Revise that: I had Dave. Now I don't have anyone.

"Can we come in?" he asks.

Yes! Yes! Come in! I think, even though I am as far from being a girl sitting on the lap of a sun-kissed, windswept boy and sing-ing at a bonfire, about to take off all her clothes and run shrieking into the lake, as I have ever been. For the record, I was never that girl, but from here it feels like I could have been or I was about to be. She was definitely the person I might have wanted to be.

Then a little golden snout sniffs his way in along the edge of the bottom corner of the door. I must admit it's pretty damn cute, this boy and this dog half in and half out of my room. And then I think: a dog! A dog. A golden retriever. The boy is really tousled and perfect in that Abercrombie-Hollister-Hilfiger way I've always both admired and abhorred. I normally like the more nerdy, booky, dark, weird boys in school. There's this one guy who wears a different flannel shirt every day and who draws all these girls as they sit in class, chins on hands, daydreaming. Everyone thinks it's creepy, but I always secretly hope he'll draw me. It wouldn't mean anything, but I have often wondered how he would see me. What would he choose to emphasize. My nose? It's long and bigger than I'd like. My hair? I do have good hair.

Why is he here, this boy? How easygoing can a boy with a dog in a hospital really be?

I look down at my gown. I have two on—one tied in front and one in the back—just like the ones I'm sure everyone's wearing to the Metropolitan Ball. Plus, there's that lack-of-showering issue, and that the last time I looked my hair was knotted, and also greasy, itchy at my scalp. My skin has developed this kind of . . . gray fog surrounding it, as if I'm here for smoke inhalation. And I'm not going to lie; there hasn't been a whole lot of teeth brushing either. I am the most disgusting I have ever been.

"No!" I say, turning away. "I'm busy?"

He cocks his head sideways. "Not really seeing the busy part," he says. The dog continues to inch his way in.

"Seriously," I say again. "I am." I cross my arms. I am actually grateful for a visitor who isn't someone in my family or a nurse with a needle. I'm not sure I want this boy and his dog to go away, like, *forever*. "Thanks, though," I tell him.

"Okay." He backs up and so does the dog, at the exact same time. I think—truly—of synchronized swimmers. "We'll try you later," he says from the hallway. "When you're less loaded down with so many activities. When your calendar clears."

I have to laugh. Everything hurts when I do this. I have to go to the bathroom. The door is already closed and I doubt he can hear me.

"If that boy was headed to see me," Thelma—she speaks!—says from the other side of the curtain. She sleeps all the time. I mean All. The. Time. "Well, I wouldn't mind seeing his boots next to my bed is what I mean. But a dog? No sir. No dogs in here."

"Hi," I say.

"It'll be okay," says Thelma.

"The dog was so cute," I say quietly, and I can hear the squeak of sneakers and the click of nails on the tiles as they make their way down the hallway together. I miss Mabel. Her dog body. Her bones. I hear a faraway knock and then a meek greeting and then the two of them going into some other lucky person's room.

There is no Wi-Fi in here. None. Nothing. No cell phones at all; they screw with the heart monitors or something. But I do have my iPod. I'd brought it for camp, because cell phones are forbidden there too. The way my phone has been banned this summer, you'd think it was radioactive. But this was all part of the "camp experience." And thank God I did bring my iPod. I imagine having my music here as some kind of soundtrack to this horror movie I'm living. Often I think of it: like the songs that would be playing while the medical students all march in (Pink, "Blow Me"), or as my mother comes walking through that door (Missy Elliott? Don't know why, but I think it . . .).

Or when I'm alone in here. For that, it would definitely be Birdy. I love her. Dee-Dee says I look a little like her, which would be amazing because I think she's beautiful—thin but not workout thin, perfect skin—but I think Dee-Dee says that because of her long, light-brown hair and her crazy shaggy eyebrows. Those are both like mine, and I still don't know why I'm so bizarrely scared of plucking my eyebrows. All I've ever wanted was to be one of those girls who, like, takes a wisp of hair from each side of her head and gently pins it back. Maybe a braid or two. But my hair and my face, and also my personality, they're not like that.

But still, if I were a singer-songwriter and I could be anyone, I would be Birdy because (a) she was, like, five when she wrote her first album, which is incredible, and (b) I love her low, pretty voice and (c) I love her lyrics. There's other stuff loaded up, too. A Fine Frenzy. Snow Patrol. Parachute. Drake. But also David Bowie and Miss E and Bob Dylan and the Beatles, especially the White Album, which Zoe got me into, probably because Tim got her into it. What if "Blackbird" was playing as the nurses came to take my blood? I think. *Take these broken wings and learn to fly* . . . Now I realize, though, that it's not just in here; I have always liked sad songs. They have always been my life's soundtrack.

So I've got the White Album and Birdy and some Broken Social Scene and I also have this Brontë novel—*Wuthering Heights*—that I'm supposed to read to prepare for school. I've been carrying it around all summer. I haven't read that much, but it's good! Like crazy dark, gothic good. But in here? I can't concentrate on a thing. And this book and the landline make it feel like pioneer times. So even if it's limited cable, I'm thanking God for television. Thank. God.

And the landline. Nora called me on it my first day in here. My mother was unpacking a few things from home—a brush (ha!), a toothbrush (ha-ha!), some underwear (well, okay), and so on, and I, who had nothing better to do than watch her do these things, answered the phone on the first ring. I imagined it was just after dinner at camp, and the campers were singing in rounds. (*In a cabin in the wood, little man by the window stood, saw a rabbit hopping by, knocking at his door . . .*)

"Hi," I said to Nora when she called.

She just started talking. I was wrong; I'd forgotten; camp was over and she was already home in Baltimore. Everything was moving so fast outside of this place. I was losing track of it. *Wait for me!* I thought before she began talking. It was a weird thought. "I'm still seeing Angelo," she said. "We're kind of dating. It's real, Lizzie. Like post-camp real."

Post-camp real. David B and I didn't even say good-bye. I had been looking to fall by then anyway, looking to finally turning my friendship with Michael Lerner into something . . . else. More. I have loved that guy since the eighth grade. Like, *loved* him, always hoping, in this crazy kind of pining-little-girl way, that he would one day change, that he would suddenly see me differently. Or see me at all. But he never has, and now it's all changed anyway. So for all these reasons, hearing Nora's good news made me insane. Insane with rage; insane with envy; insane with sadness. Had I asked her if she was dating Angelo? Had I asked her *anything*?

Wait for me.

"You know. Angelo," she said, as if I hadn't heard her the first time.

"Hmmm," I said. The nausea, which is always there now, I can't get rid of it no matter what I do, began to rise in my throat. My mother hummed to herself as she folded my underwear, piling it into neat stacks.

"So that's been, like, really brilliant. Blinding. With Angelo, I mean."

Nora and her British slang. I'm not sure if she studied it or overheard it on her family trip to London or read it in some novel, but man has it made its way into her . . . lexicon.

"Once he kissed me when we were picking blackberries," she went on. And on. "In the daytime. I'm such a tart!"

"Cool," I said. But I really didn't care. Like Really. Didn't. Care. I was impressed, though. I couldn't even imagine ever kissing anyone in the sun.

"Cheeky girl," said Nora. She actually said this, and even I know cheeky means you have to have said something . . . sassy. "So what's going on with you?" she asked.

"It's money in here," I said. "You don't know what you're missing."

Nora was silent.

My mother, bent at the waist, stopped for a moment and then resumed her organizing.

"No really, it's like the best vacation I've ever had." I thought of the pain meds but refrained from making a drug reference due to my mother's ever-presence. Better than smoking pot, I wanted to say, but that wasn't true anyway. Nora and I smoked together once this summer, and we just lay on our backs in the woods and looked up to the sky and watched the leaves rustle on the trees.

Nora cleared her throat. "Sorry, Lizzie," she said. "I'm so sorry. I was just calling to say I hope you get better soon. Everyone missed you a lot at the last bonfire. It was all so sad."

It seemed so far away from me, already. I might never be able to go back there, never again be that girl singing along to some guitar like nothing had ever happened, setting my marshmallows on fire. That's how I liked them. Blazed.

What if I'm just sad forever? I thought. It's almost like I was never there.

Nora kept apologizing to me.

"Thanks," I said to Nora.

I couldn't picture her in Baltimore—what did Baltimore look like? What did Nora's room look like? Were there Clash and Sex Pistols posters on the wall? Daniel Radcliffe? Bloody Edward Cullen? I just didn't care anymore—and so instead I pictured the lake lit with candles, paper boats flaming and then blazing bright before going out. How would I just push a boat out on the lake and make a wish now? A wish: no more pain or fear.

"Bye," I said, and hung up.

But if I had let that boy in, if I'd let him in and said hello, if he'd been mine then, *mine*, just the thought of him, maybe I wouldn't have been so angry. If I'd had him to think of and wonder about and hope and hope and hope for, maybe I wouldn't have felt that there was nothing ahead of me. And then maybe I wouldn't have felt so left behind.

Still Day 4: The Anatomy of an Innocent Frog

My mother comes in and says, "It's not botulism."

How sick am I? I want to know and I also don't want to know.

She takes the remote and makes a big production of flipping off the TV. My mother hates television. "They think it's something else, but we have to eliminate all the other things."

I ignore her. One day I will want these details, perhaps, but I decide I want to avoid them right now. I don't tell her about the boy and the dog. Instead, I say, "I was actually watching that." Someone was blathering on and on about how to talk to your boss if you're a woman and he's a man. "It seemed like useful information for me and my new life. My new life as an office person."

I hear Thelma giggle.

My mother breathes in, deeply. "I'll bring Daddy's iPad tomorrow, okay? What can I load it up with for you? Please tell me Animal Planet shows. PBS?"

Actually I love Animal Planet, especially *Too Cute*, which really is so cute it slays me, and my mother loves to make me watch *Nova* with her, even though it bores me to tears, but what I want now are the stupidest shows I can possibly get my hands on.

"I don't care," I say. "*Switched at Birth. 90210.* Old *Gossip Girl.*"

"I think I get it," she says. "But more importantly, or I should say, more *imminently,* Dr. Malik should be in soon."

Imminently.

Even though they are pumping me through with saline and antibiotics, and also an antinausea medicine that, if it's working, makes me wonder what life would feel like if it *wasn't* working, I know I'm not getting any better. Because it is really true: sometimes you just know. Outside: school is starting tomorrow. I can picture everyone in his or her first-day-of-school clothes, the hallways all bright and shining and ready. All the teachers coming out from behind their desks to introduce themselves. Lockers. Empty notebooks. That *smell.*

What I have here, all I have really, is a new hospital bracelet with my name and birth date and Social Security number typed on. That says to me, this is *permanent.* And I have my mother, who now looks around as if she's going to tell me a secret. "It's not salmonella either. Did the pain people come back? Are you comfortable, sweetheart?" She takes my hand.

She's going to tell me I'm *dying,* I think. I will never see my friends again. I will never cuddle with Mabel and fall asleep to her snoring. I will never go to Spain or any Spanish-speaking country, not Mexico or Venezuela or Costa Rica or Puerto Rico, which I know is not a country. I will never become a vet. In this moment I realize that is always what I've wanted to be. A vet! Now I know, but now, of course, it can't ever happen. Also, I will never again hit the hockey ball around in Lydia's backyard or go shopping with her and Dee-Dee, or go

out to eat with them, or even pathetically wait outside of Lolly
Adams's party until a junior from my art class finally lets us in
so I can down three beers and make out with Joris, the Dutch
exchange student.

I let my mother hold my hand, but I can't talk.

I will never wear an actual gown. It's not a word I've ever used
before—they're just dresses—but now the sound of it, a *gown*,
sounds so beautiful and so far away.

"Mom?" I say.

She covers my hand with her other hand so that her hand is
creating a hand sandwich. Ha, I think. A hand sandwich. *Cheeky.*
But really I just feel her wedding ring, cold and sharp.

"Mm-hmm?" she says.

She says it sort of distractedly, which is strange, because I'm
so sick and could be *dying* and maybe just this once she could
not think about work or what's for dinner, or if Zoe is having
sex with Tim. I know she thinks about that, because I hear her
talking to my dad about it when they think we're asleep. I don't
think they are having sex, but what I do know now is that I will
never have sex. There has been no one I have wanted to have sex
with yet, minus Michael L, but I'm not really thinking about it
because all I can hope for is a kiss, just one day, a surprise. But
we can't go anywhere from here. This is nowhere.

"Am I going to die?"

My mother looks up, startled. "My goodness, no," she says.
She brings the hand sandwich to her heart. "No, no, no. We
just have to figure out what's going on. And then they can fix it.
Dying? No." She shakes her head vigorously. "And because you

are going to live, we really have to get you out of bed. You need to move around!"

The idea terrifies me. I cannot possibly move around. Perhaps ever again.

My mother clears her throat as she looks away from me, and I believe her, but I can tell my question has upset her. That's when another doctor comes in. This one crosses his arms, and without looking at me, he says that we need to put in a central line.

"A who?" my mother asks. "What?"

He nods. "It's a tube that is connected to a vein, so blood can be taken and we can get medications in more easily without jiggering the IVs and infecting the sites."

I shiver. It's not just an expression; I really do it.

As if he's read my mind, the doctor turns toward me. He has pens in his breast pockets. Both of them. "It's a small surgery," he says. "Tiny, really. It will deliver all the medicines and saline and liquid food, and it will let us take blood for testing. So we can figure out the problem."

I wonder, if I could see inside myself, what would it look like? I imagine a map, roads of sick blood leading nowhere. Blue blood. So blue inside. What I would do now to just feel my old weird self in there.

"Now, Mrs. Stoller, can you please wait outside while we put in the line?"

"I would like to stay," she says.

He shakes his head. "Please," he says. "It won't take long."

She gets up slowly, and as she walks out, I doubt I have ever been so sad to watch my mother leave the room. She leaves the door slightly ajar, but I can't see her.

"I've got one too," Thelma says over the curtain. "There are worse things. Believe me."

A nurse comes in with a kit of some kind that she opens, peeling back the seal, and then she is scrubbing my chest with this brown antiseptic.

"I'm Alexis." She tilts her head to the side as she spreads out large pieces of gauze over my heart.

"Oh," I say. "Hi."

This is when I think of the frogs.

Okay, the frogs. Let me back up to the science lab at school. Middle school, dissecting frogs. There was a lot of human drama about the frogs. Most of the guys were super excited about the prospect of cutting into frogs; a little too excited, if you asked me. And most of the girls pretended to be squeamish, groaning when Mr. Hallibrand told us about it. But we weren't squeamish, most of us. It's just what we thought we should be.

A few days before we were set for the dissection, Zoe had told me that when she and her lab partners cut their frog open, it moved. "It totally came to life!" she said before kicking me out of her room for the night so she could call Tim. "I'm not kidding."

I knew she was just trying to freak me out, but it did make me even more worried, not so much that the frog would become a zombie, but that it wasn't really dead and that it had a soul and that soul was being tortured.

Of the four in our group, I was the one with the scalpel. I remember pinning the frog to the waxed tray. And slicing into the skin and then pulling it back from the fat tissue and muscle and bone. The anatomy of an innocent frog, exposed. My hands shook. I remember the scissors cutting, the small bones breaking when I hit something wrong. And I remember the heart. Actually, my sister wasn't lying: when we touched it with our gloved fingers, that heart jumped back, still beating. All four of us screamed.

Now the surgeon's head is turned at my chest. The nurse rubs on some anesthesia—"local," she calls it, as if she means it's like, made in America—and then he's performing his incision. I can hear it but I can't feel it.

Outside I hear my mother squeal. "Look at you!" she says. "How sweet you brought your dog."

"He's a therapy dog," the boy, *that* boy, says. "I bring him to cheer up the patients. There aren't so many teenagers on this ward, so it's nice to have your daughter here! I came by earlier, but she was busy."

"Busy? Huh. Well, it's nice that you do this," my mother says.

I remember: the frog heart jumped in my hands. It makes me think now: What does it do when you're alive? Does it jump? The heart, I mean. My heart, I mean.

"At first it was something I had to do, but now I like to come. Sometimes I even get here before school. Originally it was pretty much my parents' idea," the boy says to my mom. I wonder if he's brushing his hair out of his face with his fingertips. I wonder what it would be like to touch his hair, and I think it would feel warm, like he'd been walking through a meadow, in the sun. "I enjoy it now, though. A lot."

"I see," my mother says. "I'm Daphne." My mother always has

to pretend she's this cool mother, insisting my friends call her by her first name, letting me drink wine on special occasions, taking me to R-rated movies because my dad hates going to the movies and my mom hates going to the movies alone. "My daughter is Lizzie."

"Connor," the boy says. "And this"—and I hear his sneakers squeak as he surely squats down; also I know he's rubbing the dog's scruff, and it makes me ache for Mabel—"this is Verlaine."

"Verlaine," I hear my mother say. "The poet!"

"Yes!" Conner says. "But also the singer. From the band Television? Anyway, his name is Verlaine."

"I think that's a better option," my mother says. "The poet Verlaine was a pretty intense fellow!" She laughs.

My heart beats so hard I wonder if the surgeon can feel it. And then I wonder if it's going to make him slip and puncture it so that it can't ever beat again. Who, I wonder, would come to my funeral? I imagine Nana trying to give a eulogy, breaking down and being led away.

But no. Soon the surgeon gets done puffing into his blue mask, and the nurse pulls back the blue sheets and goes for my mother.

"Bye, Verlaine," my mother coos. "Come and visit us again soon!" And then she is through my door and her face changes for a moment. When she recovers, she throws me a beaming smile. "Well, that's a sweet pair," she says. I know she is talking about Connor and Verlaine, but I look at the surgeon, who waits impatiently to speak with her, and wonder if she means us. *Me and Mr. Surgeon sitting in a tree, K-I-S-S-I-N-G. . . .*

I'm really a frog. Frog-like. Waiting to be dissected. So there you go! Hi! My name is Lizzie Stoller. I'm sixteen years old. I've never been to Spain. Before this, I was normal outside, weird on the inside. Before this I was the kamikaze. I would have liked to become a vet. Welcome to my froggy world.

Day 5: Apparently Life Goes On

Zoe has talked to Lydia, and so now I know she's starting varsity. It's a no-brainer, really. No one's faster than Lydia. At first it bugs me—it was supposed to be my turn—but what difference does it really make? I can't even move.

My mother, however, doesn't seem to realize I can't move, and she constantly tries to get me out of bed. I'm surprised she doesn't get me airlifted. She brings me my father's scratched-up iPad, and instead of walking, I turn to what my mother has chosen to let me watch. But she did a pretty nice job. *Teen Wolf, Glee* (eh, it got pretty bad after the third season), *Pretty Little Liars*, which I linger on, but then I hit *Vampire Diaries*. Why? Because I like vampires, but I think I like them in general because being one is pretty far away from my life. Vampires have nothing to do with me, and I'm comforted by not having to think about anything real. So I settle back, and then the worst thing happens. I can't set the iPad on my belly. I can't sit up to watch it. And for the brief moment that I do this anyway, looking at the screen makes me sick to my stomach.

So. I have no cell phone, no Wi-Fi, no movies or decent TV, and I have a mother who won't stop harassing me to get up and walk around. And I have something horrible happening to me that no one can yet name. They have me on medicines, steroids, and some things I don't even know about. And now I have no iPad.

That's pretty much all there is to say about Day Five.

Day 6: And On . . .

Pretty much the same as Day Five, but add more kinds of medication that do nothing, and also add on my father trying to get me up too. And add one or two of the nurses. I wonder about the boy, about Connor, if he's going to ever come back or if I officially scared him away. I listen for him; I can't help it. It gives me a thing to do in here, in between my mother's chirpiness, the calls from Zoe, the calls from Dee-Dee and Lydia, who phone me together after school. Dee-Dee is going out for Rizzo in *Grease*. When I talk to my friends from school, there are a lot of sighs and silences. I sort of hate talking to them.

I get a package from David B. I open it up and there's a God's eye, the yarn this deep, deep purple and then an intense red, wound around and around real, bumpy sticks, not the Popsicle sticks the youngest campers use. Maybe I'm softening up in here—a lot—but it feels soulful. My heart catches in my throat when I see it and then the note: *I know everyone laughs at these, but I see them as talismans. They are like the sun. And the sun protects us in all these ways. I am wishing all the best for you, Lizzie!* he wrote.

I think that note is beautiful.

Now I have the talisman hanging by my bed. My mother hung it with a pushpin, one she found on the nurses' bulletin board out front.

And in between all that, Day Six is pretty much just waiting.

Day 7: The Wig; the Mountain

I wake up to Thelma's voice, but all I want is to put my earbuds in and just tune out.

But I don't. Yes, I say, high school. One sister. And a dog. No, I say, I don't go to church. Virginia, I tell her. Suburbs. That's all she asks.

Then it's my turn. I learn this: Thelma's married with a kid, and she's a secretary at some government office. I've seen her husband—or at least the tall man in a navy-blue jacket, gold cuffs, and collar who comes in each night who I *think* is her husband—but I gotta say, there are too many people in and out of here, and I haven't been paying a lot of attention.

When I tell her I'm in high school, she's silent for a moment.

"You'll be out soon," she says. "This is just some strange hiccup in God's plan."

"You too," I say, because what am I supposed to say? All of this is way out of the age-appropriate province.

I crane my neck and look in where the curtain is just slightly parted. I guess that's Thelma. She's smiling. Her hair doesn't smile with her, and she scratches under it.

Thelma has a wig.

"Both of us," I say, looking away.

"All right!" My mother stomps into the room with her coffee as if she's ready to spearhead some kind of movement. "That's it. You have to get out of that bed. You're going to get bedsores, Lizzie! Your muscles are going to turn to jelly."

I can tell she has talked to my father about this and that he's said, *You're absolutely right, Daphne, you have to go in there and just make her get up. Be tough!*

"I was just sitting," I say. "That counts." I roll away from her, onto my side, which causes a lot of pain in my stomach. It also tugs the wires that connect me to the IVs along the metal stand next to my bed, which feels like the lines are pulling at my heart.

Thelma makes a moaning sound from behind the curtain.

"Shall I call a nurse?" my mother calls out, but there's no answer.

Just then I hear the quiet swing of the door opening, the rush of outside activity, like the sound of a seashell to my ear.

The door opens—for a fleeting second I think it could be the boy and his dog, and then the door closes and it goes quiet, as if someone has put the seashell down. It's Thelma's husband who comes in, with a kid I assume is their kid. They have to pass through my space to get to Thelma's side of the room, and we all say hello and I see the little girl, her hair all frizzy with yellow and pink and purple barrettes and little ponytails all over her head. She won't look at me.

"Poor woman," my mother says, sitting down next to my bed.

"They're right there, Mom," I scream-whisper. "They can hear you."

"Well," my mother says.

The little girl peers around the dividing curtain. My mother doesn't seem to notice, but I wave and try to smile, and she shoots back behind her curtain. Thelma, her husband says. Thelma Thelma Thelma, and I wonder if she has her wig off, and what her daughter thinks to see her mother like that.

"I'm not moving," I say to my mother. "Really, I'm not."

I think of a cheesy television movie, the one with the determined patient who gets out of bed and struggles for life, and despite the odds, and due to all that *strength*, he wins. But can I just say something about strength? It's only an expression. You either become healthy again or you don't. Just because a person is sick and isn't dead yet, it doesn't mean she's strong. I don't feel strong. In fact I'd be happy—if that's what you want to call it— to just give up and lie here. I am the opposite of strong.

"Yes, really," she says. "Darling, there are some very sick people here." She tips her head toward Thelma's side of the room.

I get it! I want to scream. But I can't.

My mother looks up at me. She tilts her head, and I can tell she has a decision to make about which way to be: the stern, tough-love kind of mom, like on the Lifetime movies where the mom grips her daughter's face with one hand and says, "Now you listen to me, missy, we're going to kick this thing and we're going to do it *together*," or the sweet, tender kind of mom who takes her daughter's hand and tells her she's so sorry for what's happening to her, to them, to their *family*, it isn't fair, life just isn't fair, is it? But how else could she help her?

I won't deny I'm really hoping for the second option, when my mother says, "You are going to get up and walk those hallways and get that system moving, or we're likely to be in here forever."

I'm outraged. *Hello?* Maybe it's not option two, but I am *suffering* here. I don't know how to say that to my mother, though. How the suffering can take my breath away.

"Time to say good-bye," I hear Thelma's guy say as my mother sighs back into the chair.

"We?" I say.

"I know you're the patient," my mother says, softening. "But if you think this is fun for me, you've gone crazy."

At some point it just seems easier to actually walk than to listen to people constantly asking me to walk. Also, I secretly think about the possibility of seeing Connor out there in the hall and that maybe I was rude to him and now he's never coming back to the room. I think about changing out of my disgusting hospital gowns, but you are supposed to wear them in here, and also? It will take so much energy I won't be able to take the walk anyway.

So. I call the nurse to say I'm going to get up. You'd think I'd told her I'd found a suitcase full of her money, because she sprints in, her face filled with gratitude as she unhooks all my wires. When I swing my feet over the bed, my mother gets so excited it's embarrassing. As I try to catch my breath, just from *sitting*, I look at these two skinny white legs coming out of my hospital robe, and they look like they belong to an old person. I have always wanted to be skinny like you just can't be bothered to eat, like you're not *trying*, but I didn't want it to happen like this. I'm also nauseous. How many ways can I tell you how nauseated and in pain I am? There are no more words. All the words sound the same.

I just want to lie down and cry now. I can't do this. I have never before—not even as I went screaming from the goal line, hockey stick high in the air—wanted to feel strong. I think I actually wanted to be less strong then. Just regular. Smaller, weaker, girl-like, Birdy-like. Birdy. But that's not what I've become either.

I stand and grab the IV stand for balance, and holding on to my mother, I sort of stagger toward the door. I don't even care if my hospital gown is open in back, which I guess it is, because my mother reaches behind me and closes it.

"There you go," she says. "Look at you!"

I have all this rage. At my mother for making me do this, for talking to me this way; at my father for his stuffed animals; and also at myself, for being someone who might never be normal again, not inside or outside. Why can't they figure out what's wrong with me? Who do I get to freak out on for being sick like this?

I ignore my mother's excitement as she opens the door to the hallway. The nurses are bustling around at their station outside my door. An elderly man glides by, holding his IV stand; an old guy is slumped over in a wheelchair. It's like a television show about a hospital. Or a show about a bus station.

I push through. I'm out! I'm *up*! I stand, breathing in the air as if I've finally reached the tippy top of a mountain. I even smile at the nurse coming out from behind the station. And then I see

Connor and Verlaine turning the corner from the elevator banks, fresh and ready for their daily visit. Maybe they're coming for me! For me.

"She's up!" the nurse says as she walks briskly by.

"She sure is!" my mother says. "Isn't she doing great?"

I roll my eyes, but I don't mean it. Because it is true! I'm up. I can both see and feel my knuckles go white as I lift the other hand to wave to Connor. I instantly regret this—how embarrassing can I be?

Connor and Verlaine are moving toward me, and I can hear my mother smiling—you can do that, by the way, hear my mother smiling—and then, quick as a mugging, I'm down. *Down* down. Like on the floor, pain chomping a chunk from my side. I know it's no good in there. All I can wish for is that I will lose consciousness, but I don't and so I can tell that, as the nurse runs toward me and as Connor lets go of Verlaine's leash and comes flying to help me up, I'm crying. It's like a movie how much I'm crying, and my mom is crouching down on my other side, and she and Connor carefully pick me up. They handle me like I'm glass and bring me back to my bed, where I dry-heave into my little lima-bean, sad-smile metal bowl, only now I turn it around to make it frown.

Connor bows his head like he's the one who is ashamed.

"Thank you, Connor," my mother says grimly.

He nods. He isn't smiling. I can see the lines of his mouth, turned down.

At first I think, thank God he's leaving, so I can experience the pain and humiliation of this moment alone with a roommate and her entire immediate family and a mother and a bunch of nurses and techs and students and doctors wandering in and out of here. As in: privately. As private as it gets here.

A nurse hooks me back up to my tubes that lead into my heart, and she clicks open her pen and says, "It's okay, honey, we'll try again tomorrow!"

"I'll be here," Connor says, turning to go. He raises his free hand in a way that seems to shield his face.

I look at my mother when he goes, but she won't catch my eye.

Then she turns toward me. "I'll give you a minute, honey," she says, and I watch her follow Connor out the door.

I lie back. It's not relaxing in any way, but it's the most relaxed I've been. And for just this one moment, everyone leaves me alone.

Day 7 Still

But the moment of being left alone ends pretty quickly. I'm not sure about it, but I think I hear just the faintest knock. I don't say anything.

Then there is that sliver of light. The sound of outside. And Connor's sweet face.

"Hey," he says.

I clear my throat.

"Hi. Can I come in? Just for a second?"

I'm silent, which I suppose in this place means yes.

"I wanted to check and make sure you're okay," Connor says.

I look down at Verlaine, and his head is cocked to the side and he seems to be asking the same question.

I just cross my arms. I can't look either of them in the eye.

"Well, I'm glad you're all right. But I also just wanted you to know it's okay."

"What's okay? This?" I hold out my hand to the wide expanse of my luxurious room. I shake my head. "It's just not."

"No, I get that. I do. But please don't feel strange about it. About the fall."

"Thanks," I tell him, even though I feel 100 percent the

opposite of okay about keeling over in front of Connor.

"You comfortable with dogs?" He comes to the side of my bed. Briefly I forget how ashamed I am and I feel this: crazy lucky. How lucky am I, I think, that this guy works here, now? The crazy unlucky part comes back quickly, though, because here he is standing up and I am lying here, a mess, a mess who fell on her face in front of him.

Who is Connor? He is incredibly cute, but I can see he also bites his nails really, really short. Like he hardly has any nails. That is never a good quality in a boy, I think, as if a girl who just fell on her face is in any place to judge. A girl with a rat's nest for hair and a gray face that, due to the steroids, is as round as a moon. Make the actual moon full and I might just turn into a werewolf.

I nod. "I have a dog," I say, managing to do so without crying. "Mabel. A springer."

I love animals. I love all animals so much, even birds, even fish. That's why I want to be a vet, though I gather there is a good deal of math involved in becoming one. I have no idea why this could be, but it could be problematic for me.

"Can Verlaine hop on your bed? He's super careful."

I close my eyes for a second. I am not the kind of person who closes her eyes while she's talking. I can't stand that. In fact, it repulses me, but again, it's not like I'm exactly in a position to be repelled. This time it's more like a way to keep everything down. So I do it; I close my eyes and nod.

And then Verlaine is sitting next to me, so careful not to hit my body, his paw up as if in greeting. How on earth did Connor train this dog to be so perfect? I imagine Verlaine at the circus, walking the tightrope with Connor. I picture Mabel, who just jumps up on everyone and tries to steal food and licks faces without asking. It makes me smile. And Verlaine's smiling too. That dog is a serious smiler. I take his paw. The soft scratchy bottom, I feel it. Feel his *nestells*. When we were little, that's what Zoe and I started calling those pads on the bottom of dog paws, cat paws too, for that matter, but we are dog people. I feel the smooth nails.

"Hi, Verlaine," I say. I want to hug him and hug him and never let him go.

I look over at Connor. "I love him," I say.

Connor crosses his arms. He cocks his head. He smiles.

He's so perfect I almost forget how embarrassed I am. His perfectness takes over. But I feel absolutely terrible.

Both Connor and Verlaine seem to know this at the exact same time.

"I just wanted to come back in and make sure you were okay," Connor says as Verlaine hops down from my bed. "And to say I'll see you again soon. We will."

I nod.

"So see you soon!" he says brightly.

"See you," I say. "Bye, Verlaine!" I say with much more enthusiasm, because it is so easy to love on an animal. There is no shame in it.

Bye, you two, I think, as I watch them move out of my room and into the busy hallway.

Day 8: Well, Now We Know

Who knows what time it is when an X-ray tech guy comes into my room with a portable machine, covering my chest with something that resembles a bulletproof vest—if I close my eyes, I can imagine I'm a cop, with a gun I'm not afraid to use, *bang, bang!* Maybe, I think as he takes a picture—*poof!*—from outside of the room, I have some special baffling disease that no one has ever seen before? This pleases me, like maybe they'll write up my case in a special journal. They could name the disease after the doctor who has cured me.

I'm listening to Velvet Underground when my parents walk in with their *looks*, and then the surgeon too, and I take the buds out of my ears before I turn the music off. I can hear Nico singing, all throaty and drugged: *I'll be your mirror, reflect what you are, in case you don't know* . . . while I wait for them to tell me about my incurable disease.

Here it is: it is not cholera or consumption or any of those unnameable illnesses in old novels, those diseases that can, like, *take you.* I have: ulcerative colitis.

Bleh.

They're talking, but I'm not listening. Okay, so I won't be

possessed or *consumed*, though my colon, which they are saying is one of the few vital organs a person can live without, might be taken. I might have to have surgery to get it out of there. Out of me.

"The colon is getting bigger and bigger," Dr. Orlitz, the surgeon, says, moving his hands farther and farther apart. His hands are pudgy, and I think of them dissecting me, pulling back my skin to expose muscle and fat. "If it grows too large, it could explode. Do you know what happens when a colon explodes inside a little girl?"

Am I the little girl in this scenario? What happens to her? I would lie if I said I'm not totally alarmed.

My parents nod.

"It's very dangerous," the surgeon says.

"We need to *save the colon*," my father says. He says it to the surgeon; he says it to my mother; he says it to the nurse, who smiles away from him. He says it to me now as he sits on the very, very end of my bed. "Surgery!" he says, head in his hands. "Whatever we have to do," he says to my mother when the surgeon leaves. And then to me. "Lizzie," he says. "My Lizzie, my poor Lizzie," he says.

And then he has to turn away.

After my parents leave, I call Zoe. From the landline. The novelty has worn off; I'm getting sick of this no-cell-phone policy. I know that phones can interfere with pacemakers and that, a nurse told me, it can short-circuit a ventilator (what the hell? I don't even know what people are saying in here anymore), and while I have not seen a cell phone in use, it's true, I'm not exactly trolling the communal bathrooms and lounges for people using them in secret. Besides, I feel like my mother has just taken mine and made up all these rules. I feel like she has done this so I will not have access to the web, so I will not be able to understand what's really happening to me. Surprisingly, I feel a little relieved. I don't want to go into the dark tunnel of the internet, where I can find all these stories about people with this disease. It is a dark, lonely hole in there, I know that it is.

It's a dark hole outside too. I am missing everything. I am missing the beginning. Junior year. I am missing discovering all the newness. I don't want to know who else is starting during preseason. I don't want to know who's Frenchie. I already know Dee-Dee got the part of Rizzo. I am a horrible person, but I cannot stand everyone's good news.

So instead I just call Zoe to tell me the truth and deliver me more crappy news.

"Okay!" she says when I tell her the name of this thing I now have, and I can tell she's psyched to just have a task, like a concrete thing she can do to help. "It's *diseased*. The colon," she says. And then, like it's friggin' show-and-tell, she recites, "'The colon is a six-foot-long vital organ where all the water is taken out of the food you digest before it leaves the body. It connects to the small intestine, which sucks out the nutrients before the digested food hits the colon, where it sits and waits to be *eliminated*.'"

Vital. That word again.

There is a pause, and then I hear the rapid-fire sound of my sister typing. "Okay, this site is more clinical," she says.

"'Ulcerative colitis is the result of an abnormal response by your body's immune system,'" she reads. *Blah, blah, blah*, is what I hear; just squawking. My ears hurt from the sounds.

Then more artillery fire at the keyboard. "So you've just had a super-serious flare-up. You can be throwing up, and obviously there can be blood in the *stools*." Now she giggles. *Giggles!*

"Really?" I say. But it comes out teeny.

"Sorry," Zoe tells me. "So it says that some people have this for a long time and go in and out of remission and flare-ups. I think your colon is just giving out," she says. "I'm so sorry, Lizzie."

Fantastic. Why, then, does everyone want to save it?

"Do you want to know the rest?" Zoe asks. "I mean, what happens if they have to remove it?"

"Is it bad?" I ask her. Zoe. For some reason I remember the two of us flying a rainbow kite on the longest string. I know my father is behind us, steering, but I don't see him.

Zoe clears her throat. "Yes," she says.

I'm silent. I listen and I don't listen. I still can't make myself think about it. Apparently you can't just get your colon taken out and walk back into your old beautiful life. I can't let myself think about it. I see the blue of the sky, the soft white clouds; I see the rainbow kite soaring. And then I see him: there's my father letting go.

Day 9: Life Time

Now the new thing is not what is wrong with me but the thing is to: *Save the colon!* So how will we know when we've saved it? Is a bill passed? Does a school stay open? Does an innocent man walk free?

There are, apparently, a million and one ways. Several types of new medications in many kinds of combinations. Massage. Herbs.

"What about a fecal transplant?" I hear my mother say to a doctor or a resident outside. Did I hear her *correctly*?

Save the Colon. It's like a cheer at a football game, which, for the record, I'm also about to miss. I can picture the bleachers filled up with everyone, the weather turning. I can hear that stupid marching band. I used to feel bad for the kids in marching band, their tall hats always off-kilter, their heavy tubas and trombones marked with greasy fingerprints. But then, when I thought more about it, I was in awe of them. Can you imagine? Making that kind of music while walking? *Marching?* Well.

I wonder now if I'll be out by homecoming, but part of me knows that even if I am, I won't be there. At the game. I can't imagine caring. I never cared, for the record, about football, though sitting on the bleachers up from the field, hanging out with my friends, that was something that was once fun. But king and queen? It was not even a concern. Other things I'm about to miss: all the parties the seniors weren't going to let me and my friends into anyway. Preseason. Sitting at a desk with *Wuthering Heights*, raising my hand. The future. It's happening without me.

I'm having these lovely thoughts when my mother comes in with her coffee.

"Okay, lover," she says. "Up, up, up."

I have secretly always loved it when my mother called me that. "But don't you think it's best for me to save my strength?" I try. Honestly, though. Shouldn't my colon be resting too?

She sips her coffee. "When," she asks, her mouth around the lip of the paper cup, "is best for your schedule?"

My mother. And her *coffee*. I don't drink it, but still it taunts me.

"Later," I say. "God, Mom, later."

She sips.

My food goes in through an IV from the bag of TPN, a kind of milky, liquid food that's supposed to provide nutrients. Even though I know I'm losing weight, I'm convinced it's going to make me gain thirty pounds. If I get out of here, I won't even get to leave *skinny*.

I take a breath, but it's like I can't catch it. I am so weak. I am so small. I am just about to give in to trying to get up when there's another knock at the door, and I see the little snout again.

"Verlaine!" my mother says. "Come on in, you guys! You're here early, Connor."

I feel my face get hot with embarrassment, and I tilt my head and look at my mother with the biggest eyes I can muster, which she also chooses to ignore.

"Thanks!" Connor says.

I mean, the wrinkled oxford shirt, the perfect-fitting jeans. And the long, light eyelashes? The gray-blue eyes? Come on.

Verlaine's dog mouth is smiling, and his big tail is wagging. It would be nice to pet him again, it's true, but now I've got this whole, like, *layer cake* made of shame—the *diagnosis* layer and then the falling-on-my-face layer and then the layer that is me lying here practically naked—and I can't deal at all. "We're talking." I nod to my mother, who I hope will have my back.

"Oh, sorry," Connor says, pulling back on the red leash. I swear Verlaine stops smiling. "I'm just doing a quick hello before school. I like to check in and see who is up for a real visit later. But usually everyone's around in the morning for checking in."

You got that right, I think. That's for sure. We're all *around*.

"Also just checking in. After our talk and all."

"Talk?" says my mother, and I feel my face get even hotter, and so I know it's even more red.

"I'm fine," I say. "I'm totally fine. Thank you."

Why isn't this boy out playing lacrosse or sailing, knee bent on the bow of a boat on the Chesapeake? That is where he belongs, not here in the land of darkness and doom. If he were in here, though, as a patient, I bet his mother would just sit by his bed, quietly holding his hand. There would always be fresh flowers on the side table and cold filtered water on the swingy table.

"Come on in!" my mother says. "Hi, sweetie," she says to the dog, who wags his way over to her. "I was just going to get some coffee," she says, and then she, like, hides her coffee! Mortifying. I touch my head, feel the dreadlocks forming on my scalp. No, dreads would be more fashion-forward, though totally wrong for me, deeply wrong. Wrong on so many levels. But I haven't washed my hair since camp! I am a monster. Revision: I am a monster who has not bathed.

My mother is out the door before I can convince her not to go, using my extreme illness, my new superpower, for good.

Connor scrapes what I have come to think of as my mother's chair over to the side of my bed.

Verlaine sits next to him.

Thelma stirs.

"Perhaps I should properly introduce myself," he says.

I blush. Again. Can he see it on my sick, gray face? "Yes?" I say.

"I'm Connor." He holds out his hand. "Connor Bryant."

His hair sort of swishes to the side, as if it's forever being blown in the wind. His lips are the slightest bit chapped.

"Lizzie Stoller," I say, sort of sticking my hand out and letting him shake it.

"So," says Connor. "Tell me everything."

Maybe it's because my mother isn't here to watch me. Maybe it's that I can't eat this cake of shame anyway. Or that I've really got nothing left to lose here. Whatever the reason, I consider the question.

"Okay," I say slowly. But what have I got to tell him?

"It doesn't have to be a thing. It can be a feeling."

I look at him, and I know my face says *what the hell*. "A feeling?"

"Yes." He reaches down and pets Verlaine.

Who is this person? What is he doing in here, precisely? I
wonder. But I don't ask him. Who cares really? I am in a jar. I'm
like a firefly in here, bumping up against the glass, frantic, the
holes my father has punched into the metal cap the only way air
gets in. My blinking light just might go out in here.

"I'm tired," I say. But I don't mean it like I need sleep, which I
very much do. You cannot sleep in here at all.

He nods.

"Of being me. In here. I wish I could just be the kind of sick
person who is sad and upset and shows it. Who's, I don't know,
vulnerable." I shrug.

He nods again.

"That's annoying," I tell him.

"Is this you being vulnerable?"

I have to laugh. "No. It's all just coming out angry. That's what
I'm saying. I'm tired of that. It takes a lot of energy to be pissed
off all the time."

He nods.

"Okay, but it is annoying that you keep nodding! It's like we're
in a movie and you're the shrink."

"Shrink I can do," he says, pressing his fingertips together and
forming a triangle with his hands. "See?"

"I do," I say. I wonder about Connor.

"What else, Lizzie Stoller?" Verlaine has gone from sitting to
lounging. He yawns.

"I'm boring Verlaine," I say.

"Don't do that," Connor says. "You're *deflecting*."

I look hard at Connor. So beautiful and weird and in my

room. It's like he's staring at me through this glass. I'm flying around like crazy and there he is, head tilted, peering in.

"I'm scared," I say. It just comes out.

Connor stops smiling.

"I'm really scared." It's all I can say. I feel it all over. It's in everything.

He stands up. He goes to the side of my bed. He touches my arm, and I get goose bumps. Goose bumps.

I go to pull my arm away. But I stop myself.

"I understand," he says. Connor Bryant says.

I look into his eyes. They're blue and gorgeous and clear, and he looks like he's almost crying.

"Thank you," I say. And for one brief and fleeting moment I am filled up with gratitude. Just filled up and over. Brimming.

And that's when my mother cracks open the door. "Hello?" she says tentatively. "Guys?"

Connor nods. "We were just going," he says, readying to leave.

I feel deflated again. Back to the misery.

And then my mother steps inside.

Day 9, afternoon: Finally

Somehow it happens: I take a shower.

Day 10: Like Honey

My mother arrives in the morning after the nurses have taken my blood and that technician has come in for the X-ray and after Dr. Malik has come around, marching to the foot of my bed before 6:00 a.m. with a new protocol to try. His students take notes behind him in a long row. Here I am, pinned back and helpless, splayed out on the waxy dissection tray.

"Look at you!" she says. "All clean!"

I don't say anything.

"Ready for a walk! Is Connor coming again today?"

"How should I know?" I say.

My mother sets a picture of our family on the side table—a term I use here only loosely—next to my bed.

Well, I guess we're settling into our new home. We should re-wallpaper too. But when I look at the photo, I have to turn away.

There we all are. Zoe leans on my father and makes a stu-pid face. I'm looking over at Zoe and my hair blows toward my mother, who's looking just at me. My hair has started to fall out now. I try not to think of Thelma when I find big clumps of hair on my pillow.

"There we are." My mother stands back from the frame, like

she's trying to hang a picture straight.

There we were, I think.

"So!" she says. "When are we going to try a walk again?"

She barely finishes her sentence when out of the corner of my eye I see the crack of the door widen. My heart freezes. And then a plain old resident in a white coat walks in, clicking her pen. She talks about my red blood cell count, which apparently is dangerously low.

"We've gone and ordered a blood transfusion," the resident says. She has a British accent. Her words are really just more squawking sounds.

"Can I please talk to you outside?" my mother says to the resident. "Please," she says like she's giving an order.

And then there is the sound of them leaving the room, and the resident trying to say something to my mother, and then the sound of my mother interrupting the resident, and then the sound of my mother's actual voice, growing loud. "You get me that doctor right now. Right here or on the phone, I don't care. If you don't get me the doctor right now, you have no idea what you are about to see me do," she says.

And soon there is the sound of Dr. Malik.

It's the strangest, eeriest feeling to watch someone else's blood become your blood. It doesn't *feel* like that, like some kind of alien intervention, but this is what you know is actually happening.

A packet of blood drips in slowly. I had thought it would happen quickly, maybe because the word, "transfuse," sounds like a word that means "instantly," but no, it's very slow.

Nana always tells Zoe and me, *Remember, blood is thicker than water. Family*, she says, *is what's most important.* I am here to tell you, that is no joke. Blood is *way* thicker than water. And it goes in as slowly as I imagine honey would, and it makes me feel less like I'm being invaded by aliens and more like I'm a vampire, sucking the life out of some poor unsuspecting person to save myself.

So some random person's blood is dripping painfully slowly into my veins via some crazy straw linked up to my heart and I'm watching the Food Network. I can't eat, and here I am watching food get cooked. It's just so wrong. Anyway, this is all happening while my mother's eating in the cafeteria and I'm watching someone make a heinous casserole I wouldn't even eat now.

Thelma says, "Turn it up!" As if she doesn't have her own television.

I do it.

Thelma asks, "Honey, what would you eat if you could eat?"

I shrug, though she can't see me.

"Girl! I know you heard me," she says.

"I heard you," I say. The last time she really talked to me was three days ago, when she told me I'd be getting out soon. There's been like hello, good-bye, here comes the nurse to poke at us, but that's all Thelma and I have really said. And it's not like me to be rude, but doesn't being transfused give me some kind of free pass?

"Come on then!" She kicks at the curtain and I see a glimpse of her, just a flash, a wig set on her fist, and she's twirling it like it's one of those old-fashioned globes of the world. "What would you eat if you could?" Her head's bald and brown and totally smooth, something that might feel good to touch.

"All right." I let myself think about it. "Pizza. Hot dogs. Macaroni and cheese." I have to laugh; it's total kid food. "Ice cream sundaes dripping with chocolate sauce."

"Mm-hmm," she says.

"Sprinkles. Rainbow ones."

"That makes sense. Me? I'd eat ribs—dry ribs, now, none of that bottled sauce, and collards, corn bread. Black-eyed peas." She makes a sound of licking her lips. "Same as you," she says. "The stuff we ate when we was small. That's what we want. To make us feel better." Still she's twirling that wig.

On TV, the lady puts more butter on top of butter.

"Yes," I say, because it's true.

Then we're silent and the blood in my IV stand is tomato-juice red and it goes *drip, drip* into the line that feeds into my blood. Is my blood as red as this other random person's blood? *Thicker than water.* I can see the packet out of the corner of my eye, even when I try not to look, even when I stare straight ahead at the television.

Once in a while a nurse comes in to look at the drip and squeezes the balloon of blood, like she's squeezing someone's heart.

There's a knock on the door just as the butter casserole is ready.

"Hello?" he says, peering around the door.

I look away from the blood and over to the door, and there he is.

There they are.

Connor and Verlaine.

I smile big when Connor walks in.

He shakes his hair out of his face, and I look over at the packet of blood. Oh God, I think. Am I embarrassed? I have no idea. Is getting a transfusion *embarrassing*? More embarrassing than falling in front of the nurses' station? More embarrassing than making the campers put down their archery bows? More embarrassing than having to sit in the shower clutching a cord that calls a nurse if I fall down? I think of regular embarrassing things: spinach in my teeth, getting an answer wrong in class, blushing. *Duck soup,* as Nana says. Nothing.

"Can I sit down a minute?" Connor says.

Yes! I think. Then I change my mind. Or not my mind. My body is what's really making most of the decisions. Please don't sit here, my body says. Please! Go away, it says. But what it does instead is shrug.

Verlaine pants at the side of the bed as Connor gently sits down. How can I explain it? Being jostled hurts and then it is the exact opposite of hurt. Then he does this thing: he touches my leg. My knee actually. Very, very softly. How does he know that this is the single place that doesn't hurt? He knows it before I do; I only realize it as he touches me. So softly. Again.

"Hi," he says.

My heart is a thousand butterflies. My stomach is a sack of them; it counters the pain of it. "Hi there," I say.

Connor Bryant. He has slender, beautiful fingers. Connor

Bryant. Yes, you could barely call the nails actual nails, and there are some spots of blood along the cuticle. Even if I were in more of a position to be grossed out, I wouldn't be. I wonder what could make a boy like Connor Bryant bite his nails that way. But it's not like I think he's cute despite the bloody stubs; I think he is adorable because of them. "Did I mention when we talked yesterday that Verlaine and I, we're candy stripers?"

I have to laugh. Out loud. I imagine Connor in one of those white aprons the candy stripers are supposed to wear. I've never seen one here, but I imagine Verlaine in a little white apron too.

"Yup. Candy striper." He brings his hand across his chest, pointing to an invisible sign. "We're out of uniform today," he says, looking down at Verlaine. "Left our candy canes and lollipops at home." His smile is dazzling. All white teeth and then the crinkling at the eyes.

"I'm a chocolate eater myself," I tell him. "But there's not a lot of chocolate eating going on in here." Connor has his smile, but what have I got? I wasn't much for flirting before, and I can't say this is the place to start. "Me?" I say. I didn't mean it as a question. "Patient."

"I see that."

I stop laughing.

"Can Verlaine come up?"

I nod.

"*Up*, up," he says to his dog, his beautiful dog, and somehow Verlaine gets on the bed as delicately as a cat.

I pet him and look at Connor. He seems pretty strong; I can see his arm muscles through his faded, wrinkled oxford. The collar is a little frayed, which looks like he's just got better things to do than worry over a new shirt. Like he's worn it so many times it just knows him. "Okay, so now you. Now you tell me everything. Like what are you doing here?" I ask.

He clears his throat.

Don't leave, I think. I'm sorry I asked. I take the question back! It doesn't matter why you're here, I think, but I don't say any of those things.

"Let me sit over there," he says, pointing to my mother's chair. "I don't want to hurt you or anything."

"Okay," I say brightly. He probably thinks I'm disgusting. "Sounds good!" I don't want him to leave the bed, but every time he moves I feel a wave of nausea.

"I'll leave Verlaine with you, though," he says.

I grab Verlaine's scruff. I smell his dog smell.

Connor gets up gingerly and goes to sit in my mother's chair. He crosses his legs, which is actually the cutest thing. It doesn't look girlie on him. It looks old-fashioned. And elegant.

Vans. Black-and-white checkered, with laces. Slayed.

Connor Bryant: slayer of the sick and the weak.

I wait. What will he say? He could have recovered from some terrible illness and wanted to return to help others. Or he could have a sick sister. Or a mean father. Maybe he isn't going to tell me anything. Honestly, I have no idea what he is about to say.

He sighs, then gives the kind of smile that could burn a house down. I never knew that kind of smile before, but I do now. "College apps," he says. "So brutal, right?"

I feel my face do the thing where half of it mocks the other half of it. "Okay," I say. I don't know him at all, but I don't believe him.

He brings his ankle over the other knee, and sort of shakes them both. He fiddles with his laces and shakes his leg harder.

"Okay," I say again. "Got it." I can go back to anger easy as pie. I mean cake.

He stops, like freezes, and looks up at me. If nothing else: Connor Bryant is *intense*. He makes me look like I live on a rainbow and drive a unicorn.

"Sorry. No, that's not true. About the apps. Just a thing I say. But this"—he points to me, practically dead here, on the bed—"bodes well for you. Harvard, here you come."

"Right," I say.

"Oh, I don't know," he says. He joggles his ankle again; again with the laces.

"And also, not really thinking about it. About how I got this fantastic fun disease and came to spend all this time in this, I don't know, what would you call it, heaven? So I could, like, get into the Ivy League."

"Thought so," he says, pointing a chewed-up finger at me.

For a fleeting second, I don't like Connor. Like 100 percent. But then he smiles and the moment is gone. Like it had never been there at all.

He softens. His whole self. "Sorry." He shakes his head, like he is shaking back to himself. "I don't know why I said that. Like being sick means you have it made? I really don't know why I said that."

"It's such a romantic disease that I've got. I couldn't have planned a better one," I say, "for college, I mean."

Connor laughs. Full-on, head thrown back. It's amazing. Verlaine jumps down and goes to sit next to him. That's how good the laugh is.

"Fair enough. Okay, So I guess I have to ask then. What *do* you have? Why are *you* here?"

"You don't know?"

"Me? God, no. There's all kinds of confidentiality here. I know the children's hospital, where I also go, has most of the young people with cancer. And here we are, on the cancer ward. So. Cancer?"

I try not to seem self-conscious about Thelma, who's probably sleeping anyway.

I shake my head. "That was ruled out two days ago." Was it Day Eight? It seems more like seven years, seven decades, seven centuries. "They put me on this floor because it's safer than the general illness unit with all those infectious diseases. It's kind of surreal, though, being here." I nod my head in Thelma's direction.

I have turned into my mother in here.

Connor pets Verlaine silently.

"Oh, so I have this disease called ulcerative colitis. It's embarrassing, really." I could not say anything, I know, but what's the point? It is what it is here, people. But I do realize that part of the pain I've got in here is shame. It hurts me. How ashamed I am, even just when my father enters the room with a teddy bear. It's that kind of a disease.

"Being sick is like that, I think," Connor says. "I see all kinds of people in here. No matter what they have, everyone seems to feel ashamed. Bodies," he says.

I swallow, big. I wait, but that's all he says. I nod. "Bodies."

I feel like Connor knows everything. And understands.

"Also, not just bodies."

I wait for an explanation, but one doesn't come. "I'm not sure what's going to happen," I say.

This is the part I haven't mentioned, not to anyone. If the colon doesn't get saved, I'll have to have a bag attached to me. I can't say it. He will never come near me if I do. If this really happens, no one will. I will be a freak. A freak with an ileostomy bag.

Connor nods, but he doesn't look at me. And then he does. Right at me. "You're still you, you know," he says. He scootches the chair so it's right next to my bed. "I think that this place and being sick can make you feel like you're not you, but you'll be back. To yourself."

And who was that? A girl on a dock with her feet in the water, waiting to be pretty? What did that even say about me?

The thing is, I won't actually really be me. What will I even look like? I can't picture it; I don't want to picture it. Eventually the bag comes off, if I'm to believe what I hear. There will be some sort of *reconstruction*, as if my body is recovering from the Civil War. I don't know anything that will happen yet, but I do know I will never be the same.

I feel like I will choke. How does he know absolutely everything? It's like he is on the moon with me and no one else has gotten here yet. No one else is coming.

He takes my arm, which I hadn't realized was sort of dangling helplessly over the side of the bed. He turns it over, holds my hand in one of his, and then runs his eaten fingers up them along the inside of my wrist. There are veins there, and I feel him tracing them. His touch is as light as a buttercup.

I resist the urge to snap my arm back, tuck it into my disgusting hamster nest of a bed. "I bet you do this to all the girls," I say. What I mean is: now who will ever love me, come to my door with flowers, write my name in wet cement, throw stones at my window?

"Nope." Connor says. His fingertips tickle my wrist, and it's hard not to smile.

I look over at the IV stand, and I can see the blood transfusion is done. There's no timer that dings or anything, but the dripping through the clear tube seems to have stopped. There's just the residue, like that stuff along the glass when you drink tomato juice, which, for the record, I will never ever be able to do again.

Bodies.

Connor looks down at his Vans. And then he looks up at me.

"You'll be back," he says.

And for the first time I believe it might be true.

Day 11: Frog, Prince, Fairy Tale

Then it's back to the torture, back to the night rounds and then the morning rounds. Except after the morning rounds on Day Eleven, Connor and Verlaine come.

Again.

"Hey!" Connor says, peeking in. It's so, so cute because Verlaine peeks in the same way, just at the bottom of the crack in the door.

I sort of love them. I nod. I can't wait for Verlaine to jump up onto my bed, sweet as a lemon drop, and for Connor to sit at the end of it and maybe touch my feet through the blanket. Or maybe just sit in my mother's chair. Whatever.

He glides in. Today he has on a long-sleeved polo shirt and . . . wait for it . . . it's purple! He has a backpack, and he's wearing the straps over both shoulders. He's so preppy, but it's exactly right for him. He is just so different from me, different from the old me, the me on the inside, but I make a mental note to perhaps make a costume change tomorrow.

He stands at my bed, clutching Verlaine's leash. Verlaine is smiling, his tongue sort of hanging out of his mouth, waiting and hoping.

I don't want to say, *You guys! Come sit down on my bed*, which is basically a hotbed of germs and disgustingness, so I just lie there, waiting.

"What?" I say when no one else says anything.

He taps his toes.

"Let's go for a walk," Connor says.

I feel like I've been kicked in the stomach. I can't help but think that my mother or the doctors and nurses have sent Connor here to make me get out of my bed, which, while it *is* a hotbed of germs and disgustingness, is *my* hotbed. It is mine and I am its. I cross my arms and turn my head.

"Come on, Lizzie," he says.

I can't help but note that he has said my name after a sentence. I can't decide if this is more amazing or less amazing than his sneakers and his purple shirt. Just the sight of those sneakers makes my heart lurch. I try not to think that Connor is probably here in my room saying my name after a sentence because it's his job to say my name post-sentence. It's probably in the Candy Striping Handbook, right there along with take patient's wrist and run fingers along it, ever so softly. He's just doing what he's supposed to do, which is to be nice and bring his dog around to make people—sick people—happy. Connor has no feelings for me at all. He wouldn't when I was healthy, and he certainly wouldn't now that I'm not.

So I'm trying not to think that, in addition to being here and in pain and recently transfused and about to lose my colon, I could also get my heart broken. Is that irony? Someone somewhere is mocking me.

"Not today, guys!" I say in my most sparkly voice. "I'm tired."

"Yeah," he says. "Today. Now, even. I went home for Verlaine and came straight here just to get you up."

"That's so nice of you," I say, but my heart's not in it. No, my heart *is* in it, but I don't want it to be, and I'm trying to make what I say make it *not* in it. I am his job, I think again. I admit, I am crushed.

"Nice? I'm actually getting paid by the hour. In cotton swabs and alcohol rubs. So take your time."

Maybe he read my mind. I laugh anyway.

From behind the curtain, Thelma laughs too. "Go, already," she says.

She has this big, deep laugh I've never heard her use. But why would I? Who laughs in here?

"Can you give me a second?" I say, to all of them really. I can't even imagine what it would be like for one of the orderlies to pull back the blanket to reveal my . . . *gowns*. And my hospital socks.

"No problem," Connor says. "I'll go grab Collette and wait for you outside."

I smile. "Sounds good."

Not a moment later the nurse comes in, sneaking up in her sneakers like all the nurses do, which makes me realize why they call them sneakers.

Collette is fleshy and blond with really dark roots, and she's dunked herself in so much perfume I might crash from the overpowering smell if I don't stop and drop from weakness. "You're heading out!" She adjusts my wires. She doesn't unclip me so much as she untangles me and helps me sit up and swing my legs over the side of the bed. "I'll get those two cuties now," Collette says when she's done.

A few moments later—three heartbeats—and Connor is back. "Well, look who's up and about!" he says. He and Verlaine are, like, bopping together, in tandem. Connor holds out his elbow. "May I?" he asks.

Again I think of gowns, for me a long one, maybe green silk, that ends when I'm all the way across the room. I touch the L of his arm with one hand and lean the other on my little coatrack stand, which glimmers with the pouches of all the stuff that isn't curing me.

"Where are we going?" The little plastic circles on the bottom of my socks make my feet stick on the linoleum. The elastic digs into my ankles.

"Oh, everywhere." He walks toward the door. Verlaine practically hops beside him, his nails clicking on the linoleum.

Outside my room is another world inside another world. It's all like one of those beautiful Russian nesting dolls Nana once gave me. One fits in the other that fits in the other that fits in the other. But where is the end? How does the outside tell me how many are inside?

I guess you just keep walking. I do: I shuffle out into the hallway—the sock rubber seems to make this more difficult—next to Connor but falling a little behind.

"Look at you!" a nurse says.

"Hiya, Marion," Connor says.

"You got her out!" she says. "You guys heading to the nightclub on six?" She chuckles.

How amusing, I think. The humor bar in here is a little low for my taste.

"How does it feel, honey!!!" she asks me.

I cannot stand the way everyone seems to be speaking in exclamation marks. I drop what I now see is the tight grip I had on Connor's elbow.

Something small but solid whirls by us, and Connor reaches his hand up and catches it. A frog's tongue to a fly. Perfect. I can see Connor walking through the world in his own way. With power. He has it.

You know who doesn't have it? Me. What little I had—the good hair, the field hockey stick—is gone now. I'd say you really don't know power until you've got none, but that's not really true. The girls I know at school, the evil, cruel ones, they know what they've got. Lydia and Dee and I, we were never like that.

He turns the object over in his hand. A rubber chew toy.

"For the sweetest dog in the world," Marion says, winking.

Connor beams, and the light inside him somehow manages to burn brighter. "Awesome," he says. "He can't have toys in here, but I'm keeping it for him." He wags the rubber bone at Marion and sticks it in his back jeans pocket.

"Come on," he says, as if now we have the keys to somewhere. To anywhere.

He and Verlaine are just ahead.

All I can do is drag myself and all my IVs and wires along and follow behind.

Wait for me.

We walk the long hallway and then turn the corner, and there are these large orange armchairs set out in front of a big window, which looks out onto a massive construction site. We're near the elevator bank, and I can hear the *ding* of arrivals and the closing doors of departures.

I'm exhausted. I sit. I might never be able to get up.

Verlaine lies at Connor's feet. We both look out the window.

Again with the silence. And then I ask it, again. "So I told you my story, can you please tell me yours now?"

"Like, I'll show you mine and you show me yours?"

I can't tell if this is sweet—like flirting—or if it's incredibly obnoxious. "Kind of," I say. "But without the showing part." I drag my socks back and forth, and they hiccup along the linoleum.

"Damn!" He snaps his fingers.

"Trust me," I say. "Nothing good to see here. Trust."

"I doubt that, I do. But I joke, I joke. Okay. I get it. It's my turn for show-and-tell."

"Just tell," I say.

Big breath in. And then he goes, "Well, last summer, when I turned sixteen, I was walking home from the movies with my friends."

"Walking?" I say. Because it's really hard to walk home from the movies from where I live. You have to drive almost anywhere.

"Yeah, the one in Georgetown. I live just a few blocks behind it. It was afternoon."

I nod. Oh. Connor is rich. In the real world, he's all urban and private-school and probably has a summer place at the beach where he takes all his skinny, cool, private-school girlfriends. He probably has a ton of girlfriends. He is so obviously just doing his job here.

In the real world, I would never know Connor. He would never see me. Which, in my weirdo world, makes me like him more.

"Anyway, we had all sort of broken off for home. For some reason we weren't hanging at my buddy Brad's that day, which is strange, because we usually did. Or my house, because neither of our parents were ever home. It was kind of great then. Anyway, I was alone, walking home, listening to "Marquee Moon"; you know that Television song?"

I don't say yes and I don't say no, but I sort of wave the question away with my hand.

"Out of nowhere I saw this little girl." He shakes his head. "I don't like to talk about it."

I urge him on with my eyes and a little lunge of my head, which I know makes me look like a crazy person. Or a lizard. "Well," I say. "I'm not hiding much here." I glance down at myself. I am smaller than I used to be. In every way.

"I know you're not. That's why I'm telling you." He clears his throat. "Anyway," he says. "Anyway, so I saw her—really cute little girl, and then this car speeding off Wisconsin Avenue, breakneck-like, around the corner. Hits her. I mean *hits* her. This mean squeak of the brakes and then this massive thud, and she is flying. I mean *flying*."

"Oh my God," I say.

"Yeah. Then there is the sound of her hitting the asphalt. It happens in parts. It's not one sound. It's like her bones hit the ground at different times. Anyway, anyway," he says, shaking away the thought. "That girl was over a year ago, right?" Connor continues. "But I still remember that sound. And then I remember the blood, everywhere, and her mangled body. Blood out of her nose and eyes even. That's how she was when I ran up to her to help her, because the car drove away. I know I was screaming. Then it is just a big blur."

"Wow," I say. I know it's a stupid thing to say, though.

"Anyway, so people came rushing out of their houses and then her mother ran out, and then there were all these ambulances and police cars. Then everyone, like, turned to me. The paramedics, the neighbors, the police, everyone. They asked me if I'd gotten the license plate number. But I hadn't gotten the plate number. But they just kept asking me and asking me. I hadn't even thought to look or take my phone out and take a picture. I just didn't think of it."

I swallow, hard. "It's not your fault you didn't look at the plates!" I say, with feeling. It isn't, I think. I mean, what a horrible thing! "And anyway, you ran to help the girl. And also? That wouldn't have kept the girl from getting hit," I say. I feel the need to call her the girl, to keep her a stranger.

"She died," he says. "The girl."

I don't say anything.

"Like, right in front of me. I had all this guilt. I still do. It's hard not to think about it. My mother's friend, who's a doctor, suggested I do this."

"A psychiatrist," I say.

"Yeah, so he said I should get Verlaine his Canine Good Citizen certificate and take him into hospitals. That was like six months ago."

"Wow." I say it again. The situation seems to demand the word.

He's silent.

"What did he have to do to get the certificate?"

"Crazy stuff," Connor says. "I had to open umbrellas in his face. Scream at him as he heeled. He was epic. He's a fantastic dog."

I pet Verlaine's head. "I can see that." I look outside the window and watch a crane dump more dirt on a pile of dirt.

"He thought it would make me feel better to do something positive."

I nod. "So positive," I say. My heart, like, spills out. It's so big for him, big for Connor. All that gratitude again.

"It's like I get to give joy. Verlaine does anyway."

"You do too," I say because I forget to stop myself.

Connor looks me in the eye, and I don't care that my hair is greasy and flat and that my cheeks are swollen, or that I'm in these hideous powder-blue hospital robes. He's so close. I can see his soft, light lashes, almost as long as whiskers. They flutter. What else aside from lashes flutters? I think only wings.

I know I need to get back to my room, but I don't say anything about it. If it were anywhere else, even in the sun, we would kiss. Right now. But in here is a place of sickness and sadness.

I can't even picture it. I mean, I won't let myself. I'm trembling, but not from feeling sick or cold or in pain. That—this—is fear and it's also hope. I try to push it down and make it stop, which makes me swallow a lot of air, which makes me cough. Good to know this dignity of the sick you hear about will never, ever apply to me. But really, take all that away and I am trembling from possibility and panic and wishing.

"So that's the story. Okay?" Connor asks.

Is it okay about the story or am I okay, I can't tell which he's asking, but I do know this: If I don't move, maybe he won't realize I'm here and maybe I won't detonate the future.

"You're still you, too," I say.

I can see Connor swallow, his little Adam's apple bobbing along his neck. "Hard to tell," he says.

I nod.

"So!" Connor says.

"Anyway," I say.

"Anyway."

We look outside and I try to steady myself, waiting for what comes next.

Day 11 Continues! We Were Never Here

Connor and Verlaine and I walk slowly, as slowly as I have ever walked, back to my room. They wait outside while I run to the bathroom in my room, run being the operative term for stagger, lurch, stumble, lunge, and then when I'm sitting on the side of my bed, breathless, trying to untangle all my various wires, I say, "Okay, you guys can come in."

In they come, the very portraits of good health. It just kills me.

"What do you miss most in here anyway?" Connor sits down in my mother's chair.

"Well, aside from, like, my life, you mean? Like my freedom?"

Connor smiles, this time with no teeth, which, I gotta say, manages to be just as charming as the smile with all the teeth. "Yes. Aside from that."

I sigh. "Being outside. Walking with Mabel. Being near water with Mabel."

He nods.

"Also? Food."

I know I should have said friends. Or going to see bands. Or sneaking out to drink beer. Something normal.

"What kind of food? Like, what would you eat if you could eat?"

It's like Thelma!

"Ice cream sandwiches," I say. "Crab cakes. Milk shakes." So let's just say this is all in the Candy Striping Handbook. I will still play along. My heart is already in it.

"Virginia is for crabs!" he says.

"Actually, it's lovers. Virginia is for lovers," I say, slightly embarrassed by the word. *Lovers.* "Maryland is for crabs." But I get it. The District is for cool kids, and the rest of us are suburban losers. I get it. The girls Connor knows are probably all blond and tan and easy in their skin. Everything slides over them; nothing sticks. Or they wear vintage dresses and have short black bangs and wear nose rings. Or they have big black glasses and speak seven languages and have just moved here from London because their parents are diplomats.

"Don't forget hot dogs," says my roommate.

"Hi, Thelma," I say.

"Hi, Thelma," says Connor.

"What kind?" He uncrosses his legs and places his elbows on his knees. He is killing me. Verlaine stretches out, exposing his stomach, and I scratch him. "Of milk shake."

"Chocolate," I say. Easy.

"I would miss strawberry," he says.

"Strawberry!" I giggle. "Very pink."

Connor laughs and sweeps his hair—it really is strawberry blond—out of his face. His hands. They are crooked and beat-up and eaten and soulful. They have feeling.

"Books? What's your favorite book? Like, what are you reading now?"

"I can't read in here. I mean, I just can't."

"Okay then, what would you read if you could read, I mean?"

"Hmmm," I say. *Wuthering Heights* is on this swingy table over my bed, but I don't think he can see it. That's some intense love in that book. Deadly. Haunting. Dark, dark love. I'm not that far in, but I can't help but note that everything important happens when the characters are young. It's like all that matters. "I like lots of different stuff. Like Stephen King, and also *The Handmaid's Tale*," is what I tell him.

"Don't know that," Connor says,

"It's about this cult society where this woman has to have sex every month until she gets pregnant."

"Lovely," says Connor.

"Yeah, it's pretty dark. Okay, what else? Ray Bradbury. *Fahrenheit 451*."

"Oh my God, I love that book!" Connor says. "I love Ray Bradbury. Stephen King is good. *The Stand*."

My heart leaps. I've chosen correctly. "Yeah, totally. *The Stand*."

"Hey, do you have any music here?" he asks.

I can hear the sound of Thelma fidgeting, as if to say, please, please don't play music in here. She clears her throat.

"We'll be quiet!" he says to the curtain as he stands and grabs my iPod off its charger. "Promise!"

Connor knows everything.

I watch in horror as he scans through my iPod. Books are easier than music. To be right about, I mean. I have some pretty lame stuff on there. Like, "Hey There, Delilah," which I love, by the way. I've got Kelly Clarkson! Kind of as a joke; kind of serious. But thankfully, Tim loaded it up with at least some good music before I went to camp, stuff he knows I love. He put on other women singer-songwriters, mostly Brits, and I think it's because he knows I love Birdy and he must have listened to Birdy Radio on Pandora. Gabrielle Aplin, Emeli Sandé, Jasmine Thompson. Which, now that I think about it, is kind of sweet. I mean for him to do this kind of research for me. Even if it's more for Zoe. Wouldn't that be nice? To have someone who wants to impress you so much he listens to Pandora for your little sister? I wonder if they are having sex after all.

So I like Birdy, and also old stuff she was inspired by, like Nina Simone. And then I like the classic-rock stuff like Guns N' Roses and the Rolling Stones, circa *Sticky Fingers* (David B from camp listened to that album all summer long), some David Bowie, Velvet Underground. I like a lot of different kinds of music, just depending. Being in here has made me think sometimes it's better to look back. Like what has happened before—music, books, movies, *life*—maybe it was better, more important, before. *Wuthering Heights*-style. I think there are people who look forward and people who look back, and I have become a person who looks back. Maybe I always was.

"Oh!" he says. "Oasis. Bright Eyes? How emo of you."

"Well," I say. "I don't know." The music shaming. Here it goes.

"Britney!" He sort of yelps it.

Exactly.

I start to be embarrassed, but then I do the opposite. "Nothing wrong with some Britney!" I say. "Come on, she's very cool."

"And JT too. She is," he says. "They are." I can't help but think of how they met, in the Mickey Mouse Club. Like this total alt-world. It brought them together. It's all this crazy unreality here too. It's like deep, deep time and space that you have to write all this complicated code or say some wacky spell and turn around three times to get to.

"Birdy," he says. It's like a breath. It breaks a spell.

"I love her," I tell him.

"Me too. You look a little like her." He unwinds the earphones wrapped around my iPod and puts the left bud in his ear. A smile creeps over his face.

Beautiful Birdy, with crazy eyebrows.

Then he leans in, toward me. He puts the right bud in my ear. The music pours in: "Every time that I see your face I notice all the suffering. Just turn to my embrace, I won't let you come to nothing."

It's so sad and so beautiful. It makes me ache. I look over at Connor. He's just on the other end of that short wire. His eyes are closed. Even his eyelids are splashed with freckles. In one ear I can hear the shuffle of the nurses and Thelma's snoring and the *click clack* of mothers' and daughters' high-heeled shoes and I hear Birdy in the other and I don't know what's going to happen to me. I don't know if my colon will be saved or taken, and I don't know what life will look like to me either way. And I feel all that, I can't stop *feeling* in here, but I am also having one of my favorite moments, ever. I can't breathe and I don't want to.

It's getting darker, and I imagine we are on a beach watching Verlaine and maybe Mabel, too, run in and out of the waves. We both have jeans on, rolled up at the ankles. I'm wearing cool sunglasses, Wayfarers, not aviators. The sun drops. It's just like that.

As if he's read my mind, Connor says, "Let's pretend we're not here."

I swallow. Hard.

"Let's pretend we were never here."

I hear him in one ear and I don't stop listening in the other: "And I'll stay here if you prefer. Yes I'll leave you without a word."

I feel like I will cry, and I don't know if it's from sadness or happiness. All I think is this: Who would you love if you could love? Please tell me who that person would be.

Day 12: Window Seat

Day Twelve is pretty much just awful. For one thing, I wake up and shout my usual hello to Thelma, but there's no shout back. Her television is quiet. When I cock my head and look in through the crack in the curtain, I can see that the bedding has been changed, and there are new sheets pulled up tight, the IV stand empty just like a coatrack waiting for someone else to hang her jacket and hat.

Thelma is gone.

When my parents come in, I can't look at them.

"Hi," my mother says, slowly. "Hello?"

My father hovers by the door, his hands in his pockets.

I just gulp and look over at Thelma's side of the room.

As usual, they don't get it. "Are you in pain?" my mother says. "Are you okay, Lizzie?"

I nod, though there are tears streaming down my face. This is a different kind of cry. I've never realized before how many different kinds there are. But this one, it is a silent cry, the cry, my cry, for another person, a kind of cry I thought was saved for old people.

Slowly it registers. I can see the realization take over my

mother's face, first in her eyes and then her twitching nose, then her frowning, trembling mouth. She puts her hand on my shoulder, and I let her keep it there.

I am glad my father looks at the floor, because I will dissolve into one million pieces if he looks at me. I will become air. When I was little, it was always my dad and me. Superman rides, raking leaves, me sitting on his lap, pretending I was the one driving the Volvo. But that was all before. It was before high school and it was before this. I am so far from there now.

No one says anything and then, to add to this joyous moment, Dr. Orlitz, the surgeon, comes in. He stands over my bed and sucks at the inside of his cheek, which makes a crazy-loud *tsk tsk* sound.

"It's going to have to come out." He flips my folder closed. "If not today, then tomorrow or the day after, but I can tell you, it's going to have to go." He touches one pudgy hand to his stomach, which is pudgy too.

Both my parents straighten, like they're meeting with my high school principal or some head of state.

"You can try all this." Dr. Orlitz points to the IV stand, which has a zillion wires coming off it, all connecting to balloons of medicine and liquid food. "And you *should* try everything," Dr. Orlitz says. "Everything. You're young, after all," he says.

"She is," both my parents say at the exact same time. "She is very young."

"Can I have a look?" He waddles over to my bed.

For anyone who's curious, when a surgeon says to you, *Can I have a look?,* what he means is, *I am going to touch you right now.*

He places his hands over my stomach and squeezes lightly.

I scream in pain.

"That hurt?" he says.

For real? I don't think I need to dignify that one with an answer.

"You see that?" He points at my stomach and looks at my parents. "Her stomach is getting very, very hard." He shakes his head. "You know what that means?"

Everyone is silent.

"It's not a good sign at all. It means the colon isn't functioning right. It could be getting toxic. If it explodes in there, it's going to be a real mess. Your daughter could die."

Inadvertently I cover my ears.

"Well, we don't think it's going to come to that, do we, Martin?" my mother says.

"They are finding new drugs all the time. We just have to hang in there," my father says, but I can tell he doesn't believe it.

"It might be a little beyond that." Dr. Orlitz, the *surgeon*, that *asshole*, gives me a look that says, We *know what's up, don't we?*

Stupidly, I grin back at him, because, after all, he's the doctor, and I do need him on my side.

He winks at me. "We're going to have to make some serious decisions," he says. "We wait too long and it *will* explode."

My mother sits down, and my father puts his hands on her shoulders.

"See you tomorrow." Dr. Orlitz grins my way like the villain mugging at the camera in the movies. "We have some serious decisions to make then."

———

So. Thelma is gone and the surgeon is unbearable and my father leaves and my mother stays, just reading the *Washington Post* silently, and here's the other unbearably terrible thing about Day Twelve. Connor doesn't come. The morning goes by and I can hear the wheels of the lunch carts whir and squeak by, but they don't stop here. I'm getting a new roommate, I'm told. And then I guess it's afternoon, after school, and what's worst about Connor not coming to see me is that I can hear him in the hallways, swooping in to all the rooms with his sunshine and his good cheer, and I hear old people laughing and the nurses greeting him and he doesn't stop here and there is no sunshine at all in here, just the surgeon telling me my life is about to be pretty much over.

For a moment I wonder why Connor doesn't come, but then I know why. It's that I told him about my gross disease, and he went home and Googled it and decided it was so disgusting, just thinking about it, that he couldn't even do his volunteering job with me. He is letting himself off the hook now so he doesn't have to be attached to some freak with an ileostomy bag in the real world.

My mom looks up from her paper just as I come to this realization. Maybe she can see it on my face, the way it must be crumpling like an old Coke can, ripped and ruined.

"Honey," my mom says slowly.

I nod. My throat is just stitched closed. I can't swallow or speak.

"It's going to be okay," she says. "The surgery, if it happens, and also after. It's just temporary, honey."

I don't care if that's what she thinks it is. I am trying to be me. I am trying to stay me, I mean. And stay funny and also keep my sadness inside away from my mother, who will want to take it and hold it and discuss it with me and also take it away from me. She is my mother.

I see her come toward me. This one time, the first time since we've been here in this horrible place just waiting for people to come in and steal my blood and prick me and prod me and tell me what the matter with me is and also be wrong, for the first time I let all of her come toward me, and I lean my head on her chest and I feel her arms around me, her fingers brushing at my hair, and I can't help it, I start crying. Weeping really. That kind of cry. I don't think I will ever be able to stop crying, and I am also thinking about Connor, who will never come back here, and Michael Lerner, who was never going to be more than a friend, and every boy who was supposed to love me back. I am crying for the past and also for what I don't know about even tomorrow.

I can feel my mother's arm. I smell her Yves Saint Laurent perfume, from the bottle with the deep-red top that has sat on her bureau for as long as I can remember.

"Mommy," I cry into her chest, and she holds me tighter.

"Mommy," I say again, and I realize now I'm saying it and I realize now that in all of this I am just a little girl, not like Thelma's kid, who I know doesn't have a mother now, but young, like I have never seen myself before, too young for this thing, and also alone. I am crying and crying and also I am hoping my mother will never let me go.

Day 13: Not Spain

I wait on Day Thirteen. I wait for the doctors to tell me what's going to happen to me.

And I wait for Connor. I want him to come far more than I want Dr. Orlitz with his cold, fat hands to enter the room and let me know my fate.

My mom hasn't arrived yet when I hear a tentative knock at our door and my tentative heart soars. Connor! Connor. He is back and he will tell me how he had to leave the hospital early yesterday and he would have texted me to apologize but I can't use my phone in here. Also, he doesn't have my number. I will tell him about Thelma. He will sit on my bed and stroke my gross, disgusting hair and he'll tell me that he can still see down, down and into the real me—or, no!, he'll say that he doesn't even have to see to the real me because the *this* me is great just the way she is.

I know this is not a likely scenario, but it could be. It could also be this: what will happen to me is so terribly awful that he will have to love me anyway.

The door opens. And then Collette comes padding in with her damn sneakers, soft as clouds, if clouds could squeak.

"Hi, darlin'," she says softly.

"Hey," I say, disappointment practically oozing from my pores. "Where's Thelma?" Just for clarity. I want to make them tell me.

She looks at me with a face that says what I know, and then she places some pamphlets on my swingy table and for a split second I remember Thelma spinning her wig, but I try to push it back. Collette fans the pamphlets out, and it looks like they are offering a choice of places I might like to visit. A Caribbean island! The beaches of Nantucket! Three days in beautiful Barcelona! I imagine eating pot after pot of paella, which we made in class once when we were studying the region in elementary school. I imagine sleeping in a castle. But soon enough I see these pamphlets do not offer the prospect of adventure and relaxation. The one on top says *About Your Ileostomy* in a font that makes it look like it's from the turn of the twentieth century. It says, *This booklet includes guidelines to help you care for your new ostomy at home. It's important to know that you're not alone. Thousands of people have ostomy surgery each year.*

"Why are you giving me these?" I look away from these pamphlets of doom and also from her.

"Just for you to take a look," Collette says. "Whenever you're ready. It doesn't hurt to be prepared."

I am curled up in a ball, just hoping that *How to care for your ostomy at home* will remain as foreign and far away as Spain is.

"Like I said," Collette says as she turns to leave. "Just whenever you're ready."

The door swings open—that seashell; the ocean—and then it is quiet again.

———

While I'm waiting for my parents to come in for the verdict, the phone rings and I can tell by the ring that it's Connor, that he has clearly managed to get the number from the nurses or—and I can't believe I didn't think of this earlier—he just called the regular hospital operator and got transferred here. Like a hotel. This is just a really, really crappy hotel.

"Hello?" I say, trying not to sound as eager and crazy as I am to talk to Connor.

"Hey, doll!" the voice—the girl's voice—says.

"Hey, Nora." I try to mask my disappointment and gather myself up. I can feel myself, gathering. The last time I talked to Nora was, like, ten days ago, but it feels as if it's been over a century. Like cars had not been invented when I got here.

"How are you?"

So sweet of her to check in on me, I think. I mean, it's only been a century. "I don't know, Nora," I say. "Not great. I might have to get surgery, like, tomorrow." I decide right then that I'm still not going to mention Connor. Even though I don't know if I'll ever even see him again, still I have the thought that maybe he could be mine. This is my armor. I want to keep it for myself, this feeling that is almost love and could be love, or what I think love would be if I had just one more minute with him. He could do one little thing. Tell me something true. It would just put me over that invisible line into love.

"Jinkies!" says Nora.

Seriously?

"I'm sorry, Lizzie," she says.

I nod, but of course she can't see me.

"Well, I was going to tell you some stuff, but it's kind of ridiculous now. I mean, you have real-life stuff. Like this primal life stuff."

I think I give out a laugh, but it is something different. "No. Tell me. I need something else to think about. Other than this primal life stuff." Apparently I will never stop wanting to torture myself. There is a word for that, isn't there?

"Okay, well, if you're sure."

"Yes," I say. "What's happening?" I want to know and I so don't want to know.

"Well." And it feels as if she is about to tell me this secret, only for me. This is why I have not turned the lights out on Nora. There is a way she will always have of making me feel like I am the only one. "I started stealing!"

"Stealing!" I say. "Stealing what? Why?"

"Lipstick and, like, different kinds of tights. And bras I try on underneath my clothes in the dressing room. Little things."

I don't consider myself a sheltered person necessarily, but I find this information both thrilling and shocking. "Why?" I say it very loudly.

"Because I can," Nora says. Her voice has gone from excited whisper to more like she's *decided* on something. "It's terribly wizard."

"Wizard." I have no idea.

"Good stuff," she says. "But I see it's not really that important right now. I'm gutted for you. Really."

"Okay then!" I say. I know I won't be in some dressing room

trying on bras to steal or buy. Even so, I don't get the fun of it, and I guess I realize I'm caught up on it being, like, *wrong*. Also? The British crap has got to stop.

"Also Angelo dumped me."

I guess we're done with the shoplifting talk. "Sorry," I say. "But I mean, bound to happen, right? Camp is over." I couldn't imagine Angelo in the real world, dressed in regular clothes. Or maybe board shorts with no shirt and Sanuks is regular clothes for Angelo. But I can picture Connor being absolutely anywhere. I feel I could teleport him to the moon and he would be charming and sweet and appropriately attired.

"Thanks a lot," says Nora. "I didn't know you were expecting this. Me being dumped."

"Well, I haven't spent a ton of time thinking about it, actually. I mean, sorry not to have called and told you my thoughts on your relationship with a screwed-up camp counselor with no eyebrows." I realize in this moment the freedom I have. I can say whatever I want. I can relax. No one can turn on an invalid. What would that look like? I realize I can find a way to feel powerful here.

"Of course, of course," Nora says. "I'm so sorry."

Ha! Nora is sorry. I take it further. "Yeah, well, maybe you should think about other people for once. In general, I mean. Not just with me."

Nora waits a beat, like she's not sure what she's hearing or that I've actually *defied* her, and she isn't sure how to react to this new phenomenon. "You're right," she says. "You're so right."

Power.

"When do you find out about the surgery?"

"Today," I say. "I should go, actually. My parents are here. Everyone is waiting for everything."

"I'm so sorry about what's happening to you," Nora says, and I know that she means it. I can't blame her. In fact, if it were me, I might do what Dee and Lydia are doing, which is kind of not doing anything. Their mothers sent really nice flowers. At least Nora has had the balls—the *bollocks*?—to call me.

"I'm sending you some music," she says. "Like on a CD. Old-school. To your house. Where I know you're going to be soon."

Suddenly I feel bad that I was mean to Nora, because I am filled up with gratitude. She is a hard friend to have, but she is also a real one. We have all these years behind us. Summer years, I think. That is a different kind of time. "Thank you," I say. "Can't wait to get it," I say, and I really mean it.

"Tell me what happens," Nora says. "Okay?"

"I will." I am getting used to talking about it without wanting to cry. I am hardening. And softening too. You can, it seems, get used to anything.

Nora and I say good-bye, and then I do what I always do here: I wait some more.

My parents are back, pretend-smiling so much I think I will die not from my exploding colon but from just having to look at them while we wait for the surgeon. My mother thinks that Dr. Orlitz just wants to cut everyone open. That he, like, gets some kind of commission or something. Here's what I think: just let him get it out and stick on that hateful bag and then we can all just go home.

Home. Lily pad, I think. Big and wide and floating in the sun. Just then, the phone rings again.

"Oh, hi!" I say to Connor. It's like I'm home, lying in bed, phone under the covers, volume low, waiting. It almost feels normal. *Everything* is almost. I cup my hand over the receiver like they do in old movies with old phones and I look at my parents, *hard*. For once they get it, and together they stand and together they leave.

"Okay, hi," I say. I try not to sound as excited as I am that he's called me.

"Hope you don't think it's creepy that I'm calling you," Connor says.

"Not at all," I say. I wonder where he is; I wonder about his room. Does he have posters? Are they of soccer players or surfers or bands or girls on sports cars? I'm really hoping it's not girls on sports cars, and I'm pretty sure it isn't.

"They connected me from the big hospital hub." He laughs. "There's still this whole cloak-and-dagger thing here. Like, I can't know your room number, even though I've hung out in your room."

"Nice to know I'm protected!" I say. But of course I'm not protected at all. Against anything.

"I was getting reviewed yesterday!" he says. "So they followed me around and made sure Verlaine was cool and that the patients were cool with Verlaine and me."

"Oh," I say. "How weird." I don't add about the *devastation* of hearing him in every room but mine. That would make me seem crazy, but that's what it was. *Devastating.*

"I thought it would be embarrassing to go to your room. Like maybe I haven't been the way I'm supposed to be with you."

He just said, when I'm *with you*, I think. Or something very close to that. I swallow. I wonder if he has a big room or a small room. What his window looks out onto. What color the walls are.

"Hello?"

"Sorry!" I say. And then I realize something. It's just our voices. He can't see me now, my gross dry skin or the hair that's starting to sprout on my cheeks from the steroids. I look like a hamster. So it's just us talking, the two of us, with only the usual inequality of me wanting him to like me and the possibility—probability—that he will not like me back. "I hope you got a good review."

"I don't know yet," he says. "I mean, you probably have bigger things to think about right now, but in case you heard me walking around, I wanted to tell you why I didn't stop by."

"Thanks," I say. "Yeah, I did hear you guys."

"I'm not coming in today. I've got to study, I'm so behind. What's going on in there?"

Without thinking, I blurt it out. "Thelma died!"

"Oh my God," Connor says. "I thought she was just getting chemo."

"I don't know. I don't know." I swing the swingy table back and forth, slowly. The pitcher wobbles. I only wish it was glass and that it would fall and shatter.

"Are you okay? About Thelma, I mean."

"I have no idea."

Connor is quiet for a moment, like it's that moment of silence at the Oscars for all the movie people who have died. "What else?" he says.

I tell him about Dr. Orlitz and his hands and I tell him about waiting to know and how sad I am for my parents and how jealous I have always been of Zoe, who is older and has a, umm, I drop the boyfriend part, but she's older and doesn't have a disease, and I tell him how stressed I am to miss school, I mean academically even, because I am into school, and I tell him how nervous I am that I'm going to be so behind. I tell him I'm a walking time bomb.

"I just really need to get the hell out of here," I say.

"I know. I mean, I like the hospitals now. They're these really safe places for me. They're where I see people I have come to . . . know so well. But I'm not sick or in pain or facing what you're facing."

He just *gets* it. I want to ask him if he thinks I am disgusting. I want to ask him how he feels in general about me. I almost feel like I could.

But I don't. "Yeah," I say. "It's kind of safe for me too. People are taking care of me, and my parents are here and not fighting in front of me, barely even bickering. It's nice in some ways, it's true." Why me, I can't help but think. Why has he chosen me?

"Sometimes I feel like outside of the hospital is the real prison part."

"But you get to go to school and go on walks with Verlaine and maybe drive to the beach or something. I want to get outside! What I would give to just be free for a minute from all this."

"I hear you. I don't like to drive," Connor says. "But yeah, our summer house is on the Eastern Shore. We used to call it the visiting house. It's close to DC, so my parents can go to and from more easily. I used to go sailing all the time there. Not anymore, though."

Duh, I think. Sailing.

"The only time I feel good is when I'm here. Like when I'm here with you, just for example. I don't have to be this person who's supposed to be all happy. Who I was before that accident."

"I understand."

"So, not sure if I actually said this, but she died," he says. "The girl."

"You did," I say. "You said."

"She was wearing a green dress," he says. "I never talk about this. I swear. It must seem like it's so normal for me, but it's not."

"It doesn't seem normal. I mean, it doesn't seem like you tell everyone. It seems totally normal, though. In the regular outside world, I mean. To tell people what happened. I'm sorry."

"This sounds so cheesy to say, but I feel like you're sick on the outside and I'm sick on the inside. No one can see mine. But it's really there," he says.

"Sick?" I say. "You don't seem sick."

"But I feel it," he says. "I don't know why or how I'm even having this conversation with you. But I guess for me the sick part and the conversation part is why, umm, I like hanging out there so much with you, I mean."

I cannot make my breath start again. He is telling me something important.

"You have this hard shell. Like what you were saying that first time we really talked. The angry part of you. But there's also this sort of soft inside part of you. It makes a person want to get to that inside part."

"What, like I'm an Oreo?" I say. I can't stop myself.

Connor is silent for a moment. "No," he says. "I didn't say that. But that is what I'm talking about."

For some reason I felt that until this moment that I could say and do anything. That everyone but me was unharmable. Like, how could I ever hurt this perfect boy? Before it felt like I was the only one who could get damaged here. Who could be wounded. But I can see now that maybe Connor could be hurt too. Maybe I'm not just his job, or some sick person he has to save, a dead girl he has to bring back to life. Because I'm here. I'm alive.

I don't need to be saved.

"Sorry," I say. I pick at an invisible stray thread on my gown. "I'm actually kind of sick inside too. I want to hide that."

"Me too," he says. "Blue inside. Guilty."

Blue inside. "Guilty?" I ask.

"Oh, I don't know. Also? You have fantastic eyebrows."

I laugh and run my finger along them, imagine it's Connor touching my face. I wonder what is really wrong with Connor, if what he's saying is true. If he's that sad.

"I think you're beautiful," Connor says. He sort of whispers it. He sort of coughs it. I think of his chewed-up fingers moving toward his mouth to cover it.

I want to believe Connor with every cell of me. That he could want me, now, later. But buried deep is also this: why is it always the girl waiting for the boy to tell her she's beautiful? Connor is lovely everywhere. I imagine even his blood is sun-kissed and windblown. And it seems like he might need to know that too.

But I don't say it. Because that's how it is: the girl waiting for the boy to tell her.

Connor says, "I do, Lizzie. I really, really do."

When my parents come back in, my mother says, "Well, don't you look like the cat who ate the canary."

We all laugh.

For some reason we are all sort of tinkling and popping and giddy and strange. We don't know anything bad for sure yet, and we are all exhausted, and I guess because I am light and smiling my parents feel it and they are happy too. They are smiling and holding hands. I'm propped up on my pillows, kind of rubbing my feet together like I used to do at night, right before falling asleep. That's when they all come in. The team. My team, which of course has nothing to do with hockey sticks and dribbling and making sure you're not offsides, but I guess there is still a goal.

Save the colon.

Dr. Malik and Dr. Orlitz and some others I don't know and some students I recognize and some I don't all stand at the foot of my bed in their lab coats, their arms clasped before them. They look like a string of paper dolls.

My father clears his throat.

Here we go.

Part 2

Day 13: Lite-Brite

The colon could not be saved. That's what the surgeon told us. Looking back, I see that moment as a frozen image. The paper dolls. My mother with her hands over her face. My father turning away from us both. I can't see myself. I can't remember what I thought or what I knew or who I was about to become. It was just the happiness of Connor's call and then the horror of this scene. Best and worst. Always, at the exact same time.

I'm not sure if the hospital gave us a private room, like some kind of frequent-flier or reward-club points for being there for so long and still having to get operated on, or if my parents ponied up the extra money, but finally I had both the window and the aisle. We moved to this room, and Zoe came in after school with a Lite-Brite and a deck of cards and some crappy magazines and she climbed into bed with me and we read about the worst thing that was happening to people, which was cheesy shoes or being photographed in see-through dresses. Zoe held my hand under the covers. I rested my head on her shoulder and slept a little bit, but at the end of that day, like at the end of all twelve of the days before it, everyone went home.

I watched them all leave. I looked at the Lite-Brite. *Sleep well,* Zoe had punched in the board before she left. It shone now—in all the colors—through the dark.

Day 14: The Lone Ranger, Alone

Did I think I was going to die? Or that my life as I knew it was ending? My life, *whole*. It makes me sad how scared I was and how hard I tried to pretend that I wasn't. I didn't know who I was about to be. I didn't know any of it, but I thought about it a lot that day, moments when my parents were downstairs in the cafeteria getting coffee, and the nurses were on break or busy or maybe they were just giving me a moment free of their pinpricks and blood pressure cuffs and checking line connections, and techs had just done everything there was to do. Being alone then just felt like everyone had given up on me. Just me and Zoe's magazines and that novel and crappy TV and the Lite-Brite, whose lights had all gone out.

Now, though, I know. How great would it be if we just knew the endings? Well, most of the endings. Even if they were awful. I suppose that's why people go to psychics. There weren't any setting up shop in the hospital, though you'd think they'd make a decent living visiting the sick and the dying.

But you can't know a thing about the future really, and I didn't know anything at all about mine, not even what would happen that afternoon.

That afternoon, Connor came. It was the first time I had seen him on his own. It was like the Lone Ranger without Tonto, though yes, I do realize that movie is totally racist.

"Hi, Connor," my mother said as he came in. "How are you, honey?" She seemed so tired and, well, resigned.

"I'm good, Mrs. Stoller, thank you!"

"Call me Daphne," she said.

I mean really? In all this, with all this?

"I was just going!" my mother said, and because they were in fact just going home for a few hours, it wasn't terribly mortifying. "We'll be back in later this afternoon, Liz," my mother said, turning to me.

It's funny how she called me Liz when she was being light-hearted and Lizzie when she was serious. It seemed like it should be the other way around.

"Okay," I said. "See you later." But I wasn't entirely happy to see them go.

I was, on the other hand, entirely happy-thrilled-amazed-delighted to see Connor.

He hovered by my bed and we both watched them leave. When they were gone, their voices fading in the hallway, he gingerly sat down. He set his backpack down carefully on the floor by my bed. He leaned in to me. His body was touching my body. It felt like I was being shocked in all the places our bodies met.

"So," I said. And then I told him about the surgery. That the colon could not be saved. The saving was finished. There would be no saving. What is the opposite of saving? This.

"Lizzie!" Connor said. He clutched my hand.

"It's okay," I told him. But it wasn't. It was, though, nice to offer comfort to someone else, even if it was comforting him about me.

I could see him swallowing back tears. I wondered if he was getting ready to book. I mean, who wouldn't want to run after hearing such a thing?

But instead of getting up to go, he leaned in closer. "Okay," he said, like he was now resigned, like he'd decided something. And then he came even closer. "I have an idea."

Day 14 Continued: Pumpkinhood

I estimated that we had about two hours before my antinausea medicine was finished. And the pain medicine too. Before the insane pain, as I called it then, would return.

The others packets were less important, and so I disconnected them. I had seen it done enough times. It was just a little plastic tubing coming out, and with a twist I was severed.

I was not thinking that I could barely stand on my own and that I was only good for about twenty minutes before something disgusting happened to me. I was only thinking about getting out of there with Connor.

I took the pouch of antinausea medicine and the pouch of pain med and placed them next to me on the bed. They were like water balloons. They didn't seem serious. And yet without them I basically turned into a pumpkin.

Considering these logistics made me not think of things like: Would I throw up? Would I need to go to the bathroom? Would I *make* it to the bathroom? All this fodder for potential humiliation got pushed way down as Connor waited in the hallway. I slipped on my jeans—enormous on me now—and a light sweater because I was always cold by then and I also wanted to hide the IV lines, which sprouted and bloomed out from my chest, evil stems. I carefully pulled the pouch through the arm of my sweater, cautious not to tug too much. My hospital bracelet got caught in the sleeve, but still I brought my hand and arm through it. I can do this, I thought, as I went to the closet and sort of toed my Converses. I kicked them over to the side of the bed near Connor's backpack, but I couldn't lean down to get them on, and then I got scared for the IVs and for a moment, I seriously doubted our plan. Connor's plan.

I don't know why I did it. I sat back down on the bed, out of breath. I was so . . . sick. That is just the word for it. And I don't know why when Connor looked in and asked if I needed anything, I told him yes. But I did tell him this and so he came in and he got down on his knee and put on my sneakers as if he were placing my feet into glass slippers. He held my heel and glided each foot in (which makes it seem as if it were easy, but those damn hospital socks, those plastic grips, they made the whole thing a lot less than graceful). He tied my shoes slowly, his head dipped in concentration as he ever so gently turned my laces into perfect bows.

Okay, I know *why* I did it, but I don't know how I did. I think it was like I became superhero strong, or for this single moment my sickness—my evil kryptonite—disappeared. My pain faded like invisible ink, like magic, and with it my fear. At my instruction, Connor took my L.L.Bean backpack from the closet, the one I'd taken to camp almost an entire lifetime ago, and I placed the balloons of medicine carefully inside. You could barely see the line connecting me to them; just two teeny plastic tubes.

And then he just walked me out the door. He managed to be casual, waving to the nurses, saying stuff like "That's great, Lizzie, you can do it," as he looked at the floor just ahead of his feet, indicating that was about as far as we intended to go. I saw Collette look up and turn her head for a moment, thinking, and then I saw her shake away her thoughts and turn back to her papers. Had she thought someone else had disconnected my lines? Was she just letting me go? Either way, Connor guided me, silently, his hand gentle but also sure at the small of my back, radiating heat, as we moved toward the elevator. It lingered there as we went *down down down* to the first floor. I was just so caught up in the moment I felt the opposite of pain and fear and sadness. Joy and happiness. Bigger than ever before. Big, big joy and no fear.

I was all adrenaline then. Or maybe it was just running on fumes. Whatever the case, for the first time ever I was outside in the real world with Connor.

It was a perfect day, weather-wise I mean, *great walking-around weather*, as my father would say. Sunny and not too warm, not too cold, not a cloud.

When we emerged from the lobby, the sun was blinding. Connor still had his hand on my back, still! I got the chills. Like in a shivery good way, not like all the shivering I'd been doing in the hospital. It was like that game Zoe and I once played where she would pretend to crack an egg on my head and make the pretend yolk drip down my neck. *Let the yolk drip down,* she'd say, her fingers along my scalp and neck, and I felt that same shivery weirdness now.

"Wait here one sec." Connor let go of me, and I watched him disappear around the corner.

I waited and started to feel myself begin to turn back into myself again. Cinderella at the ball, time ticking. A werewolf sprouting hair. I could feel the pouches swishing at the bottom of my pack now. I had like an hour and forty-five minutes left until they were done. I could manage without them—I wouldn't die or anything—but things would turn seriously . . . negative without them.

And then there he was, in a blue BMW as shiny as a bowling ball, pulling into the hospital drive.

He shot out of the driver's seat. "If I'd known this was happening when I'd parked, I would have paid for the garage." Connor laughed. He opened the passenger-side door for me, and then he bent down and brought my legs in as if I was suffering from polio or he was tucking me into a pre-pumpkin stagecoach, about to place a blanket over my lap to keep me warm for the cold journey ahead to the next kingdom.

Then he went back around and got in. He put one hand on the wheel, the other on the gearshift.

Of *course* Connor could drive stick.

Then he winked at me.

I cannot wink without looking like I'm having a stroke, so I just smiled instead.

And then we were off.

"So," I said. "Where are we going?" I tried to sound, I don't know, *game*, up for any adventure, but it came out too soft for that to be believed. I breathed heavily. I was losing my superhero strength, and my fear was swiftly returning, a train pulling into the station. Where *were* we going? And so where would we be when I went down, when I bent over in pain? Because, I suddenly knew, this would happen for sure.

Connor put a finger to the side of his mouth to illustrate that he was thinking. "Nothing too special." He smiled.

I saw his freckled fingers on the gearshift and I wanted to touch his hand. As if Connor had read my mind, he removed it for a moment and grabbed my pinkie. It felt like he *needed* my pinkie. His grip was urgent, and he braided his fingers with mine.

He extricated his fingers from mine to switch gears and then tied himself to me again.

I brought my free hand to my chest and felt the tubing of the central line. It was still connected, but I could feel the entry point getting irritated from all the jostling and from the weight of my cotton sweater. Connor kept driving, and I don't remember what we passed or any of it because what was happening for me was our hands.

That love I had for Michael Lerner? That was not love. That was intense like. That was crushing. But it was not this. It was nothing remotely like this.

Because Connor was coming to the other side. The side of loving me back. I could feel this *then*. And I couldn't say how or why then, but by the time we'd sped beneath a canopy of trees and slid into a dirt parking lot, he was mine. Of course that had been my wish. Always.

"Here's good!" Connor stopped the car and cranked the parking brake and got me out of the car—again with the legs as if he were transferring me to a wheelchair—and then he took my hand as if instead of putting me in a wheelchair, he was asking me to dance. Two pouches of medicines in my backpack, two IV lines coming out of my chest, a ticking clock, and I was a girl at the ball. I didn't need a gown. I thought I did once, but now I know you just need someone you love to take you by the hand.

Gently, he guided me over to the boathouse. Fletcher's Cove. It's part of the C & O Canal, built many, many years ago (how many? I have no idea), with two paths alongside the canal for donkeys to pull boats carrying cargo. This we learned on a school field trip.

"I sometimes come here on my own with Verlaine." Connor had his hand at my back as we walked ever so slowly down to the dock. "It's peaceful."

I couldn't even nod.

Boats rocked against the old wood, and I could see the trees and also us mirrored in the water. He went in and out of the boathouse briefly, and then we were headed to one of those bobbing rowboats.

I knew this was misguided as we stepped into the boat, just from the wobble of my footing, but I didn't care. I wouldn't have traded it in for *not* going, even though the truth was I couldn't and I shouldn't have and this was about to end and it was about to end badly.

Connor, the mind reader, said, "We're going to hug the shore. Just a little ride for a few minutes. To get the hospital off us.

Being on a boat used to always make me feel so much better."

This one with the sailing, I thought, as I gingerly sat down. I had become a girl who, skinny as a nail, sat down gingerly. Whodathunkit.

I looked up, trying not to be sick. Why did I look up? I have no idea. I was glad it was happening, that Connor had taken me away and that in that moment of taking me he had started to love me back.

We pushed off. I turned to watch the sun behind me, shining down in golden rays, when I felt the boat teeter a bit. Connor reached for me then. He turned me toward him and knelt down on the wet, leafy boat bottom, and then his hands were cupping my face, and then he was leaning down toward me and he kissed me. It was long and deep. It was like the movies, the two of us in this red rowboat, Connor's lips finally on mine. I could feel myself blushing as his hands brought my face closer, I was so happy inside. There is no other way to say it. And I wished that I would never have any other kind of feeling ever again.

My heart was in my ears. I was in the moment, and I felt all that happiness and newness and there was a terrible ringing in my ears that I refused to answer. It's not like I hadn't been kissed before, or hadn't kissed back, but this was different. I saw stars. It was just us in this small, special world. It was the kiss and it was Connor but it was also sickness and pain. And the world began closing in.

"I have to go." I pulled away when I realized the stars were not from happiness. They were not sparkly glitter stars. "We have to get back," I said. The boat was turning around. The leaves were swaying on either side of the canal and the sky above them was as blue as a robin's egg. The boathouse became a tiny pinprick. And then it all went completely black.

When I came to, Connor was carrying me out of the boat. I remember the boat rental person saying we needed an ambulance. "That girl is very sick," he said, and then I snapped awake and both Connor and I told him "No!" I was just fine. I remember getting into his car and then waiting and waiting, unable to speak, gripping the leather handle as we sped back to the hospital.

Where did Connor *go*? All I remember was being alone in the room with Collette. She stood over my bed, reconnecting my IV lines.

"I don't think you understand," she said. "I don't think you understand your situation here."

I swallowed. It made me feel nauseated again. As punishment for my five minutes in that boat, I was never going to live another moment without feeling as if I would puke.

"This could have been so serious. What on earth were you two thinking?"

"I'm sorry," I said. Why was I apologizing to Collette? "Where's Connor?"

"I understand," she said, acknowledging my statement but not my question. "And I won't tell your parents. Someone else might but I won't, which is just crazy, but you do need to know that was really, really stupid." I was all clicked in, all connected, a plug to a socket. I wanted to use my illness superpower, the power that let me say whatever the hell I wanted without consequence, but she was also keeping our secret, so . . . "I mean disconnecting your own lines! You could have had an embolism."

I didn't know what that was, and I didn't ask.

"Which, just so you know, is a blocked blood vessel. Which kills you. Boom," she said, smacking the curved part of her palms together. She had dark-purple nails with a layer of blue glitter over them. "Killed."

So now I knew.

That was when I heard the other nurses greeting Connor. Connor, they said with none of their usual enthusiasm. Hello. That's when I realized Connor wasn't going to have a job here anymore. Collette might not tell my parents, but everyone else here knew. There would be no more Verlaine and Connor making this place a better, more livable world.

Soon there was a knock on the door.

"Hello?" Connor peeked his adorable head in. His face. His freckled face. His face with the lips I had just kissed.

"Hello, Connor," Collette said grimly.

He bowed his head. It was like his whole body was apologizing. When he looked up, he looked at me and his face changed. I couldn't decode what he was telling me or what he was exactly sorry about.

"I left my backpack?" Connor said.

I felt then the familiar fear that getting his backpack was the only reason he'd come to my room, that I'd been wrong and he had not come to the other side at all but had in fact been unmoving on the non-love side of things. Perhaps that kiss had only been a way to tell me good-bye.

But I smiled meekly. And in my smile I was totally, subversively happy about our day. I hoped he saw that.

"By all means." Collette mock ushered him in. "You do know, though, that this girl has a very difficult day ahead of her tomorrow. I expected more from you, Connor. Really."

Oh God, the I-expected-more-from-you tack. That was almost as bad as the bad-judgment tack that might have been utilized here were it my mother speaking.

"I know," he said. "I was just trying to help. Her mood, I mean." He looked at me, hopefully, and in that moment I realized Connor really had no idea. And yet I would have followed him anywhere.

Collette slipped out the door, and then Connor went to stand at the side of my bed. His hands rested on its bars, which were up now, a prison cell. He rocked back and forth, toe to heel, heel to toe.

"God," he said. "Can you believe we got you out?"

Really? I thought. This is the takeaway? But what I said was, "I can't." I looked out the window. I was starting to feel the embarrassment of the day move through my body. Shame. My crippling kryptonite.

He moved to the other side of the bed and crouched down. And then he unzipped his backpack and gingerly removed something from inside.

It was a Tupperware container filled with liquid.

"This is only going to get us in more trouble," he said, standing. I heard his knees creak and crack. "But I brought you something. I had it for you earlier."

What was it? I craned my neck to look closer. WHAT HAS CONNOR BROUGHT ME! WHAT IS IT? WHAT IS IT? I thought. And then I saw it. The little, well, legs I guess, frantically doggy-paddling the water. A tiny head strained from beneath a hard green shell.

"A turtle!" I gasped. It was so teeny I could have fit it like a quarter in the center of my palm.

"Shhh." Connor put a chewed-up finger to his lips. "I got her to keep you company," he said. "But obviously they're not allowed in here."

Was he crazy? Not even Nora so blatantly broke rules. Or maybe he was just lovely.

I sat up a little and looked into the container, squinting at the turtle. It was so green, and it looked like it was outlined in gold. With a little snake face, its contoured eyes made it look as if it were wearing a mask, it looked so determined to swim. I stared at it through the cloudy plastic.

"No, you have to leave it!" I said.

"I think it's a she," Connor said. "And you need to keep the container open. She won't last long in there, but you'll be out in a few days, and then you can get a tank for her at home."

I slid the top off and looked in at the turtle. The shell had these striations of gold and a tile-like pattern, like the wallpaper of those French kings we read about when studying the French Revolution. "Thank you." I looked up at Connor. I thought of all he had done for me that day. Or tried to do. I mentally scanned the room for a place to hide the turtle.

"She's just hatched," Connor said. "I was getting Verlaine

some pig ears at the pet store and I saw a bunch of these. They reminded me of you."

I didn't know what to think of the fact that I reminded Connor of a reptile. "It could be a he, though." Why do we always refer to animals as he? Unless it's like a lioness or a mallard, it's usually a he.

"I wonder what's beneath her shell. I wonder who she'll grow into. Like I said, she's just hatched."

I could see the turtle's itty-bitty nails. I imagined peeling back the shell and seeing what was beneath. I'm still not sure how you tell if a turtle is a boy or a girl.

"I'm going to call her Frog." Can you dissect what's under a turtle's shell? I remember thinking this.

Connor shrugged. "Sounds good to me," he said. He didn't ask why. "She's yours. To keep you company."

"Thanks, Connor." I wondered then if he liked when I said his name after a sentence as much as I did when he said mine. "I love her," I said.

He took the Tupperware and sort of set the blue top over it and then he opened the drawer by my bed. He carefully placed Frog inside it. "I'll leave her there," he said. "Okay?"

"Okay," I said.

I heard my mother greeting the nurses. "What?" she said. "Did something happen?"

I braced myself, but nothing happened.

"Everything's fine!" I heard one of them say.

That said, I knew my mother could just open the drawer and find Frog there. But I didn't want to let her go.

"Hi!" my mother said, opening the door.

"One minute, Mom!" I said. Did no one knock? *Ever?* Suddenly I felt breathless. Connor was leaving. And tomorrow morning I would get wheeled away and into the operating room. Dr. Orlitz would be ready and waiting. I imagined a butcher knife in his fat hands; it would be a horror movie I would never be able to watch, not even the preview.

My mom disappeared, but I could hear her waiting. You can hear my mother smiling and you can also hear her waiting.

"I guess I have to go," Connor said. But he still stood there. "Hey, can I get your number?"

I had to laugh. I gave him my number, and Connor punched it into his phone.

"I'm calling you now," he said.

"No phone." There had been a brief moment today in the car with Connor when I'd remembered and, if I'd had it on me, heavy in my hand or my pocket, I could have finally used it, but mostly I loved the emptiness. The way no one could contact me.

"Well somewhere, wherever it is, it is getting my call," Connor said.

"Hello?" he said. "Lizzie."

I looked at him talking to a me that wasn't there.

"Voice mail," he mouthed, pointing at the phone.

"Well, this is Connor," he said. "The guy from the hospital? The guy with the cute dog? Call me sometime." He clicked off his phone and grinned at me.

It felt amazing on this side, this other side of love, and then I felt that horrible aloneness again, like I was in some big, dark void. Is that what it's like for everyone, even those girls who won't turn into hideous freaks to the boys they love? What it felt like on this side was: wonderful and terrifying. Breathtaking.

"Okay," I said.

He grabbed my hand. "Let's pretend we were never here," he said, and I remembered him telling me that before, when we'd gotten back from our first walk outside the room together, just three days ago. But in hospital days, it was a lifetime. And now, Connor leaned down and kissed me on the cheek.

It happened so fast. I didn't get to kiss him back or to thank him, or to even just say how much he'd done for me in that place. Because then he was gone.

Just gone.

And then, almost instantly, my mother shot inside my room.

"You okay?" she asked brightly.

I couldn't look at her. I remembered walking outside with Connor, and for a moment, it was just us. That was the reason we left.

I nodded. "Just a minute, okay?" I said.

I heard the ocean call of her going back into the hallway, and only then did I bring myself up to sit. Again, that makes it sound easy, but it was not easy. The day had nearly ruined me. I didn't know it then, but it would be awhile before sitting was easy, before moving in my body was normal again. I thought I knew so much already, but I didn't know anything then. Nothing.

I sat up and I leaned over and opened the top drawer of my bedside table. I slid the top off so Frog could breathe. I looked down and watched her struggle, even in the smallest stretch of space.

Hard shell or soft center. Which is the best way? This I know from biology class last year: a turtle dies without his shell. Her shell. That, I remember.

I thought of the frog heart, the way it jumped beneath my hands during our dissection, and I didn't know what the next morning would bring, or what would come after, or after that, but I did know now that somehow my heart would miraculously keep beating.

Cutting

I remember Collette cutting off my hospital bracelet four days after the surgery. What would that have been? Day Twenty? Day Twenty. I was like a dog freed from her leash. But it was also like I didn't *need* the leash. Like I was going to be fine on my own. I left it there on the swingy table, along with that horrid plastic pitcher and the plastic blue box with these three Ping-Pong-like balls I was supposed to raise up by sucking in air ten times an hour to keep the fluid out of my lungs. I didn't look at my IVs, the connections dangling from the stand like alien tentacles.

Zoe had taken Frog home, and I left everything else. Pulled back my thin, unwashed hair in an elastic band, tugged on my way-too-big jeans, tied my Converses, walked into the hallway, and waved good-bye.

I was so weak and stooped over from all the incisions, but I was so strong.

I could feel the bag pulling at my stomach, a mysterious tug as I stepped into the elevator with my mother. I had been on the twelfth floor. Who knew? I don't recall ever noticing, I thought, as I walked out of the hospital and into the sun. My father was waiting there, the car idling in the circular drive, like he was picking us up from a hotel. I wanted to drive, and I did have my learner's permit after all. It was the oddest thing how much I wanted to drive, but even I knew I was too weak, that if anything happened, I didn't have the reflexes to prevent an accident.

"Can you imagine?" my mother said when I brought up the idea. "After all this?"

Yes, that made me think of Connor. Every time I got into a car after leaving the hospital, I thought of Connor watching a car crash, over and over again. It was good, I thought, to think of someone else for once. So: I tried to be in Connor's head for a moment, seeing the world as he saw it, watching that girl die like that. And then, as my mother helped me into the front seat where she thought I'd be most comfortable, I tried to see me through Connor's eyes. Here he is watching me put on my seat belt, here he watches me buckle it, so carefully, my stomach still stapled. It's all I can do to sit up straight. So what does he see? Someone who is leaving way different than when she arrived. It's like I was in transition, not yet hatched, waiting to be this new fixed and damaged me.

I thought of Connor watching me pull up to my house. My house! I had left it before camp, in *July*. It was almost mid-September, already fall, and my father's rhododendron had already flowered, petals fallen, and waxy leaves flanked the house, along with the flowerless little branches of the azalea bushes. Zoe came outside, pulling the door shut behind her, just after Mabel ran out barking wildly in the front yard. I got out of the car, slow as an old person. After the surgery, my stomach hurt differently. It was like a wound now, something healing, becoming a scab that is becoming a scar. I ignored the crinkling of the bag and the fear I would always carry that it could come undone.

I focused on the healing part, on being out of that hospital with its smells and its sounds and the needles and thermometers and the heart monitor I was hooked up to after the surgery. I focused on the surgery being over, not on the pain of waking up from it. I focused on Mabel, moving toward me, her ears swinging, her dog smile and dog sounds.

"Mabel!" I bent down with considerable discomfort and let her lick my face. "Mwah!" I said. "Mabel!" I could still be a vet, I was thinking. If I got super into physics (this year) and dissecting the fetal pigs, which were next year's victims, maybe I could do it.

That's when I saw him, his red-blond hair catching the afternoon light, as if a halo hovered above him. He had on his wrinkled jeans, a frayed blue-and-white-striped oxford, unbuttoned, a Sunshine House T-shirt peeking out beneath. My jeans were so loose on me, and I pulled them up as I placed my hand over my eyes to shield them from the sun.

Bright, glowing Connor. In a surf shirt.

"Welcome home," he said, helping me to my feet.

My mother got out of the backseat and gave a hard look to Zoe.

"What?" she said. "He just showed up here."

Everyone looked at Connor, including my dad, who, feigning exhaustion, sort of threw himself across the car hood that ticked with heat.

Connor smiled. How can I describe it? Cockeyed, charming,

devilish, mocking, sweet. Cocky. All in one boy's crooked smile. "Hi."

My mother inhaled deeply. "Connor," she said. "Darling. We have to get Lizzie settled in. We've just arrived, as you can see. You have to give us some time."

He nodded quickly, swallowing. "Can I just take a minute with Lizzie? I'm sorry," he said. "I'm so sorry to barge in like this."

I saw my mother go from really hard to really soft in one moment. "Of course," she said. "We'll just be inside."

My family walked up the steps and into the house. I sat down on the steps and scratched Mabel's soft scruff. Connor said, "Why, hello, Mabel!" and then he sat down next to me and I felt like I'd known him forever.

"I wanted to see you outside of that place."

I nodded. It felt like we were now equal. I was dressed, for one, and upright, but also I felt different. I leaned my head on his shoulder. Because I wanted to. It was as natural as breathing. I breathed.

He shook me off him. "Hey, so, I just wanted to see you, okay? I'm just saying."

I looked at him. His eyes were so blue, but they were very far away. It was almost like I could see clouds passing across them. "Okay." I righted my head.

"I have to go now," he said. "Anyway, your family is waiting."

"That's okay," I said. "They understand."

"I have to go," Connor said. That's what Connor Bryant, on my front steps, said.

"Go where?" I looked straight ahead at the Dominicos' house

across the street. They had painted their shutters green while I'd been gone.

Connor kissed my cheek and got up. "I'm going. I just have to go."

I could hear his keys jingling, the key chain twirling around his finger, as he walked down the drive.

I touched my cheek. I did! Wait for me, I thought, my heart in my throat.

Before I'd even said hello, Connor was telling me good-bye.

Girl Groups

Everything changed then. All my good feelings. All my power. Who was I to say I didn't need my bracelet, a leash? Okay, the colon was gone, but who was going to save *me* now? *Save me save me save me*, was all I thought as I struggled up the stairs to my bedroom. Well, save me and why me. *Why me why me why me?* I felt that power drain out of me, like I was an old car leaking oil onto the road.

I heard my father at the bottom of the stairs, and I knew he was looking up to me, both hands on the banister. I was sixteen years old and I was winded when I reached the top.

I went into my bedroom and shut the door.

My room. That hideous blue, those purple venetian blinds. *Zip.* I opened them. The sound like the Velcro of the blood pressure cuff. Dust motes in the light. A *Moonrise Kingdom* poster hung lopsidedly on the wall across from my bed. My Velvet Underground banana poster.

Two twin beds. One I slept on, a headboard slapped with stickers I couldn't remove. Hello Kitty. Butterflies. Orphan Annie. Also the Beatles and Wonder Woman and dancing bears. The string of dusty lights I hadn't yet turned back on. The other bed, covered in old teddy bears and ugly dolls I couldn't, for some reason, throw away. Because I'd once loved them? Perhaps. I threw the new one from the hospital on the heap as well.

My little bag from the hospital had been unpacked. David B's God's eye was on my desk, laid there sweetly by my mom. She had also fanned out the pamphlets from the hospital on my bed. *About Your Ileostomy: Guidelines to Help You Care for Your New Ostomy at Home.* So there won't be paella or nights asleep in Spanish castles, I thought.

Frog was there too. Zoe had taken good care of her, and she had this big tank on my desk, and a heat lamp, and I could see her hiding beneath one of the fake ferns.

"Hi," I said, peering in.

She slammed into her shell.

"Okay then, bye." I backed away to get a better view.

My phone! Someone had taken it out of my camp stuff where I'd been storing it, uncharged, and I plugged it into my computer. I felt that almost long-ago buzz of it charging, which instead of making me happy and relieved, made me anxious. How many messages? How many ways would I have to tell people what had happened to me? This was also why Connor was so important. He had been on the moon with me. Why hadn't he just left me there?

I heard a soft knock at the door. "Honey?" my mother said. "Are you okay in there? Do you need . . . help?"

I closed my eyes. For a while, but again, not like I was going to speak and close my eyes. I will always despise that. "I'm good, thanks," I said.

"Is *it* okay?" she asked.

I knew she meant the bag. I think she wanted to see it. But that was never going to happen.

"It is, Mom," I said. "I am."

I could still hear her hovering.

"I'm just getting settled here," I said. "I'll be downstairs soon." I'm not going to lie: the thought of walking down those stairs was daunting.

I heard my mother pad away and then I opened my Mac. As I turned it on, I took a moment to praise myself for having it password protected, and made my way in. (Mabel 1/2/05— anyone could have figured it out.) There I was. There we were: Dee, Lydia, and me on a class skiing trip last year. It was the last time we'd do a thing like that; we were too old now. I think we were too old then, too, but I still remember the hum of the bus wheels beneath us while we sat on the bus together, me across the aisle from them. In the back row two couples were making out, and someone was passing around a bottle of Coke that was also half rum, but we were only listening to music and braiding one another's hair and talking shit about Nelly R, who had hooked up with someone's boyfriend that weekend. We were so stupid then. And Lydia still had her braces. My hat had a pom-pom on top.

While I waited for all the news of the real world to pummel me, I shuffled through the mail on my desk. There wasn't much; my mom brought most of the stuff I'd be into to the hospital, but she'd left the brown envelope from Nora that said: *Do Not Open Until Home* blazoned in red across the back. I opened it. *For the strongest girl,* Nora had written with a silver metallic Sharpie on the plastic of the old-school CD case. She'd pasted a picture of a woman cut from a magazine, overly tanned, with pumped-up muscles in muscle-woman position on the song list folded inside.

Nora.

I slipped it into my computer, which sucked it in like it was starving. And then: "Close your eyes, give me your hand, darlin'. Do you feel my heart beating." I had to smile. Girl bands. We listened to them at camp when we were campers, hairbrushes and pretend beehives, jumping from bed to bed.

Girl bands.

I unfolded Nora's handwritten song list. The Supremes, 7 Year Bitch, Sleater-Kinney, Spice Girls, the Go-Go's, TLC, Sister Sledge, the Bangles, Le Tigre, Say Lou Lou.

Nora.

I turned the song list over: *Girl Groups: Because no one can do it alone,* Nora had stenciled. She'd drawn these really delicate birds and butterflies and also these skull and crossbones, a string of dancing bears.

This was what I thought then: there are different ways to be saved. There are the doctors and the nurses and the parents and there is the boy who comes and sweeps you off your feet and then there is the girl who comes and lies on your bed with you and tells you everything, makes it seem all her secrets are only for you. Who cares if they actually are? You can't do it without the girl. Without a girl. So I ask you: How could I ever turn off the lights here?

———

Downstairs I could hear the clank and crash of my parents making dinner together, crab cakes and baked potatoes, my favorites. I had just started eating solid foods—it had begun with broth and Jell-O and then rice and then a vegetable or two. It all seemed to be working. It. It seemed to be okay.

But Connor was gone. He had left.

I opened my closet, to face the mirror hanging on the door. How many hours had I spent in front of this mirror? Leaning in, learning how to put on eyeliner. Backing up to see if a skirt was too short because before all this starvation stuff, my thighs were never an asset. How many times had I changed and changed and changed? I wanted different clothes and better clothes and cooler clothes, and I wanted to be thin and easy in my skin and casual in everything, but I was not that. Now I could see the faint smudge that had once been Dee's lip gloss kiss.

I stood back. I could see all of me and I was tiny. My jeans folded over at the zipper, so much extra fabric. I'm not going to lie: I liked being that small. I liked feeling like I had slipped into these jeans, a delicate, pedicured foot into a glass slipper, as opposed to the way I had to force myself into them at camp, like a rag-wool-socked foot being shoved into an old muddy duck boot.

Who wouldn't rather wear a glass slipper? If you were going to the right place, anyway.

But it was the first time. The first time there was a full-length mirror with me alone in front of it.

I did it: I unbuttoned my jeans and let them fall to my ankles. My hip bones jutted out and my stomach sank in. But that's not what I saw. What I saw—all I could see—was the bag, which hung just to the right of my belly button. It was just a regular plastic bag, stuck to me. One end of it was tucked into the Gap boy shorts my mom had brought to the hospital. When I lifted up my T-shirt, I could see the top of it, to where the small intestine came out of my stomach—the stoma—and into the bag. There were so many powders and tapes and creams and flanges I would need to change it and make sure it didn't get irritated or open unexpectedly, but I'd had to deal with none of that then. All I had was the visual, and it looked so not a part of me. Of myself.

Sleater-Kinney screamed out from my computer. "Why do good things never wanna stay? Some things you lose, some things you give away."

I dropped my T-shirt and the fabric covered it. It was almost, for a moment, like the bag was gone. I pulled up my jeans, buttoning them carefully so as not to jostle anything. I felt the staples of my incision against the rough denim.

"Lizzie?" my mother called up, like I had been here every night, my mom calling me down to set the table or peel these carrots or grate this cheese. "Lizzie!"

I opened the door and Mabel was seated outside, quietly, waiting.

"I'm so sorry!" I said, bending down with considerable effort to pet Mabel. I'd had no idea she'd been waiting for me. "I'm coming," I called down, shutting my door and picking my way slowly, gingerly down the stairs.

The smell of alcohol and urine and starched sheets, the scent of the hospital I only now realized I'd been smelling for just about three weeks, was gone. Here was garlic and butter and chives and vinegar.

"Okay!" I said, walking into the warm kitchen. "Here I am."

Peel Back the Skin . . .

That first night I woke up all night expecting fluorescent lights and thermometer probes, and I was met instead by Mabel on my legs, snoring. That morning a plant arrived from Dee's mother, who had driven me to and from soccer practice for all of fifth grade when my mother was at work, that said, *We are all wishing you well!*

Really? I thought. Another plant? I had no idea what I wanted, but I did not want another plant.

"This looks nice," my father said, rubbing the waxy leaves between his fingers.

"Take it." I shoved it in his direction.

He looked up at me then, pausing. "Okay, Liz," he said. "I'll plant it in the garden."

Dee texted me all day that first day I was home. *How are you when can we see you do you want to go to the movies to see some music?* I wanted to do none of those things. *Family time,* I wrote back. *Family, family.*

But there was nothing from Connor. Not the first day or the second or the one after, on all the days where I sat in my room and did my homework and got caught up and watched *Party of Five* reruns in my parents' room and just listened to music. I binged on *Animal Planet* and *Teen Wolf* and *Friday Night Lights*. Also *Gilmore Girls* and *Daria*. Old stuff like that made me feel so old and ahead of my time. My mother, who had taken time off work to be home with me, brought me lunch upstairs that whole first week.

It was maybe my fourth day back and she came upstairs, a plate of scalloped potatoes and chicken left over from dinner the night before wobbling on a wicker tray. But truth was, the onions from the potatoes didn't agree with me—which meant they didn't agree with *it*—and so I had gotten scared to eat. Also, just putting these four days of solid food in me was already making me gain weight. I needed to, but I'm just saying, it was happening.

"What?" she said as I dragged my fork through the food. She rubbed my legs and I let her. "No good?" she asked.

"It's good. I just can't eat all this stuff yet."

"I know," she said. "I'm just trying to make up for all that time without real food in the hospital. But maybe we should just go back to beef broth and Jell-O. What do you think?"

I gagged at the thought.

"Hey," she said. "I hate to do this again, but we have to talk about getting you out. We have to talk about you seeing your friends again and getting back to school. And walking, Liz. You need to be walking now."

"My friends?" This was what I chose to focus on. "I don't know, Mom," I said. I wanted her to ask about Connor, and also I really didn't want her to ask. Before all this, she might not have even known about some guy I liked. She had no idea about Michael L for instance, though there was a period in ninth grade where I talked to him every night for hours. Literally. Half the time he talked about Rachel P and Tracey B, and all the things he wanted to do to them, but this was how it was. Friends. I had come in as a friend and I was going out as one, if that. Friends. Say it enough out loud and it sounds so awkward on your tongue.

"Nora might be coming," I lied, sort of. Though we were emailing—she didn't email in British really—to find a time for her to visit, it wasn't going to be this weekend.

"Really."

"Hmm," I said.

Nothing from Connor. No news. He wasn't on Facebook, and I confess I looked for him there. He didn't seem to be online at all. It was like he'd never walked here on earth. Like I'd dreamed him up. I held my phone close, all the time. It was back, and I hated it but I knew I needed it because it connected me. To the possibility of Connor. But the connection was cut now. Whatever you want to name what it was we had, what we were, it was gone now. He didn't call.

I listened to his voice mail. A lot.

Hello, Lizzie. His voice.

The guy with the cute dog.

Hello, Lizzie.

Hello, Lizzie.

Hello, Lizzie.

What was he trying, all these times, to tell me? Once he'd told me: We were never here. I had been too dumb to realize that this meant we would never have met. If we were never here, we were also never there. And so we would never meet again.

How many times, how many ways could we say good-bye? "It will be nice to see her."

Who? Oh yes, Nora. Sure.

My mother gave me a last pat on the knee. "Mabel needs a walk, and maybe, just this once, it can be someone else who takes her."

I nodded. "Got it," I said, moving the potatoes around on my plate. Just because I knew I shouldn't eat them didn't mean I wasn't dying for them. I was so hungry then.

The guy with the cute dog, he said to me, over and over. *Hello, Lizzie,* he said. *Hello.*

Hello.

So: that first week home I tried to eat; I tried to avoid getting up; I tried not to think about Connor. I tried to catch up. And I trolled every social media site I knew to find out what was going on with everyone. Did you know everyone was amazing? They looked amazing and they went to amazing places and they did amazing things there and they ate the *most* amazing things with their amazing friends and amazing boyfriends. You know who wasn't amazing? Me.

You know what was better than looking at everyone else's amazingness? Petfinder. All the beautiful dogs no one wanted. I couldn't bear it, but I couldn't help it. The pit bulls everyone thought were aggressive, the beagle who was too old, the Lab with three legs, the matted puppies rescued from mills. I can't explain even now the way those animals hurt my heart. And I really couldn't stop looking.

I was coming off all the steroids and pain meds and my hair was growing back and my face was getting back to my face. After I got my staples out, I could stand up straighter. But what did it matter, really, I thought, with all these sick, sad dogs and Connor gone?

Tim was really sweet. Sometimes he'd stop by my room on the way to Zoe's and lean in the threshold, wave, ask me if he could drive me anywhere. "I wish I could help you get better," he said, and it was so nice I couldn't bear that either.

I listened to Birdy. Basically, I tortured myself, and if there was a soundtrack to that torment, it was Birdy.

Birdy. It's just that it's the words, the sound, the girl. The feeling. Just over and over and over: "Where I am (A stranger with your door key explaining that I am just visiting.) Where I am (And I am finally seeing why I was the one worth leaving.)"

Oh! And I finished *Wuthering Heights*.

The first weekend I was home, in mid-September, Dee-Dee and Lydia called to ask if they could come over. What could I say? Sorry, I'll be out at the beach? And so I watched from the window as Dee's mom dropped them off—that same Toyota Camry we drove to soccer in—and they came bopping up the front stairs. They whispered to each other and straightened their cardigan sweaters and swung their hair as they rang the doorbell.

"Girls!" My mom was so excited to see them. "Dee and Lydia are here!" she cried up to me, as if I didn't know it was them.

I don't know why I didn't go to the living room before they came, because everyone turned to watch me as I walked down ever so carefully, clutching the banister. Their smiles, which had been so real at seeing my mother, changed. I could see them holding on to them, their eyes wide. Why me? I thought. Why the hell did this happen to me?

What did I look like to them? Did I still look like Birdy? My hair was not as thick, but it was still long. I had a cold sore on the side of my mouth, I know that. My immune system was just shot. And while my face looked a lot better to me, I imagine to them it looked a lot larger than before, rounder. My eyes were puffy. I was twenty pounds skinnier.

"I made it!" I said, as I hit the bottom step. "Hi!" I tried to steady my breath.

For a moment they just stood there. Dee-Dee all WWRW (What Would Rizzo Wear) style, had on a yellow pencil skirt and a purple cardigan. I half expected her to pull out a cigarette and burst into song. And I had no idea what the hell Lydia was up to. Her hair had once been really cute and natural, and now it looked like she'd curled it into ringlets or something. She also wore a ton of eyeliner, and it was all smudged. She kind of looked like one of the poor children hanging out in the dirty pub in *Les Misérables*, which I'd seen with Nana at the little theater near her house in Florida. *Our little bit of culture in the sun,* she'd called it.

Then, as if someone had prodded them with a hot iron, both of my friends leaped forward. "Hi!" Dee went in for a hug, as lightly as she could. I had become so fragile. I could tell that was what they saw.

Lydia had a big bag with her and she set it down, also hugging me softly.

"Poor Lizzie," she said, pouting. "Poor thing." I pictured her without all that makeup, zipping in and out of the orange cones on the hockey field. Lydia was always the fastest one.

What is it about young people trying to sound like old people? I mean, we are teenagers, I thought. How can she be talking like this?

My mom ushered us over to the couch. "Something to drink, you guys?" she asked. She was beaming. Her face was like throwing sunbeams.

"Thank you, Mrs. Stoller." Lydia crossed her legs. "Do you have Diet Coke?"

Well, Lydia just lost a lot of points there. Did she not remember that *Mrs. Stoller* was against soda? Like, full-on against it. And I couldn't drink it now anyway. The bubbles. Don't ask.

"Nope," my mother said. "No soda in this house. How about some lemonade?"

My friends agreed on a lemonade, and then Lydia reached into the bag.

"So," she said. "We have stuff from school, which your mom asked us to bring. We've got your assignments from English, your physics textbook, your Algebra Two textbook."

"Algebra Two," I said. I mean, Algebra I had been enough for me. "Physics." It had been a stretch when I'd registered for it, and now, even with this new prospect of vethood, it just seemed ridiculous.

"Sorry," Dee-Dee said, probably realizing how depressing a

math textbook would be for me. "Okay, so other things." She bent into the bag. "A card from all of us. Everyone signed it," she said, handing over a sealed envelope. "And this is from your hockey team." Also a card.

"Not my hockey team now," I said.

Everyone squirmed.

My mother brought out the lemonade, and then she went upstairs to her study to work.

"And this," Dee said, holding something at her chest and smiling at me coyly, "is from Mr. Michael Lerner." She handed me a little white box.

What would I have once done for a teeny-tiny box from Michael L? But now? I mean, was it a lifeline? A turtle? Was it even alive? That, I now knew, had nothing to do with love.

I set it aside.

Dee-Dee looked at me, dumbfounded.

"What?" I said. I looked back at her.

"Open it!" she said.

I did. It was a little dangling heart necklace. It was sweet and very Spencer's or Laila Rowe, from our mall.

"So sweet!" Lydia said, falling backward on the couch.

I closed the box and placed it on the wooden coffee table in front of us. How could it mean so little to me now? It just sat there with the magazines and books scattered all over the surface. Just another thing. A thing that was not from Connor.

"Hey, so, some news," Dee said. She told me about a tree catching fire in the quad, a friend I'd been close with in elementary school who was moving away, the fight for green vegetables for lunch.

"And homecoming," Lydia said, leaning forward. "It's soon."

Dee-Dee nodded.

"Don't care," I said. "At. All."

They looked at me, and I will say it was sort of blankly. Did they do anything separately now?

"I mean, do you guys *care* now?" I asked. Our freshman year we had laughed about the whole thing. King Queen Prince Princess. It was all so ridiculous and petty, and the prize never went to the right person. Even when there was some interesting or weird choice, like, I don't know, the *chess* champion, or the girl who everyone loved despite her eye patch, it always seemed pretty misguided.

"I don't know," Dee-Dee said. "Well, there's also hockey? There's a home game that weekend too."

"Don't," I said. "I can't even."

"Can't even what?"

"That was the end of my sentence, Dee."

They were both silent, fidgeting in their seats.

"Anyway," said Lydia. "We're older now. It's kind of fun. I mean, who do you think it could be this year? For queen, I mean. Who do you think?"

I felt the tug of my bag and the tickle that tells me something is going into it.

"Also, I do have a pretty big part in the play this year. Just saying," Dee-Dee said.

Lydia nodded. "She really does, Lizzie. Can you believe?"

"It's very cool, Dee, about the part. But I don't know," I said, both hands on my knees. "Maybe it's just that I've been in the hospital for, I don't know, like, three weeks and then, like, I don't know, had a vital organ chopped out of me, but I really, really don't care."

They sat up straight and silent.

And I will admit now that for a fleeting moment I thought, I *could* get the pity vote. Perhaps I could be princess. . . .

I could hear my mother shuffling in the study. My poor mother.

"Sorry," said Dee.

Oh, what did I care. I was also sick of people apologizing to me for just living their lives.

"Okay, okay," said Dee. "You. Tell us about you. How are you doing? Like, what does this mean now? For you, I mean. How is it . . . different?"

They looked at each other. They had clearly talked about it on the way over, how to act, what to say, or what I might look or seem like, and here it was, upon them: me.

I closed my eyes. Suddenly I felt these people were strangers. Had I ever spent the night at Lydia's, slathering our faces with her mother's beauty packs, playing "light as a feather" and trying to contact the dead with Dee's old dusty Ouija board?

Was I different or were they? And I couldn't help but wonder, why did this not happen to one of them? Like, why was I here and why were they over there, all intact and shining and (tediously) the same?

I started to say it. *I met this boy.* It was on the tip of my tongue and then I stopped it. It was like talking about camp or summer—yeah, it was a lot like Danny and Sandy in *Grease*—and what I had with Connor just seemed so different and special and otherworldly really. And now it seemed so over.

"I'm so tired, you guys." I wasn't lying.

My mother came out of the study. "It was so great to see you two," she said, walking down the stairs. My mother didn't use the banister. Just me. The old lady of the house. "Come visit again soon, okay? Lizzie doesn't head back to school for a few more weeks. Not exactly sure when yet."

They both stood up. Did they do *anything* separately?

"I'll call my mom," Lydia said.

"That long?" Dee-Dee looked at me. I saw her again, the girl she used to be, a tomboy with a bowl cut, dribbling a soccer ball, her tube socks pulled up high. She was there, inside, I could see down, down, down to it. I could tell she was thinking, she must be really sick. Me. I could feel myself soften toward her, toward my Dee-Dee from patrols and soccer and sneaking out through her sliding glass door.

I crossed my arms before anyone tried to hug me.

"I guess we'll wait outside," Lydia said.

I was headed up the stairs again, slowly, slowly, when Dee-Dee said, "We'll come by again soon, Liz. We'll see you again soon!"

Here was my first assignment:

In three to five pages, please write a critical essay that examines one of the three topics listed below.

1. Is Heathcliff's gradual decline the result of delusion, insanity, or a supernatural haunting?
2. What are the features of older gothic novels that Emily Brontë adopts and/or reconfigures for her use?

3. Does Heathcliff love Catherine Linton?

(Be sure you back up all your assertions with textual evidence! Also, work that is not double-spaced and paginated will not be accepted.)

Okay, option three: Does Heathcliff love Catherine Linton? Because Heathcliff, as repulsive as he is, and also as enthralling, clearly loves Catherine. His whole life is affected by her and by their love. By this time they had together when they were young.

But Heathcliff never says it. I looked through the whole book again, did an online search for the word "love," and there was no evidence. All I could see clearly was that Catherine loved him. Here's what she once wrote in her journal: *"Whatever our souls are made of, his and mine are the same."*

He never says it, but we know. But how do you really know if someone loves you? Or loved you. Catherine dies before she ever knows for sure.

I decided against that essay and went with option two. The gothic novel. I thought it would be much easier to write about ghosts, but how can it be that ghosts are more of a sure thing than love?

Ghosts: the girl who died. Did she haunt Connor? I imagined this little girl in a green dress scratching at Connor's window. Was she covered in blood? Or was she the girl she was before she was killed?

Did he try to save her? Was he trying to save me? Would that make up for something? Could it have been anyone? It could have been anyone.

As I wrote my first essay for my junior year, I asked myself all of this, and this is what I came up with: I was only there to help Connor with his guilt over not being able to help that little girl in the green dress. And maybe, just maybe, he was only there for me to get through that time with something sweet to, well, live for I guess.

But Connor, now, was gone. All I had was a turtle named Frog growing bigger every day, and a haunting message on my voice mail. The turtle needed a lot of taking care of. Sidebar: Who knew how much trouble turtles were?

Fake gold dangling hearts. No love and care needed there.

As I wrote about foggy full-mooned settings, about the wind along the moors, about ghosts and blood and the way we say the names of the dead, I took a break from Birdy and listened to Nora's CD.

The Ronettes: "The night we met I knew I needed you so, and if I had the chance I'd never let you go. So won't you say you love me?"

Say Lou Lou: "'Cause I nurtured the clouds in my eyes, and all of those times I lost myself in lies, it was you I was trying to find."

TLC: "My outsides look cool, my insides are blue. Every time I think I'm through, it's because of you."

Sleater-Kinney: "I'm your monster, I'm not like you (peel back the skin, see what's there), all your life is written for you (I'll never show you what's in here)."

Girls, the soft ones, the angry ones, the sweet, the cool, they all know how to say it.

In how many ways, how many ways?

The Shelter

The following weekend, after Dee and Lydia marched in and marched out, some kind of squadron, when I was finishing up my essay, my father knocked on my door.

"Can I come in?"

"Of course," I said. "Enter!"

He cracked open the door à la Connor. But it was just my dad. "Mabel wants to go for a walk," he said.

"Really?" My computer was on my lap, on my knees really, to avoid, like, *melting* the bag. "Mabel does?"

"Yes. Mabel does."

"Okay, Dad." I set my computer aside on my bed and went for my sneakers.

When I opened the front door, it was way colder outside than I'd thought, and so I took my father's jean jacket from the hook in the front hall closet.

My father put Mabel on her leather leash and we were off.

Which makes it sound easy. It took me a while to get down our stone steps. So it was more like: after ten minutes of my tottering down those and then finally reaching the driveway, then! we were off.

"You okay, honey?" he asked me as we made our way up our street.

"I mean—" I start.

"No, I know," he interrupted. "I know you're not okay, but how not okay are you? How okay aren't you? How are you handling this, honey?"

I gulped, trying to get my swallowing done even though my throat felt blocked. "I don't know."

He nodded and we kept walking, Mabel stopping to pee every five seconds, an excuse for me to secretly try to catch my uncatchable breath. One of the many charms of a girl dog.

"Why did we end up with Mabel anyway?" I asked after a period of silence.

"Why?" he asked.

"I mean, how did it end up being her? Why a breeder? Why a springer?"

"Well, your mother had done all this research on dogs, the best ones with kids, the ones who are adaptable. She and I went to some shelters. We didn't want to bring you and Zoe, because we knew you'd fall in love with every dog! And there were so many ones we wanted there. But in the end, it was always the springers that had our hearts. I had wanted one from the start. We had them when I was growing up."

"You did?" I asked.

"We did. I had a springer named Daphne. Can you believe it?"

I looked at him. My father. He was graying, and I only noticed it then. I'd seen so many pictures of him young, with a mustache, wearing army pants and tie-dyes, and then when I was born.

Now he looked like a professor. Like a dad.

"That is hilarious." I pictured him as a kid, calling *Daphne! Daphne!* and my mother in the form of a dog running up and licking his face. "I'd thought you rescued Mabel."

My father shook his head. "No. That would have been nice, though."

But then she wouldn't be Mabel.

"You okay?" He turned to look at me.

I nodded. "I just have this eye thing," I said, touching the corner of my eye. "You know, Mabel is seven," I said.

"She is."

I stopped walking and turned to him. "Okay so, I really want to rescue this dog. She's like, part beagle, part border collie, a little Lab, I think. She came from North Carolina, from a batch of puppies just left in a Dumpster in the horrible heat. Her hair was matted and her skin was raw from hot spots, but she's doing really well now, with some of her siblings at a shelter. A kill shelter. In Manassas."

"She needs to be rescued? I see."

"She does."

"I see," he said again.

"It's a kill shelter. I don't know how much time she's got. She needs to be saved, Dad."

"Okay," he said. "Let's save her then."

I was stunned because it's usually, let's talk to Mom, let's see, let's see if Zoe is comfortable with this, *blah blah*, but not today, apparently. Post-hospital rules.

"That's great."

"It is," my father said.

My dad stuck his hands in his pockets and I stuck my hands in mine. Well, his. There were some kind of strips of soft plastic, and I fingered them for a second and then took them out of his pocket to see what they were.

My hospital bracelets. The one that was handwritten and the typed-out one. The one Collette cut off only a week before.

I looked at them, flat on my open palm, and then I looked at my father.

"You know, when you were born, your mom wore a bracelet just like that. It said 'Baby Stoller.' We hadn't named you yet. We were waiting to meet you. I have that one too."

Mabel had her face in the bushes, sniffing deeply and loudly.

"So this first one I took because I was scared. Really, really scared. The second one I took because I wasn't, but you had worn it every day in there, and you had left it behind. All your bracelets," he said.

I just rubbed my naked wrist as we made our old loop around the long, tree-lined blocks of my neighborhood.

"So when do you want to go get this puppy dog?" he said, as we turned the corner for home. He looked at his watch. "Don't know about you, but I'm free this afternoon."

Next thing I knew we were all in the car, heading to Manassas for Greta. We were heading to her to save her.

"We're getting you a sister!" I said to Mabel, to explain why she wasn't coming with us, as we left her, stunned, behind.

In the car I stared out the window along the highway.

"Want to play I Spy?" my mother said from the front seat.

"Um, no?" Zoe put in her earbuds.

"How often are we all in the car together?" my father said, turning to us.

I peeked over at Zoe's phone. *Revolver.* I motioned her to give me a bud, and when she handed it over, we both leaned back: "I will be there and everywhere. Here, there and everywhere."

"Play it again," I said, and she did: "To lead a better life, I need my love to be here. . . ."

At the shelter Zoe and I knelt down and gripped the metal of her caged-in kennel and watched her. Greta. It means pearl. And that's what she was, once we got to her, pried her out of that sad, abused shell of hers. The eyes. Such sad, hoping, long-lashed eyes. She jumped and jumped and then she growled as the human at the kennel opened her cage.

"She just needs love and some training." The human leaned down and scratched her on the neck. "Love, love, and then some more love," she said.

"Well, we sure have that aplenty!" my mother said, and Zoe rolled her eyes.

They called the puppy Blue Eyes then, and I swear she bent her head and smiled.

Dog smiles. Like no other kinds of smile. It made me think of Verlaine. I would have liked to tell Connor about it.

I also wanted to tell him what I decided on our way back to the car, which was that I was going to take her to get her Canine Good Citizen certificate. So she could go into hospitals.

Like Verlaine. Because maybe Connor would come back and maybe Verlaine and Mabel and now lovely Greta, who wasn't a stranger to suffering either, and I could all go visiting—go candy striping—together. I would finally get the handbook! I would finally see all the secret instructions that were written inside.

Of course, there was no Connor, and it's not like I didn't know this when we got into the car, Greta freaking out in the backseat, Zoe on her knees leaning toward her, trying to calm her down. I knew all this. But it is still possible to unknow what you know.

"A new family member," my father said.

"Perfect," my mother said. "She's clearly gotten the memo about how being rabid is an important feature in our household."

"We're not going to hurt you!" I placed my hand palm up for her to sniff and then petted her softly on her back, the way the handler had shown us.

"We're here to save you!" Zoe said.

Poor Greta. Even though it wasn't even an hour home, we had to stop at a rest station to let her get some energy out. Trucks were idling at the stop as she ran in the little stretch of grass. And she looked so beautiful, all her kinds of dogs inside her, her spotted fur, her pointed face. Watching her, I thought how maybe Connor hadn't left me. Because maybe, just by coming home and being with my family, by not being so sick anymore, so blue inside, maybe I had left Connor. He could feel that way. That he was the one who had been left behind.

That's when I decided I would try to find him. I would find Connor the way Connor had found me.

Returning

That's what I tried to do, anyway. I called his phone and only got a voice mail on the first ring, the kind of VM that is just a robot reciting a number: you've reached blah, blah, blah. Blah. I didn't even get to hear the sound of his voice—that old voice mail he'd left me in the hospital was getting a little stale. I didn't have an email address for him, and when I searched for him online again, this time, like, *hunting*, with places I knew he lived, with names I thought might be his parents', all I found was his mother. I'm pretty sure it was his mother, and she seemed to be a powerful lawyer. But nothing else. Connor was a ghost.

Or that's what I hoped, because it meant that he could return somehow, scratching at my window maybe, slipping out from my closet door, *Wuthering Heights*-style.

He could rise up behind me in any mirror, I thought, but still I avoided looking at myself in the mirror then. I only looked at myself in segments: here is my leg, here is my face, my arm—like a chicken cut up for frying maybe—because all of me, I couldn't. Sometimes, though, I would look in the near distance of the mirror to see if he was standing there maybe, leash wound around his hand, Verlaine smiling beside him.

———

Of course Connor was the one who found me. It was how it worked with us. He would always be lost and I would be found.

But it took a while.

It happened when I least expected it, just like when he showed up in the hospital unannounced. How random was that, how lucky, that in that big old horrible place this perfect person showed up? This time, I was already back at school. It felt like it had been forever, but really I had just missed six weeks. October 7, just in time for homecoming that weekend, which I found incredibly annoying. Also annoying? Dee-Dee and her Rizzo attire, her constant back against the locker, notebook at her chest, her boyfriend, who of course was playing Kenickie, panting at her side. It was all so 1955; I was surprised she didn't have a chiffon scarf around her neck, like the green one Nana gave me from her drawer when I was a kid. I loved the feel of it on my face, and the smell of her lingering perfume, but it did not, I repeat it did not, belong on a junior in high school. Also? Lydia was practically stitched to Dee's side. Also annoying.

I guess I was in costume too, though. That first day back at school I felt I could be anything I chose, but there were basically two options: (1) I could be dressed up now, lipstick, nice clothes. I could cover myself up that way, I guess. Or (2) I could match up my insides and outsides better, wear my father's old sweats, his T-shirts. Old ripped jeans and some Vans of my own. Never be seen.

I went with option two.

What's to report about returning? Mostly weirdness. I don't

know why I thought people wouldn't know. Or that they wouldn't know the specifics. But they did. They were either overly nice, smiling at me in the hallways the way I always smile when I see kids in wheelchairs or on those metal crutches with the arm grips. Teachers welcomed me back as if I'd been lost in space, and in homeroom I received a summons by the school nurse to let me know that she—her office—was my safe place should I need it. That was nice, I suppose. I didn't think I'd ever take her up on it though.

And Michael Lerner.

"Hey," he said, like, sliding up beside me while I was at my locker.

"Hey!" We had been such good friends once. Now? Nothing really.

"Did you get my gift?"

I had totally forgotten about the necklace. "Yeah," I said. "So sweet. Thank you." It was nice to have his attention, I will admit.

"How you doing? Like, what was it *like*?"

"What was what like?" I pretended to be looking for something important inside. But there was nothing in there. Nothing even hanging on the door.

"The hospital. Surgery. Now."

I shook my head. He was saying: Like, what is it like, what are you like now? Now. Now. "It was fucking fantastic," I said. He wasn't really interested in me. He was interested in what had happened to me.

He looked stricken. "God," he said. "I was just asking."

"And I was just telling you." I slammed my locker closed.

You know the person who wants to be close to the sick person, the person whose mom died, the person who has seizures in the hallways? The one who will have all the inside info on this person's . . . *stuff*? That person was Michael L. And oh yeah, the sick person in this equation, that was me.

"You're welcome for the necklace!" Michael said as I shuffled away from him and down the hall.

Down the hall: flyers for the homecoming weekend hockey game. A color printout of everyone in their plaid skirts and polo shirts, their shin guards and cleats, two hockey sticks crossed in front of the first row. Correction: a color printout of everyone but me.

Anyway; Connor. I had just gotten in from my third day of school, a time that was always of note because of the mad relief I felt. Nora and I were trying to make a plan to actually see each other.

"Luv, luv," she said, "you're like a little lag in there, never going out, after being all pent up with the gerries. Totally jammy for me to come. When works?"

We agreed on the weekend. She would take the train up.

"We'll meet you under the clock at the station!" I said to Nora. "Text me when you get off the train."

"Under the clock," she said. "Chirp chirp!"

Was that even British? No idea, but didn't have much time to think about it, because as soon as I'd hung up, my mother came up the stairs. It was sweet that she worked afternoons from home now, but it did always take me by surprise to see her.

"Mail call!" she said. Mail call, when it happened, usually involved a postcard from Nana or a letter from Tim for Zoe. He wrote her letters! That guy was so in love with Zoe; it was kind of sad but also kind of beautiful. I think Zoe actually loved him back. I'm sure of it.

My mother lifted her eyebrows and tilted her head as she sliced the air with an envelope.

Plain white, handwritten address.

Connor. It had to be.

How can I explain? The fluttery weird crazy in my chest. What *was* that?

I snatched it from her. I ran into my room. I closed the door. I brought Frog out from her aquarium and set her on the floor. I put Birdy on, "Fire and Rain." I sat down, back against my bed, and closed my eyes to calm myself. I opened the letter and it was true. Finally it was news from Connor. He'd been found.

Letter 1

October 6, 2013

Dear Lizzie,
Dear Lizzie,
Dear Lizzie,

Sorry. I can't figure out just how to start this letter. I've got a lot to tell you. I wanted to write a letter to you so I can think of what to say and how to say it. And because where I am we're not allowed to use our phones and there is only one public phone.

Remember landlines?

What am I saying? Of course you remember landlines.

Okay. Let me back up. First of all, I'm sorry I didn't tell you when you came home from the hospital that I was leaving. I have been craven. This is a word I have learned here, and it's a good word and it applies to me because I meant to tell you I was going, and then there you were with your family, almost back to the person you must have been before you got sick. It was so strange to see you out of the hospital. Like a person. It's not that I saw you as a nonperson before, I just saw you differently. You like rose up into yourself, or maybe out of yourself.

It was great to see you, both ways. All the ways you are. I mean that.

*That day was my last day home. I'm at boarding school now.
This place in New Hampshire. Stone Mountain. As if. My parents
sent me here after the semester had already started—so it was a lot
of hurrying and packing and throwing things away. I had to say
good-bye to Verlaine. I can't really even write about that.*

*That's part of why I didn't write or call, but mostly it was
because I didn't know how to tell you and everything was so
chaotic. Basically, I couldn't get the girl out of my head. I saw her
everywhere. I had this feeling that I was . . . breaking apart. So I
started skipping school. And not doing my homework. And also, I
was smoking a lot of pot. Alone. We never talked about this stuff, so
I'm not sure how you feel about it, but I'm just trying to be honest.
So my mother caught me and then my parents sent me to Dr.
Farrell, who said I was self-medicating, that I was finding a way to
make those thoughts stop.*

I was at sea was what he told me. And I really felt like that.

*And now I keep thinking about your surgery. How I know it
must have been horrible, just awful and painful, but now it's gone.
The sickness. I feel like my thing is unfixable, like I can't get it
out or something. I was so stupid. I think I really thought going
into the hospital, I could save people. I think I truly thought that
visiting you would help—like you would get better. But you had to
get that surgery anyway. And patients like Thelma died.*

*So here I am, at this place. It's teeny. There are, like, twenty-five
kids, all boys. It's super strict. Everyone has their own little garden
plot! The theory is that taking care of a garden teaches you about
growing and tending and caring. I know a little bit about that
already, but just a little.*

It's all kind of complicated.

I just wanted to write you, now, to tell you where I am. I want to say that I miss our visits, my visits to you. I want to say that I miss everything about everything. I see you everywhere. But I don't want to keep you from starting over. From beginning your life all over again.

Your first day home was my last day home. So it goes.

I think that's all from me for now. But more from me soon.

Yours always,
Connor

Blue All Over Again

I was shaking as I read that letter. It was in Connor's handwriting. And Connor's handwriting? ALL CAPS. Little blocky neat all caps. Beautiful and perfect.

Of course.

As I read, Frog sat there as if she were deciding if she should walk or just enjoy the break from her usual home, but I was having *feelings*. So many, all over. I was happy to hear from Connor and shocked to hear what had happened and then I was so, so, so sad. Like blue all over for him.

I went downstairs and found Mabel and Greta. There are strange ways you realize you're getting better, and one of the goofy ones was that I could take them out together now. (The bad ways involved, sadly, my thighs starting to get back to my prehospital thighs.) Greta was so manic and crazy, and Mabel was kind of over it, sort of looking at me like, *This is how I'm going to spend my old age?* But as I untangled their leashes and made my way up the rise of our street, I tried to picture Connor all alone at some freaky boarding school and all I could think of was some *Vampire Academy* place where the school seems like this place of safety and protection but really it ends up to be the worst place of all.

I imagined him alone in his bed in the country in the dark like I was alone in the dark.

When I got home, I did this strange thing I still don't understand. I put his letter in my top left desk drawer, just underneath David B's God's eye, where my pens and scissor and Scotch tape were. And then I shut the drawer.

I didn't write Connor back.

It just *happened*. Connor wrote me when he was ready.

And so I would write him back when I was.

School Spirit

I went to the damn pep rally.

Oh sweet Jesus, the pep rally. I ask you: Is there anything worse? I only mention it to say, if it wasn't clear already: I was not voted princess. No matter what, there's always that crazy secret hope, isn't there? So pathetic, but true. But Michael Lerner was, of *course*. Voted prince, I mean, which just seemed so, I don't know, *ironic* I guess. Yes, ironic, because here he was paying attention to me finally and here he was all *validated* in the world and I didn't care. Our class princess was actually an amazing girl, Leandra Robbins, who had built houses in West Africa this past summer and who was also really into all kinds of equality and always got people to march on the Mall when there was something important about equality to march about. It made me feel kind of sorry for Michael L. He looked so, well, empty compared to her.

King and queen were two assholes who were dating and who had parties in their gated communities that were seniors only. They both drove to school, one in a Lexus, the other in a Jetta, and it was pretty nauseating. It was just so *expected*. I was tired of all that by then. The bad teen movie. I kind of hoped it was the movie where some crazy person comes in and takes out the whole lot of them. I wished that it was just me and Connor, here to save the world.

Connor and I couldn't even save ourselves. So I sat there, sneaks toeing the wooden gym bleacher in front of me, watching the hockey team, everyone dressed for the rally in their little plaid skirts, their collared, numbered shirts, all seated up front with the football players, the lacrossers, and so on. I knew that everyone but Annabelle Loughton was wearing boxers beneath her skirt. Annabelle? Well, her father left when she was young; that's why she was so needy, we all told one another as we watched her skirt fly up on the field.

I felt that tickle in my bag, and the always accompanying panic that something had come undone, but nothing had, and I just sat there watching the king and queen smile absurdly, doubting seriously that these two would ever be crowned in Georgetown, at Connor's school.

But now he was gone.

King, Queen, Prince

Lydia did not seem to care about my lack of . . . enthusiasm for the evening's sanctioned activity, which was the homecoming dance.

"I won't take no for an answer," she said when she called again. Still she sounded like she was forty-five years old.

"Fine," I said. "Whatever. Fine."

She showed up and sat with me while I got dressed. I changed in the bathroom. By changed I mean took off my big jeans and put on some that had once been "skinnies" but were now regulars. A nice three-quarter-sleeved striped cotton shirt from when I cared. Flats. My hair was coming out in clumps. The things I now know: first your hair gets crazy long from the steroids, and then it falls out a few weeks after all the anesthesia. So I just braided it and circled a rubber band loosely around the end.

So: homecoming.

The walls of the gym were streaming with long strands of colored lights, some kind of a rainbow that Leandra R had orchestrated, representing equality for all. It was all terribly cheesy, and then everyone in these huge clusters, just masses of people, fists in the air, freaking. *Uh-huh, uh-huh, uh-huh.* I never would have been in the middle of that, sweating, dancing, laughing, anyway, but now? No way. Not 1 percent of a way. What took the cake, though, was Dee-Dee, who along with Kenickie was trying to get the music changed so they could do a whole *Grease* dance-off. She had a corsage on her wrist and wore a strapless taffeta dress (it really *was* a gown), and then all the hand movements—the bumping of closed fists, the thumbs-up—with her boyfriend was incredibly ridiculous.

So there was that and then the people making out beneath the bleachers, and then there were all the haters, who sat around lurking in dark corners. Like the guy of many flannels, the one who drew everyone. He was there, wearing a flannel, with another guy in another flannel.

"Hey," I said, walking over to him, way out of the fray, practically in a cave. The refracted lights from the twirling disco ball moved above us, occasionally dipping between a bleacher seat.

He nodded at me, his long black hair flopping over his face. He had a bunch of deep red zits embedded in his cheeks. They call them craters for a reason.

He handed me a flask, and I took a swig from it.

"You've been gone a while," he said.

I liked the feeling of whatever that was burning down my throat. I handed it back to him. "Yeah," I said. "Thanks for noticing."

"Sure thing."

His friend was silent and looked straight ahead, just tapped his foot—not to the rhythm of the blasting Demi Lovato at all—while looking at the ceiling, bored.

The guy from last year's class passed me the flask again and I took another swig—bourbon or whiskey or scotch, I think, something brown for sure—and then I crossed my arms and leaned against the cold tile wall. Everyone . . . *trying*. Thumping and laughing and freaking, and shifting and trying and trying. It was nice, I thought, to be done with all that, just above it all for once. I liked that feeling of invulnerability.

Oh, Dee-Dee. She was doing some kind of fifties thing where she swung under Kenickie's legs and came up kicking, jumping and smiling brightly.

"Jesus," I said, sort of pushing back and forth off the wall with my toes.

That's when Michael L came sauntering up. It was before his prince status had been officially conferred upon him, but his princeliness emanated just the same. As in, there wasn't a lot of insecurity in his strut: skinny jeans, Pumas, plaid shirt, shock of long hair, a serious saunter. What was it about him? Because now he seemed regular to me. Or more: I was in control of myself around him. This, I liked.

Then again, what did Connor seem like? Preppy. Rich. Golden. I can't even remember. Sometimes you stop seeing what the person is to the world. You only see what the person is to you.

Sometimes. Because I could see everything about Michael L. And yet . . .

"What assholes." He stood next to me, looking out at the dance floor, back against the wall. Flannel shirts one and two scooted away as if they would catch whatever disease the prince-in-waiting had.

"Bye," I said, extra loud. "Thanks for the drink!" I could still feel the harsh, thick taste along the roof of my mouth, my throat.

The guy from last year's class gave me a backward wave as he walked away.

"Who?" I said.

"I don't know, the cast of *West Side Story*."

"*Grease*," I said. "That's the play they're putting on. I can't imagine how you've missed it. I could hear them singing from my bedroom."

"I know," he conceded. "Believe me. Bedroom, eh?"

"Please." I stood there, watching.

"Hey, so you're barely speaking to me," Michael L said.

"Yes I am."

"You're not. I don't get it. We used to be amazing friends."

Amazing friends meant me biking over to his house and hanging out in his backyard while I pigged out on Oreos and he told me about whatever girl he loved. "I guess." I shrugged.

"You guess?"

"I'm kind of wondering about this instant change in you," I said.

"It's not instant. You know what they say: absence makes the heart grow fonder."

"They? Who is that? Please, Michael. Please. Anyway, I'm not talking to anyone really. I'm just on my own right now."

"You've changed, man," he said.

I turned toward him, now just my arm touching the wall, if it were a lifeboat and not having some kind of contact with it would mean sure drowning. "You think?" I said. My eyes were leaking tears. I wished they weren't, but they were. That's the way it was then.

"Yeah, I do."

"Because everything's different now! I was in a room with a lady who *died*. I almost died. I'm all fucked-up!" I said. "I am totally different!" I tried to tamp down everything. Everything. But it was untampdownable.

"Hey," he said, softer, sweetly. He brought me close to him and hugged me.

I stood there stiffly, but I let him. It was difficult not to remember the way I would once have thrown myself in traffic to have him.

"Lizzie." He brushed my hair out of my face, which felt like he was doing something he'd once seen someone do.

I looked down.

And then he brought his face to mine, his lips.

We kissed. He had such full lips, and I could taste my tears on them. It felt good to kiss him, actually. He was an excellent kisser, his mouth open but his tongue pretty much staying put there. He was holding me so tightly and I felt myself relax, my shoulders sort of sigh back to their normal position, and then I felt him run his hand lightly across my stomach.

I went rigid. "What are you doing?"

"Kissing you," he said. "Finally."

"And?" I pushed away from him.

"And nothing."

"Okay."

"What happened exactly, Lizzie? I've heard stuff, I'm not going to lie. What does it feel like?"

I rolled my eyes. "Drop it," I said. It used to be the girl with the eye patch, and then it was the kid who had to be in a wheelchair after falling off a horse, and now it was me. I was the freak. Here he was in the closest proximity possible.

"I just wanted to know what happened," Michael said. Michael L, who I'd loved forever and who I didn't love at all anymore. How does that happen? One second you think you'll die and the next you can't even remember it.

"Then just ask me." I pushed him away. I knew what he was doing. Be close to the person everyone's talking about. The one who might be princess even though she's never been princess material. Be the one who *knows*.

"I think I just did," he called after me as I raced out of the gym.

"What Now" was playing. "I don't know where to go, I don't know what to feel, I don't know how to cry, I don't know, oh, oh why." The high school gym. Rihanna. How cliché can you be? Can I be? Either way there I was rushing out of the gym, and there I was being met by Mr. Gallagher patrolling the hallway.

"Hello, Ms. Lizzie Stoller! Having fun? We're so happy to have you back!"

I ignored him, which was rude because Mr. Gallagher was the nicest teacher and he also organized the poinsettia sale and the ski trips and trips to Disney World.

But I ignored him anyway and ran outside and called my mother and then I sat on the bike rack in front of the gym entrance, waiting for her, and then she was there, pulling up in her green Subaru, and then we were home and I ran into my room, Greta and Mabel following behind me, and then I closed my door. Greta chewed on one of the legs of my bed and Mabel climbed up on the bed with me and we lay down facing each other and she licked away my tears.

Dogs. Dogs. Dogs. Way better than humans.

"Honey?" My mother.

"I'm fine!" I said. "Really."

"Okay, honey," she said. "I'm downstairs if you want to talk."

"Thanks, Mom," I said, though I knew that wasn't going to happen, not tonight anyway.

What was going to happen?

This: I put on my father's sweats, soft and old and enormous, and one of the school T-shirts I'd been fool enough to buy as a freshman, and I got out my ridiculous study buddy, red with white stars, and I put it on my knees. I took out some typing paper.

Hi there, I began. *Hi. I got your letter. Where do I begin?* I wrote. But then I began so easily, as easily as I had talked to Connor in the hospital that very first day I told him how tired I was of being me. I wrote about school. About Dee and Lydia and how they didn't understand me anymore. Or maybe I didn't understand them. I wrote about the pep rally. I asked him what it was like there. And if he felt lonely. Too lonely.

What I didn't write: how wrong I felt it was that he hadn't told me he was going. That he was gone. What I also didn't write: anything about the dance.

And then: I debated. I debated saying it. I wrote it and I crossed it out. I ripped up the paper and started again. And then I wrote it. *I love you,* I wrote. In the end, I left it in.

Under the Clock

When I woke up on Sunday, I decided I would discuss Connor—finally!—with Nora when she visited. I had told nobody. It was the opposite of me, but I hadn't figured out how to talk about it, maybe because I hadn't figured out what exactly it was.

What was it? Maybe Nora could help, not define it necessarily, but think it over. Like I had with her so many times. So I decided I would tell her everything. I wouldn't show her the letter but maybe I could just tell her about him and us and, maybe, see what she thought.

So that was my plan for Sunday.

My mother and I went to pick her up at Union Station. We parked and then we went inside to wait, which makes it sound like we just pulled up and got out, which we did not because, *parking*, but after all that: slipping my letter to Connor inside the mailbox. After that: fluttering heart. And then waiting beneath the clock for Nora.

We waited for a really long time, though. Like, twenty-five minutes. No text from Nora. We checked the arrivals, and her train had come in, but Nora did not seem to be among the passengers. She wasn't answering my texts. So Nora. Her world and we just happen to be roaming around in it.

"I hope everything is okay," my mother said. Was it only recently that my mother went first to that bleak, bad place where no hope lives?

"Of course it is. She got on a train for half an hour in the morning on *Sunday*. I mean, what could happen? She's probably got no phone service is all."

She's off being Nora is what I didn't say, but after ten more minutes of loitering, I called her house.

"Mrs. Branford?" I said when her mother answered.

"Yes?"

"It's Lizzie!"

"Hi, honey," she said. Here's the thing with camp friends. You barely ever see their parents. They just come to get us, throwing our massive bags of dirty laundry and our army blankets and our hideous birdhouses into the minivan and turning back for home. So as long as I'd known Nora, I think I'd maybe said thirteen words to her mother. Now, on the phone, she let out this massive sigh.

"Nora was supposed to come," I said. "I mean, my mom and I are waiting for her. Under the clock. At the train station, I mean. Where we'd arranged."

"I see," Mrs. Branford sighed. Mrs. Branford, by the way, sounded the opposite of British. She sounded, I don't know, like she was Canadian or from Cleveland or something. Her consonants were pronounced *really* close together. And the sigh made it seem like I was supposed to ask her about why she'd made it.

"Is everything all right?" I didn't look at my mother, who I could see out of the corner of my eye was plaintively giving me a nervous, knowing glance.

"Nora's been arrested," Mrs. Branford said.

"What?"

"Yes," Mrs. Branford said.

I waited, breathing. I pictured her in the dressing room, layering bras over her big boobs.

"Yes. She was arrested for shoplifting last night, out with some friends. I'm sorry she didn't let you know she would not be coming. Obviously."

"Oh my gosh," I said.

"Yes. She's home now, but she has no access to phone or computer. The store is deciding if they'll press charges. Obviously we're hoping they won't, but Nora will not be visiting anytime soon either way."

"Oh," I said. "What store, if you don't mind me asking?"

"Oh God, some tarty place. The Bottom Drawer."

I giggled.

"It's a lingerie store here," she said. "Very expensive."

"I see." Oh Nora.

"Yes. We are all disappointed. In Nora. I will let her know you called, Lizzie. How are you feeling, by the way? Nora was so worried about you."

"I'm good. Thank you."

"Glad to hear it. Okay, I will let her know you called."

We said good-bye, and I slipped my phone in my back pocket. There were two ways to do this. (1) I could tell my mother what I once would have told her for sure: Nora had food poisoning.

She was so sick she couldn't call, and her mother forgot. Bad fish. It will do it every time. Or there was option (2), what actually happened. Which would make being friends with Nora pretty hard from there on out.

I looked at my mother. "Nora got caught shoplifting," I said.

The moment ended. Very abruptly. "Oh my," she said.

I nodded grimly.

"Well!" she said, taking me by my elbow. "Let's give ourselves a treat and have a nice lunch!"

Not the response I was expecting, but a better one. Only apparently there are no nice lunches in Union Station, and so we walked a few blocks to E Street into a restaurant in a really swanky hotel.

"Two," she said to the waiter.

"The brunch here is supposed to be fabulous, but I only come here during the week," she said when we were seated. "I just love this place." She smiled at the bar and the other tables.

"Looks yummy." I peered over the enormous menu, waiting.

"What did she steal?" my mother asked as she placed a starched white napkin on her lap.

"I have no idea," I lied. "Her mom didn't say."

"I wonder," she said. "How does this make you feel?"

"Can you please not do that?" I asked.

"Yes. I can not do that."

"Thank you. It was lingerie."

My mother shook her head and her eyes widened. "Don't quite know what I was expecting."

"Truth is, Nora did tell me she was stealing. It was recent. She got some kind of odd rush from it. I don't think she's, like, wanting for bras and underwear."

My mother nodded, trying to quell the evident thrill of my decision to go with option two: truth telling. Which, she couldn't have known, was also a way of not telling number three, which was the truth about Connor.

"Don't worry; I don't get it at all."

My mom paused. "You know, I was caught stealing once."

I looked at her. Anything my parents told me about who they once were, before Zoe and me, like when my father got drunk and threw up at some Neil Young concert, or when my mother kissed a famous actor, always shocked me. I didn't really want to hear about it either. I wanted them to have always been just this. My parents.

"I stole a ChapStick when I was with your grandmother. I got caught stealing *ChapStick* with my mother. In a drugstore. I was ten."

"That is so bizarre!"

"It really was. I'm sure my mother would have bought it if I'd wanted it. But I wanted to *take* it. I understand it, shoplifting. Who doesn't want to just see if she can get away with something?"

"I'm not sure that's it. But the stealing part doesn't appeal to me at all."

"Well, that's a relief!" my mother said. "Obviously that was not an endorsement."

A waiter was making his way over to us.

"I mean I have other things . . ." Like fleeing hospitals, I thought.

"I'm sure," she said. "So strange, that day, with the ChapStick. My father was a judge. It was fairly humiliating for him. I still feel this terrible, terrible guilt. To this day."

I looked at my mom. I felt terrible guilt as well. For all that I had put her through. But, I thought, at least I hadn't been arrested for shoplifting.

"Two chardonnays." My mother grinned at the waiter, daring him to question her.

Well, this was new. I tilted my head at my mom. I'd had wine with dinner before with my parents, on holidays and such, but this public display was a whole new level of Daphne's . . . liberalness.

"Yes, ma'am," he said.

"Ma'am?" She was horrified. "Call me Daphne," she said into her menu, she really couldn't help herself, as he turned to leave.

The wine was fun and it put me in kind of a mellow mood, and then Zoe was waiting when we got home. I guess she had heard what had happened to Nora from my dad, who must have heard from my mom, who must have called him while I was having the charming experience of dealing with my bag in a public bathroom. I guess I really needed to finally talk about Connor and then Nora got arrested, so whoever was sitting in front of me was who it was going to be.

So Zoe.

"Hey!" she said brightly, trying to corral Greta. Was it only then I noticed the half-eaten couch and the dust bunnies—more hair bunnies—twisting along the old Oriental carpet?

"We need to crate train her," my mother said to no one in particular.

Connor. Connor. It was all I could think about.

I miss you, I'd written. *I can't believe you're gone. It feels like you weren't real.*

When would he get my letter? I ticked off the days in my head.

The dogs bounded with Zoe into her room, and she waved me in.

Zoe's room: How was it so much better, cooler, older than mine? Maybe it was that she had framed pictures—of her and Tim, us as little girls, a sepia-toned one of Nana as a baby in little white baby shoes and a bonnet—and also a framed poster of the Calder mobile that hangs in the National Gallery. Her books— huge art books on Impressionism and Neo-Fauvists, also little books of poetry, the kids' books that she loved, like *Madeline* and *Many Moons* and *Sylvester and the Magic Pebble*— were all neatly shelved. A canopy bed. I don't even know how we came from the same parents, really.

The dogs jumped on the bed and we all lay back, even Greta.

"Crazy about Nora. What a freak," Zoe said.

"What's that supposed to mean?"

"The stealing, Liz. That's crazy."

"I guess," I said.

"I thought Nora drove you nuts anyway."

"She does and she also doesn't. I don't know, she seems a lot better than Dee-Dee and Lydia, that's for sure."

"That is truth," Zoe said.

I petted Mabel and didn't say anything.

She closed her eyes and sighed.

"Yeah, everything's different now," I said.

Zoe nodded.

"I miss Connor." As I said it, I realized how badly I needed to talk about it. Then I said it: "I think I loved him."

"He was a sweet guy," she said, but I could tell she didn't mean it.

"*Was?*"

"You said 'loved.'"

"Okay, love."

"Do you still see him? Do you guys *talk*?"

"God," I said. "I just told you I *loved* someone." I shook my head. "Love someone."

"Sorry," she said. "Tell me."

"It's okay. So, don't repeat this to Mom and Dad, okay? But he got sent to boarding school."

"I heard that," Zoe said.

"From who?"

"Just around."

"What are you talking about?" I felt a new kind of panic. That something had been going on behind my back with the people I had once been closest to.

"I know I should have said something earlier, but we have a few mutual friends. I knew someone—a friend of Jake's, Tim's friend from swim team?—who dated him. Well, more like hooked up with him, I guess. And he never called or texted or emailed her again. I think they did a lot," she said. She wouldn't look at me. "The girl was really upset."

I was dumbfounded. "Well, don't you always have all the information."

"They were drunk. Lizzie, he's one of those asshole private-school boys. We hate those kids."

Was this in fact *West Side Story*? I recalled not a single conversation that was about how much we didn't like private-school boys. I didn't even know them. "He's not, though. He's not like that."

"Lizzie, he *is*. I'm sorry he got sent away, but maybe it's just for the best."

"I'm really glad I have you to talk to," I said, extricating myself from the pile of us. "So helpful."

"Come on." She grabbed my wrist to pull me back down.

I twisted it away. "No, Zoe. That is messed up."

"Liz!" she called to me when I was in the hallway. "I was just trying to help!"

I went into my room and closed my door. I took out the letter from Connor, and I have to say, I loved it. I wanted to press it into a book and save it forever, like a flower or pretty leaf. I wanted to kiss it and hold it, open, to my heart.

And yet. And yet!

Now I couldn't stop picturing Connor with another girl, someone perfect, either perfectly cool or perfectly tanned and blond. Who would it be? No matter where he was, Connor always found someone. After all, he had found me.

Who would Connor love? If he could love.

I wished I could take my letter back, reverse the day and just suck it out of that mailbox, go back to my bed, undo writing it on my study buddy covered in stars, put the paper back, the pen. Be the kind of girl who just one time waited patiently. Be the girl who didn't say everything all at once.

I heard Tim arrive yet again and I heard him go into Zoe's room and I heard the dogs leave, and the creak of the bed, and I heard them talking and then after a few minutes I heard silence.

Fuck Zoe, I thought, with her perfect room and her perfect intact body and her perfect boyfriend, and all her *information*. I had been so humiliated—by doctors, by my body, by Connor. And by Zoe, who chose to deliver this kind of important detail way later than was ethically correct. She was my *sister*.

Why was I the only one with shame around here?

I knew they were doing it, even with my parents right downstairs getting Sunday dinner ready. I wondered if they were naked.

I tiptoed out of my room and into the hallway and leaned into her closed door, placed my fingertips against the wood. It was silent but for Nina Simone playing softly from her phone dock—downloaded from Tim's Pandora search for Sounds Like Birdy, no doubt—and an occasional creak of the bed. I hesitated, but my worst self got the best of me. I grabbed the handle and opened the door as loudly and shockingly as possible.

Zoe, who was on her bed, leaning against the perfect unstickered headboard, jumped. And Tim, who was seated on the floor, his back against the bed, just at her feet, looked toward me slowly, imploringly.

"What the fuck, Liz?" she said.

My hand was still on the glass doorknob. It always fell off, but no one ever fixed it. They looked so sweet. Like they'd known each other forever. "Oh," I said.

"What?" Zoe knocked her pencil against her notebook, which sat on her knees.

"Nothing." I shook my head.

"Do you need something, Liz?" Tim asked.

"Sorry." I shook my head again. Love is just sitting in your room studying together. You don't even have to be touching. It could be that easy. Who knew.

Who would you love if you could love? I thought, closing the door and heading downstairs. Maybe, for Connor, it was no one. Maybe he just couldn't. It really is sometimes best to cut the bad out. My colon. Just get rid of it. Before it explodes inside me. Perhaps Connor had been right. We were never there. We were not here either. Pretty much, we were nowhere.

In Ether

If this was a different kind of story, a kind where time could bend and split, where we could hurl ourselves across time, if this story—my story—let me turn time backward, it would be to before I opened Letter Two. It would be to the time when all I feared was that Connor treated a girl who trusted him badly and that he might not love me back or that he might get a letter from me that laid my heart bare and crumple it up and throw it away.

But I couldn't bend time, and Letter Two arrived while my letter was out there in the ether. It's a feeling I remember so well: wanting to reach out into the universe and snatch my words back. Impossible, of course, and here was Connor's letter anyway.

Letter 2

October 12, 2013

Dear Lizzie,

First of all, Lizzie, I miss you. I won't go on about how it is here, how strange and how dark it gets at night. Like the way you said the hospital got. No city, no stars really, just black. I miss Verlaine most then. Poor Verlaine, all alone in my house. My father takes him out, I know he does, but he's not there all day.

I guess that's a whole other story, for another letter. A letter that can just tell you about life here, like the record player in the lounge area donated by some kid's famous music producer father, who believed you needed to hear the scratch of the needle, watch the record turn, and it is a whole other experience. It is true: you really do just listen.

But that's not for this letter.

I haven't told you all of it, because I didn't want you to lose respect for me. Or stop . . . liking me. I want to stay the special guy who, when he walked into your room, made you smile.

But I need to tell you now, and this might be the hardest thing I've ever had to write. The accident was not a hit-and-run. I did not just witness the accident. People did blame me, but that was because I hit the girl. I was the driver. I had my learner's permit, and I was driving with my friend's older sister, who was seventeen and an underage person to drive with when you only have a permit. Anyway, that isn't really the important thing. The thing is I hit her. I didn't just hit her. I was also stoned. Which is horrible, I know. She just ran out in front of the car and I couldn't stop in time. She just ran out into the street. She died. I hit her. I totally hit her. I lied to you. I killed the little girl in the green dress. It was always me.

So I fell apart. I became someone I wasn't. I treated people like I shouldn't have. Until you. You made me need to be good again.

I am so so so so so sorry I lied to you, Lizzie. I wish that I could take that back too. I know it's not an excuse, but I couldn't bear you knowing this horrible thing about me.

I wanted you to see me as the good person I wanted to be, the person I know I am, inside.

I will do anything for you to forgive me. Anything.

I hope you can forgive me. I hope everyone can.

Yours always,
Connor

Closet of Lost Toys

What can I say. Stunned, shocked, bowled over, horrified, sad, angry, shaking, betrayed. Did I mention horrified? I was all of these things all at once. It was like my body was just storage, a closet of lost toys, and instead of the tennis rackets and hockey sticks and old karaoke machines and beach balls and pails and shovels and old hats, it was stuffed with every kind of emotion available to humans. Just open it and everything would tumble out. And go where? Where do those old discarded things *go*?

What I didn't feel then was sorry for Connor. When I got that letter, I just shook and crawled up into a ball and cried for all of us: the girl, for me, and also every other person I'd ever known. Connor too, I guess, even though I almost hated him. I felt this suffering—everyone's suffering—move through me. It was awful. I even felt it for the flowers dying in my father's garden. I thought I was going insane, because there I was thinking plants had feelings and that they were suffering too.

Why me? I guess I thought this a lot then. Why did I have all this stuff to deal with—body stuff, life stuff, *death* stuff—while everyone else was just making out at dances and singing in the school musical? I got ahold of myself. I was able to, without picking up the phone and calling . . . who? Who was I going to call? That was the thing. Connor was my connection to my self. I realized that only then, that he was the only one I could talk to about what he'd done.

Was Connor a bad person? Was Nora? Nora was reckless, but nothing really bad had happened to her yet. It could. It might. What happened to Connor was an accident. It was, like Collette said that day we came back from Fletcher's Cove, poor judgment. I couldn't think of her family, of her mother, holding her dead hand. I thought instead about Connor: it was a bad thing, but it was an accident. In a way, Connor was not unlike me. We had both been so unlucky.

But the difference between Connor and me was that he had lied. Was he a liar? Or was it just this one thing that he was keeping from me to make me love him? I had told him everything. Everything! And everything he had revealed had been a lie. Maybe the emotions were the same, maybe he was telling me his *feelings*, but the facts were plain old dirty lies.

Did that make him a liar? He was trying to talk to me. He was. It was hard not to think of the reasons he could have lied. Fear. I know the way fear works now—what wouldn't I have done to make even some of my fear go away?

What had he done to Zoe's friend? Was that what he meant by treating people badly? And driving stoned? Who was the girl he was driving with anyway? The girl me took over, the one who even then could not stop thinking about how much better all the other girls were, in every possible way. The girl me who could so easily lose sight of the rest of it, the real story.

I would never be strong enough, I thought.

So many lies. He was as far from that boy I had once thought he was, straight off a surfboard, sauntering in with his golden dog, as far beyond my reach as he could be. Imagine my luck, I'd thought then. Of all places, a boy like Connor Bryant. Was this the same person who had taken me out of the hospital and kissed me in a rowboat like it was the end of the world? Who had given me a turtle and let me call her Frog?

Yes. He was all those things. Did I love him despite what he'd done? I was learning that you had to take all of it, the whole person, whatever was left of that person, see everything, want everything, accept it all. People needed to do that for me and my new hacked-at self, my new bitter sparkly personality, and maybe one day I would have to do that for Connor. But I also had some power now. I was standing up and out of bed, and for better or worse—worse actually, in that here I was shoving myself into my jeans again—the staples had been taken out and I was standing up straighter and I could do the choosing. Would just having loved Connor be enough? Did I still? Could I? My letter hadn't reached him yet. But it would so soon. I couldn't take it back, so: What would I choose?

Warm Phone

It was the day the letter came. On the fifteenth, well actually just a little after midnight on the fifteenth, so, I guess if we're documenting things, it was technically the sixteenth. A call from a 603 area code came in, and I just knew it was him, that it came from a place where the leaves were changing and it was getting colder and it was like what I imagine college would be. That was what I got from the 603. All of that.

But I couldn't answer it. I had been waiting for Connor to call since the day he came into my hospital room. How many nights had I waited? But the letter had only come that day. I could not talk to him about what was in that letter yet.

I let it ring and ring until voice mail, so he could still think that maybe I just had the ringer off to sleep. I waited, the phone lighted beneath my comforter, and then I waited again for the red 1 to come up on my voice-mail widget.

There it was. I listened, but there was just dead air. Nothing. Was it breathing?

And then the 603 call again. The going through the waiting again. And then this time, Connor spoke.

"Hi, Elizabeth Stoller," he said. Still, he stopped my heart. No matter what, no matter anything. Heart stopper. "Hi. I think you got my letter by now. I'm sure you have. I wanted to call you because, as Dr. Farrell says, it's good to be direct. I want to talk to you about everything. Will you still talk to me?" he asked. "This is our only line, and we have sign-ups for when we can use it. I will call you again. I will try to reach you. Hello, Lizzie. It's that guy from the hospital. Remember me?" he said. "I remember you."

How could that message have been more beautiful? Forget that he had waited this long to call me. Forget that he had killed a girl and lied about it. Forget that he was sent away. Remember our hands. I remembered Connor. The feel of him.

I scrolled down, listened:

Well, this is Connor. The guy from the hospital? The guy with the cute dog? Call me sometime.

I held my warm phone close. The voice was a stranger's voice and yet it was the same voice, the boy was the same, I was the same.

So how had everything suddenly changed?

Good Citizen

The Bottom Drawer didn't press charges. That's what Nora emailed to tell me, anyway, and what now did she have to gain by lying? Did they even have email in juvie? I didn't think so, but what did I know? *We need to make another plan,* she wrote. And then? *I will say I've got some killer new skivvies.* I ignored this when I wrote her back. *We totally do!* I wrote, regarding the plan. *Smiley face heart kiss pink elephant yellow flower.*

But I knew we wouldn't. Maybe we were just camp friends. The gum tree. The moldy old cabins. The flashlights shaking through the woods. Kid stuff. Summer things. Maybe it's not turning off the light. Maybe it's just letting the seasons change.

I couldn't help but think that about Connor too, our season. The hospital—not camp—but this eerie alt place. Maybe the real world was not for us. We were all about parallel universes.

I didn't write him back. I didn't try to call him or email or find a way to talk to him. His voice was the same, but still he felt like a stranger.

I will try to reach you. Remember me? I remember you.

As sad as I was, I could feel myself getting stronger, everything healing, the scar sealing things in securely, like a change purse.

I never liked it, that would be insane, but I had gotten used to changing the bag, all the ointments and contraptions I needed to make sure it didn't get too irritated or worse, come undone.

I was transforming from werewolf back to human. And from human it was like I could spin three times and there were my bulletproof bracelets, my lasso. My superhuman Wonder Woman speed and strength. I felt like that sometimes, like I was some girl superhero now. My dark, sad alter ego, felled by kryptonite, was the girl sick in bed in the dark, waiting for a nurse to take her blood, a girl I hope never to meet again. I wasn't much for meeting the girl I was before I got sick either. She didn't know anything. She was ashamed of everything.

I knew a lot by then. I was smaller but I was bigger. What was my special power? I didn't know. But I did know that Dee and Lydia were off on a different path. Mabel and Greta were my sidekicks now.

That's when I decided it was time to take my sidekicks in for proper training.

We went to Petiquette because, I mean, it was called Petiquette. Also it was the closest dog training place to us. We'd missed a class, but I didn't want to wait until the next session, so I drove Greta and Mabel and me to our first class, my mother in the passenger seat.

I looked in the rearview at Mabel and Greta, scratching and scrambling.

"Do *not* get distracted, Liz." My mother turned around in her seat. "Girls!" she said to the dogs. "Oh my God!" my mother said. "Center *lane*, please!"

Just then a text came in with a delicate *ping!*

"You're driving!" My mother was borderline hysterical.

I gripped the wheel. "Mother. I'm not looking at it!"

My stomach clenched and I felt my bag. I really never didn't feel it, but sometimes it was more . . . *pronounced* than others. My mother gripped the door handle like she was in a movie. My mother was always acting like she was in a goddamn movie. Or maybe I just made her act that way. Whatever the case, we managed to arrive at Petiquette, and early too, and we signed up and I headed into the Good Citizen training, ready to go.

I checked my phone. The text was from Michael L: *One more try? I really did miss you. How about the movies with Dee and K on Fri? Wink wink clapping hands smiley face.*

K. He's going by Kenickie now. I don't even remember his actual name anymore.

K, I wrote back, but I think the irony might have been lost. Why the hell not, I thought. What's to lose here?

Think better of it was just one of the things I learned that night. The others? Greta and Mabel could not be in the same class. They were barely even the same species. And Greta could not go into hospitals and nursing homes, both places that don't have a lot of use for dogs that jump up and bark and get down on front legs to play and then whimper when they are dragged away. The trainer, a tall woman named Esther who had long hair with so many split ends it looked like she'd been plugged into a socket and who introduced herself by saying if she were a dog she'd be a whippet, gave me some serious stink eye and told me this was a class for dogs who have already had training.

Oh. So this was the *AP* class.

I went to get my mother.

"That dog is way too young for hospitals," the trainer said. "Think about it. How will she be soothing? How could her visit possibly be a comfort to someone?"

I didn't say how it totally would be, but I did think that was what we were here for, to train the dogs to be a comfort. Maybe it's not the Petiquette we need to be working on, I thought as I handed Greta over to my mom, who was reading in the waiting area, where she thought she'd be the whole hour we "trained." She took Greta into the novice class. Like so, so novice.

As soon as my mother walked out with Greta, Mabel got on her doggie smile and sat perfectly and gave me her paw and generally was her best Mabel self. I imagined bald kids smiling when she walked into their hospital rooms. I imagined old ladies motioning to her with their gnarled old-lady hands.

That was the night I met Stella B.

Stella and her pit bull, Samantha. Stella with her Clash T-shirt and her bicycle chain bracelets and her blue suede creepers, her dark black eyeliner. Her hair—kind of like a mullet—stuck out in all directions. She had three safety pins in each ear. She waved at me and she smiled, not angry like her clothes or, like Connor, all dark and menacing, a *killer*, beneath his beachy face. Me with my bag, scarred up, no one knew what was there. Once my weakness but now, maybe my secret armor. My Superman *S*— that scar—beneath my regular clothes. None of us are what we seem. Stella Sammy Mabel and me. Twice a week at Petiquette. Mom and Greta trailing, tangled, behind.

Who knew I had been waiting for someone like Stella?

Finally, my own girl band.

House of Wax

I guess I was expecting him to call me and chase me and try to win me back, make me understand what had happened and why he had lied. But no call came. There was no mail call either, just a strange and quiet void, snow falling, as silent as before those letters had ever arrived.

I wondered if he'd gotten my letter. And since it didn't mention anything about the accident, I wondered if he was angry. Or maybe he'd moved on already. Found some prep school girl in a plaid skirt and a crewneck cashmere sweater and expensive boots who'd also been sent far away from home. A girl as perfect on the outside and as blue inside as Connor was. I pictured them listening to My Chemical Romance late at night on the school record player and cutting the insides of each other's forearms with razor blades.

I pictured them needing each other.

No call, all lies, so why not go to the movies with Michael? My parents were thrilled when I told them I was going out. They practically pushed me out the car door onto the street when they dropped me off.

So here we were: at a horror movie from the fifties. *House of Wax.* Chosen by Dee-Dee, of course. (WWRW: *What Would Rizzo Watch?*) So: A wax museum, a house on fire, a crippled, burned man who rebuilds the museum by killing people and using their dead bodies. First one ever in 3D. Did that make it scarier? It was all lost on me. Once it would have sent me to the café next door, but now it just creeped me out. I had lost most kinds of fear.

What made it even less scary was that we had to go in the daytime. Because after 9:00 p.m. it turned into a place where you could drink beer while watching the burned man kill people.

I felt Michael's hand reach for mine, and I took it. Perhaps, I thought, I could live my life in the old way, at school, feeling lucky that princely Michael L might pick me, even if it was because I was the sick girl. Hadn't that been why Connor chose me? Sickness: a magnet. Our fingers interlocked. I could feel Michael's smooth nail with my thumb, normal nails, not ripped at the cuticles and bitten to the quick. He put his other arm around me and I leaned into him.

Michael's hand on my shoulder. He brought me closer and we started to kiss. It was long and slow and I will say this again: Michael L is an amazing kisser. Not a lot of slobber. A little tongue, just enough. I think we kissed well together, actually.

It was nothing like with Connor; there was nothing serious about it. And then I sensed his hand along my shirt again. I sat up straight. I looked up at the screen at some girl realizing her dead friend was already dead, and then at Kenickie, who was practically nailing Rizzo to the seat, fifties drive-in style.

"Hey," I said to Michael as he leaned back into his chair. He snapped his head in a way that moved his hair out of his face. Michael was all-over adorable, and I don't know what he was doing with me. "I'm going to wait outside."

"Are you joking?" he asked me.

"I scare easily!" I said, laughing.

"That," Michael said, "is truth."

"Ha-ha. Come on," I told him. "I just can't. Understand."

I feel like the entire movie theater was listening to us as they gazed at the display that was Dee and "K."

"Is it because you don't feel well?"

I shook my head, but not sure he could see that in the dark. I know he was thinking, why else would freakish Lizzie Stoller not want to be felt up by me?

"I'll go with you." He looked over at our friends and rolled his eyes, which caught the light of the gruesome scene. "What, I'm supposed to sit with these guys? Please."

I shrugged. "Sure."

We grabbed our jackets and shuffled out of our aisle and went out the side of the theater. Momentarily blinded by the shock of the sunlight, I heard the door shut loudly and permanently behind us. I turned my face toward the sun.

"Okay, Lizzie, spit it out."

"Spit what out?" I shielded my eyes.

"What's up? I know you like me."

"Oh really," I said. I kept my eyes shielded and now looked up at him and smiled. My first post-hospital flirt. I admit it felt nice to be free of everything, what had happened to me, what was happening to Connor, what would happen to us both. "I know you never liked me." Post-hospital rules: say anything.

"That's not true," he said.

"It's not like there weren't other opportunities. For years. So why now?"

"It's just now for me," he said.

"Hmmm."

"You know the thing I said about absence."

"Hmmm."

"Is it because you're still sick? Like, do you feel sick now?" Again he swept his hair out of his face with a flick of his head. It was starting to look like a spasm.

That's how it is, right? So easy to flip over. Michael from beautiful perfect to freakish and hideous. One small move and anyone can cross a line.

"Nah," I said. "I feel okay. I'm just not ready." Connor lied and he was sort of a criminal, but I couldn't let go of the thought of him, the maybe of him. I didn't mention him to Michael, though. If I'm being perfectly honest, I think I was also keeping my options a little bit open.

"Well, the night is young," he said.

"So young it's day." I kicked at the building with the toe of my sneaker.

"We could still hang out. What do you want to do? Where should we go?"

"Hey," I said. "Michael? Can we go to a pet store?"

Scars Make the Body Interesting

Michael's older sister, Jillian, picked us up and we all went to Pet Planet. I got a new tank and an aquarium light for Frog and some accessories for her new aquatic universe. Jillian got a guppy in a plastic bag, and Michael got one of those Siamese fighting fish for himself. "Pow, pow," he said, old-school evil-fighter-style, punching me when we stood waiting at the register. "Pow."

When Jillian pulled up in front of my house, I hopped out. She held up her fish to the light. "Thank you," she said, leaning over the passenger seat. "For making little Oscar possible!"

Michael got out and unlocked the trunk, bent down and took out Frog's new world. "It's heavy."

"I got it!" I tried to take the awkwardly large box from him.

"No, Liz," he said. "Chill, okay? If I take it into your house, I don't get your firstborn."

I felt everything relax. Shoulders, thigh muscles, stomach, heart. "Thanks."

I followed Michael L up the stone steps and unlocked the door. He set the box down in the hallway and placed his hands in the pockets of his jacket. He might as well have been holding them up to show me he was unarmed.

He cleared his throat. "We can just be friends, you know."

I nodded. "Okay." I really wanted to be friends with Michael again.

"Let's just go back to before everything."

"We can't really," I said. "But I totally get what you mean."

"Lizzie?" my mother yelled down from the top of the stairs.

"Hey, Mom." I sighed. I unzipped my jacket. "I'd invite you in, but your sis is outside."

"Well, she has her new guppy to keep her company."

I laughed. It's a funny word. "Thanks," I said.

"Sure." Michael cuffed me on the chin. He totally did this! Like I was his little sister. It felt awesome. Then he put his arm around me in this I'm-about-to-mess-up-your-hair kind of way.

I looked down at the Moroccan rug and laughed again. It turns out Michael Lerner really was a prince.

"A'ight. See you later!" he said, and then he was out the door, and I watched him go back down the steps and make his way to his family Volvo. I knew I might regret sending him away, but that was how it was for me now.

My mother was halfway down the stairs. "How was the movie?" she asked me.

"Fun, Mom."

"See?" she said, hands on her hips. "Told you so."

I made sure Frog's new tank was the right temperature, with all the perfect amounts of UVA and UVB light. I added my purchases to the scenery: little rocks and fake and real ferns, a piece of driftwood for her to bask on or hide beneath.

I sat on my bed and watched her. Actually, I sat in my bedroom for a long time that night. I listened to Birdy, but she felt so soft and sweet, too good and young and pretty. I had this thought: What if all of us Birdy fans—all us girls, really, who wanted to be good and young and pretty, too—were sitting here in our rooms, looking at our turtles or our hamsters or our parrots, whatever live thing we had here, separately listening to this thing that connects us all? But we couldn't find each other. We were alone in our rooms, invisible in the world.

In the hospital I wasn't alone. Those nurses checked on me all night long. I had a roommate. She might have pretty much only slept and watched television, and we might have been divided by that disgusting curtain, but we were connected too. And our room was connected by Connor and Verlaine, an unbroken line. In a way, me there in my bedroom, my parents downstairs, my sister off at Tim's studying for the SATs yet again, I was more alone than ever.

Maybe that's why I got so happy seeing Stella B at Petiquette on Tuesdays. Every week I looked forward to seeing her.

The first time I really talked to her was the next week. All the sessions began in a circle, our dogs at our feet, underneath the glare and hum of the fluorescent light. That night it was me, and Stella B and gray Samantha, and then a bunch of older ladies and their little King Charles spaniels and Havaneses and then two guys, one with a beagle, the other with a Rottweiler. Looking around the room, I could see the truth: dogs really do resemble their people. If I was going to resemble a dog, I was lucky to look like Mabel.

There was some monitored dog socializing, and then we were off to train. What were we doing? I think we were still at sit and stay then.

"Look at you. Heeling," Stella said, eyeing Mabel.

I hadn't heard her approach us. I straightened. How did she know? "Well, I've been sick," I said. It just came out.

"Oh! Okay."

I then saw that Mabel was in fact heeling. I laughed, but I could feel heat rising to my face.

"Flawless," Esther said, her split ends silhouetted in the evening light. "Heeling is extremely difficult for dogs. True heeling, that is."

I looked at Mabel and she was looking at me, part of the heeling process.

Stella's pit bull was pretty close to her side, and I watched her arrange her leash in a way that would get her at her hip, on the left side. She did it with such ease.

I'm telling you: she trained with ease, but Stella *looked* crazy. Her hair, so black it was practically blue, those black-lined eyes, which were bright blue, a faded wife beater with a huge men's short-sleeve striped polyester vintage button-down over it, and so on and so on. She was giggling.

"What are you going to do with her?" Stella said when we'd all sat back in our circle, our dogs subdued by our feet.

I placed my hand firmly yet gently on Mabel's back, and she sighed.

"If you guys get the certificate?"

"'If'?" I said. "Please, sister. Does it look like there's going to be an 'if' here?"

"True. Okay. When."

"Children's hospital?"

"So were you that kind of sick? Or like flu sick?"

"That kind of sick." I looked down at Mabel.

"That's shitty," she said.

I nodded. I didn't laugh at the second pun she didn't know she was making.

"I understand you might want to help little kids now," she said.

I pictured Mabel smiling at a bald five-year-old. I pictured him smiling back, cured of sorrow and maybe even cured of cancer.

"But man, that sounds fucking depressing."

I don't know why. Maybe because she was a stranger or because she was a girl or because she was truthful or because she had a velvety gray pit named Samantha, but that night, after training, when she waited with me for my mother to finish up with Greta, I told her everything about the hospital.

It didn't take that long. There was something calm about her that made me want to talk.

"You said it's going to be removed?" she asked. "The bag?"

"Supposedly by summer," I told her. We were on a bench outside Petiquette, and the night was dark and super starry.

"Are you glad?"

"Of course I'm glad," I said. "Why wouldn't I be? This thing is no fun. At. All. And it keeps me from things."

"From what things?"

"I don't know. Being close to people." Is that what had kept me from Michael L? Maybe a little.

"I would think it would filter the bad people out."

I thought about that. I thought not just of the people who might actually see it, but the ones like Dee and Lydia, who really weren't there anymore. I could filter them out.

"I see your point."

Of course I thought of Connor. He was, then, in everything I thought. And I also thought how much I liked Stella's point of view. You think you've heard everything about being sick or getting better, all of it. But then, it turns out, you haven't because Stella tells you something new.

"I don't know." She fingered her bike chain bracelet. It was rusted.

"Did you buy that?" I pointed to the bracelet.

"Buy? God no. My friend made it for me," she said. "It's ridiculous. I don't know. Anyway. I think if it were me, I might just keep it. I mean, I'm sure it's a total pain and uncomfortable and surreal to have and life changing, but now you've got another surgery, and if you remove it, it's like the whole thing is over."

"That's what I'm going for. Overness." Inadvertently I brought my hand to my stomach.

"I'm all for war wounds," Stella said. "I wouldn't want them taken from me."

"Well," I said. "You have no idea."

"I don't," she said. "I've got no fucking idea, but I think scars make the body more interesting."

"Scars, maybe," I said. "This is not a scar. I could deal with the scars. I could." I will.

"See this?" She pointed to the corner of her eye. A fine line slashed diagonally across her brow. "I fell when I was a kid."

"That's not really the same thing." Seriously? That she equated my experience with falling *down* might have ended it with Stella B, which would have been a shame, because I could tell I really liked her.

"But I didn't tell you that I was being chased. It was really bad. Chased by a neighbor. Who caught me. If I hadn't fallen and gotten blood everywhere and had to go to the hospital, which gave me this scar, it would have been a very, very bad thing."

I was silent.

"Let's just say this reminds me of a lot of things. Mostly about being lucky."

"I've been lucky," I said. "But I think I can remember that part without this."

"Can you?"

I could.

That's when my mother came prancing out with a crazed Greta straining at her leash, trying to get to us. "Wait, why am I doing this again?" she asked me. "Wasn't this your and Daddy's idea?"

"Hi, there," Stella said, standing. "I'm Stella."

"Hi," my mom said.

"Daphne," I said, nodding my head toward her.

"Hi, Daphne," said Stella.

My mother looked stunned. Finally! Then she turned to me, and trying to get hold of Greta, she flashed us both a massive grin.

Fruit

I could tell this about Stella B: that just a few months before, we never would have even noticed each other. But now, hanging out with her made me think of all of us, a string of girls, connected as we lay in our beds listening to music in our lonely bedrooms by laser beams of pink light. And I pictured my beam crossing over Dee-Dee's and Lydia's house and making my way to Stella B. What was Stella B's room like? Stella, who had a license and who was waiting to hear about early decision. Stella, who looked all beat up and punked out and biker and broken but was sweet and straight A's and smart and also *wise*. How did she get that way? And what did she see in me?

What was Stella doing tonight?

But beneath all that I was as always thinking of Connor. If Stella was right about my being sick and having this bag sort of filtered out the soulless, and I think she *was* right, then I was keeping him. Keeping Connor. But why had all this happened? Why did he have to make it so hard to see the good? How was I supposed to pretend it never happened? Was Connor also filtering out the bad people? Maybe I was also being tested.

What, I wondered beneath all of that, was Connor doing tonight?

Laser beams of light. Did they reach Nora all the way through the tunnel to Baltimore? Possibly. I put her music on. Le Tigre: "Oh, we could rock, or we could bomb, or we could try, like super hard. . . ."

Kathleen Hanna versus Birdy. Like rip open a pomegranate or bite into a sweet red apple. Which would you rather? This is what I was thinking about when, at 11:55, the phone rang again.

202!

Washington, DC. Connor's cell.

202.

This time I was ready.

Making Plans

"Hi!" he said. Connor said. Connor on the other end of the line.

"Hey," I said. Both so happy and so . . . sorrowful. Both at once. Always.

"I got your letter, Liz." He seemed so happy.

"I got yours too." I leaned my head back against that stickered headboard, right on Hello Kitty. *Bump. Bump. Bump* went my head against the wood.

"Did you get mine before you sent yours?" Connor asked me.

"No," I said. "Your letter, it came after."

"Oh," he said. "I knew that, but I was still hoping. Because your letter said I love you."

Really, I thought. Because of course I knew that. I had written it and crossed it out and thrown the paper away and then written it again. All this is to say that I knew what I had written. I knew what had made me write it too. Everything was different now. But I didn't say any of those things. What I said was, "That was before."

"Before what?" Connor said flatly.

I was silent. I could hear myself breathing. I got out of bed and went to my desk, sat down. Leaned in and looked at Frog from her level.

"Before the letter, you mean," he said.

"Yes, Connor. Before the letter."

Now it was his turn to breathe.

"It was before I knew the truth! Which was that you lied to me," I said.

"I see," he said.

"You see? Oh, good!"

"You don't have to be cruel."

Now I didn't say anything. What was cruelty, really? I always thought about it in relationship to how people treated animals. How beings treated beings who were weaker. I wasn't cruel, but I hadn't known I had the power to be either. "I'm not meaning to be cruel," I said. "That's a harsh word."

"Sorry. You're right. This isn't about you."

I gave out a fake laugh. "Thanks!" I said.

"No, I mean the past. What happened. But can I just ask? I mean, I know there is so much to say about how sorry I am and how much I want—no, need—you to forgive me, but I just need to know: Is it that I didn't tell you the truth, that I lied, or is it the thing? The thing that happened?"

"The accident? You mean the girl dying? *That* accident? You mean the time you hit her with the car you were driving when you were high?"

"Yes that. And that's also what I mean by cruel."

"I think it's both. It's a little bit about the Thing, but that was this single thing. It's more the crazy lies, though. Those were for so long."

"Okay," Connor said.

"I see what happened really clearly." I don't know why, but I opened the drawer and picked up David B's God's eye. My talisman. "That it was like a moment. And then it was over." I tilted my head and twirled it a little in my palm, felt the rough bark of the sticks that held the softest purple yarn together. "It all makes me feel really bad for you, actually. And for her. And her parents." I set down the God's eye. I looked in on Frog, basking on her log beneath the fake sun.

"Me too," Connor said. I think he was crying a little.

"Sorry."

"Sorry?"

"Yeah. That this . . . *happened*." I stood up.

"Thanks," Connor said. "In a way, it never really happened. I didn't mention in the letter that my mom is this incredibly famous attorney. She gets people like congressmen and actors out of trouble. Once a senator was found drunk and cheating, and she got him off by blaming Ambien, and then she sued Ambien and he got a zillion dollars. So all this? It doesn't exist. I was never even there. But of course I was. I hate myself. No cutting that part out, right? All the ugly stuff."

"That's crazy. Because it happened. And you lied to me about it. I told you everything!"

"I'm so sorry, Liz. I would do anything to take it back. To sit next to you in that awful hospital room and tell you the truth and have you still be there waiting for me the next day. But you can see that wasn't going to happen. If I told you, you would have hated me."

I didn't know what I would have felt, if I was being honest.

He had a point. Maybe I needed to love him first for him to tell me the truth. "You know, I looked for you online," I said. "You really *aren't* there. Like at all." I went back to my bed, lay back. *Bump, bump.*

"She got rid of *everything*. It's disgusting. You looked for me?"

"Of course. You fell off the surface of the world." I remembered just searching and searching and coming up with nothing. Like I'd totally dreamed Connor. The whole thing.

"I know. I'm so sorry," Connor said.

"Also? You're not ugly. You are so wonderful! Like, seriously wonderful. I gotta say, you're not the guy I thought you were, but I know there is nothing ugly about you."

Connor was silent.

And so was I. If the conversation had been different, I'd be mortified to have said such a thing. But not in this conversation.

"Thanks, Lizzie," he said.

"Well, I wouldn't want you to be the guy I thought you were anyway. That guy was just this perfect private-school boy who partied in the day and had no problems at all."

"Ha." It came out a little bitter.

"When you and Verlaine first came into my room, I barely remember what I thought. That was so long ago, in sick years." I sat up.

"Right?" Connor said. "Verlaine. I miss him."

"Sorry," I said. I wished Mabel was near me.

"How's Mabel?" Connor asked, because he will always be able to read my mind. Always.

"Perfect. And we got a rescue. Greta. Totally bat-shit crazy."

"Perfect," he said, and I could just tell he was smiling. "Are you still listening to Birdy?"

"Mm-hmm," I said.

"And the Beatles? There's an old-school record store near here, and I've been buying a bunch. Old stuff. But I keep looking for new-pressed Birdy for you."

"Thank you," I said.

"I didn't want you to hate me," Connor said quietly.

"Are there other lies?" I asked him.

"No."

"To me or to anyone else?"

"What do you mean?"

I took a deep breath. "Have you lied to other people?" I was thinking of Tim's friend's friend. Of her. The one who Connor never spoke to again.

"I don't know what you're talking about, but yes, I've lied to other people. But I'm not lying to you or to anyone else anymore."

"Other girls?"

"I haven't outright lied. But I haven't always been a good person. No. I know that. I am not that person anymore, though. I am up here at school and I'm just alone a lot. And sometimes at night in this garden, harvesting the fall stuff other kids planted, I feel like a fucking carrot. Like I'm tearing myself out of the ground too. It sounds so cheesy. As you can see, I'm in therapy!"

"I see!"

"Gardening at night. Heh. R.E.M. You know?"

"No, don't know that song," I said. I never was going to know the right song. Like, ever.

"You don't? That's crazy. I thought everyone knew that song."

"No, I don't. I just said I don't."

"Okay," he said. "I'll send it to you."

"I can look it up on my own, Connor."

"All right then," he said. "How's Frog?"

I looked up at the ceiling. Everything in this room was blue. "You know I do love you," I whispered, ignoring the question, even though my answer seemed connected to it.

"You do?"

"I do." And I did. I just felt it so big. Out of sadness, maybe. So much was coming from me from that place then.

"Me too," Connor said. "Since before I ever met you." He said that.

"What does that even mean?" I asked. I was teasing him, but I also wanted to know. I really wanted to know.

"It means." He was quiet. "Let me think. It means I went in there—to the hospital—looking for you and I didn't even know it. Not looking for *a* you, but for you. Because I loved you."

"Click," I said.

"What does that mean?"

"That's us just fitting together. Just being perfect."

"Okay," Connor said. "Click, click, click."

I burrowed under my covers like some kind of hamster and watched my alarm clock's digital face make its way toward late, late night. Connor was lonely and alone and sent away and fearful, but I was those things too, minus the being-sent-away part. And finally there was this person on the other side with me. Here

I was on the moon, and who knew someone else was suited up and waiting for me there?

When my clock read 2:00 a.m., I panicked a little. Connor was talking about reading *Hamlet*. "Hey, Connor? It's so late. And I'm already so behind," I said, but this time I only meant in school.

"I'm not supposed to be on my cell anyway."

"What?" I said. I was shocked. How many rules could Connor break?

"It's okay. It's a minor infraction. No one will ever know. My roommate's at his mother's house tonight."

"Oh, okay, I guess. I have no idea."

"It's all rules. There are so many."

Rules. I didn't have that many, actually. Just the ones I was making for myself. I said, "Okay, so how about this. Let's pretend this never happened. I mean not ignore it totally, but, like, what would we be from here? Without all the bad shit? Like, what are the good things? About us? Let's just be them and have them."

"I love that," Connor said. "I wish I could see you and tell you in person."

"I know. Me too," I said. "Soon, okay?"

"I have another idea," Connor said.

"Where is it again?" I said before we hung up again. I wrote down the address.

"I'll be there waiting," Connor said.

"But are you even allowed to leave school?"

"I'll arrange it," he said. "I'll take care of everything."

That's what he'd said the last time, when we snuck out of the hospital together like thieves.

Thick as thieves. It had to have been from some song I was supposed to know.

But I didn't. What I did know was this: we were thieves. But what were we stealing?

I thought of it more like we were taking our lives back.

Our lives together. The very least I could do was see Connor again.

Lost and Found

Halloween was coming. There was not a holiday I hated more, other than perhaps Valentine's Day. Costumes. Pretending. Covering up the covering up. Thank God for Petiquette.

Another night at Petiquette. And: another funny thing about Stella B? She drove a white Ford Fiesta.

"Don't." She shook her head when I watched her park. She rolled down her window. "It's my mother's car. It's totally my mother's."

Greta and my mother were already inside, but I waited for her. I laughed. I mean I covered my mouth and full-on laughed.

"I added the accessories," she said. A hula girl hung from the rearview. And one of those bobbing dogs was on the dusty dash.

"But anyway? This is kinda who I am too." She sort of cackled as she poked the hula girl's skirt, making her dance, and then unlocked the door to get out.

"I get it," I said as we all four went inside, entering the hall-way of paper pumpkins and chunks of white cotton that were somehow supposed to represent spiderwebs. Who decided that? Because they don't look like spiderwebs at all. "I totally do," I said, and it was true, I really got Stella B. She was just so clear to me.

Greta's novice class always went at least ten minutes long, and it's amazing how much of getting to know a person you can pack into those ten minutes when you're not in school or near school or with people from school. It's like being on a plane with someone. Or a hospital. Alt universe, enclosed space, anything goes.

We waited on the bench outside and we both kicked at the pavement. Stella was going through a breakup with this guy she'd been with since her freshman year. "Forever," she said. "Before I was even a person. I was an unhatched egg. A little downy chick."

I couldn't picture it. Stella all sweet and yellow and soft and breakable. "Why'd you guys break up?" I asked. "I mean, in three sentences or less?"

"He's in college."

My heart skipped at the thought. So old and far away. And so close. Stella was just so much older than I was in experience years, though I supposed I'd gained some time in sickness years. Though I do think I got some time in there with the sickness. Serious sick years.

"And just away," she said. "He's away now. That's all."

I nodded.

"And he started dating someone at school."

"What an asshole," I said.

"Yes and no. I mean, I'm a little relieved. It's been a long thing. Complicated, I mean. What isn't, right?" She laughed, but it was a dry, brittle laugh, branches cracking.

"I see," I said. "Where is he?"

"UPenn."

"Name?" I said.

"Jared."

College. It really wasn't like where Connor was. It seemed like such a faraway magical place. Oz-like.

I told her about Connor then. About the hospital and about how far away he was. In all ways. What I left out was the Thing. I left out the part about the Thing.

"I'm going to go see him," I said. "This weekend. My parents are taking my sister to look at her last few schools. I'm supposed to stay at a friend's, but maybe I won't."

"That sounds like a shaky plan. I've got some experience here, and that is a weak plan."

"I know. I haven't thought it through exactly," I said. And I hadn't. I just knew I wanted it to take place.

"Shaky."

I wanted to talk more to her. "Hey, should we go out for, like, hot cider or something?" I asked.

"I *guess*," she said. "Why not?"

"Well, this is a little embarrassing, but I'd actually need you to take me back. I live just over the bridge. Is that a total pain?"

She squinted at me, her head tilted. "It's okay." She rolled her eyes. "The one thing about the mother's Ford Fiesta is it loves to be driven. And me? I love to drive it. It's such a bizarre thing. I just fucking love to drive. So now I have somewhere to drive to tonight."

That's when my mom came trotting out with Greta. "She's doing great!" she said.

"We're going to go get tea, Mom, okay?" I pointed at Stella and then back to myself.

"You said hot cider," Stella said, pretending this was a deal breaker.

"Cider. Hot cider, Mom."

My mother was not laughing at our joke. And I could see her gears turning. She was thinking: Hmm. Where will they go? Will it be tea or will it be cider? Why have I come all this way only to return home alone? And then, I saw her settle on something. Post-hospital rules, I was sure.

She shrugged. "Sure," she squeaked out.

"Great," said Stella.

"Greta, sit!" my mother said.

But there was no sitting. Just a lot of tail wagging.

"Sit!" She pointed her finger at Greta.

Stella B laughed. "I can tell it's really working, Daphne!" She stood up and eased Greta's leash out of my mother's hand. Her rusted bike chain bracelets clinked together. She had the teeniest stick 'n' poke at the tender place between her thumb and her index finger: a crescent moon. Without touching Greta, she lowered her hand a bit to indicate a sitting position. And Greta sat and stared at Stella, stars in her pearly eyes.

"Dog whisperer," my mother breathed, clasping her hands together.

"It's about authority," Stella said, and we all nodded our heads. "Confidence."

Stella had this power. It was a different power than Nora had. Far as I could tell, it was being used for good.

"It really is," my mom said, taking back the lead. Instantly Greta jumped up and strained to free herself.

My mom was untangling herself and Greta. I looked over at Stella. She was a mess. I mean a cool mess, but still a mess, all smudged and smeared and cut and pasted. And yet I don't think I knew a being more together than Stella. Who was more together than Stella B?

Maybe Mabel, but anyway, we were all together now.

Well, we were . . . *existentially* together, because my mom took the dogs, and I went with Stella and Samantha. "There's a Starbucks near my house," I said. "I mean, since you're going to drop me there anyway."

"I don't do Starbucks," she said, opening the car so Samantha could jump in back. We both got in front, and Stella started the car and then scanned her music with purpose.

"I'm queen of the world, I bump into things, I spin around in circles, and I'm singing, and I'm singing, I'm singing."

"Okay," I said.

"This good?" Stella eased out of the lot, and as she waited to get onto the road, she hit the gear shift with her ringed fingers. The Ford Fiesta was a *stick shift*. Lame car and so not a lame car at the exact same time.

"The music?"

"You don't know Ida Maria?"

"Nope." When would I actually know the right song and the

right band and the right, right, right way?

"She's good."

"I like," I said. I did. Queen of the world was a good strong person to be.

"In a punky, poppy way. More pop than punk, right?"

"Sure," I said.

"Anyway, Starbucks, it's just gross, you know? There are a million. Let's go somewhere where there is only one or two of them in the world."

"Let me restate," I said. "There's this café not so far from my house. Since you have to take me back anyway."

"That sounds great!" Stella said. "Where?"

"I'm looking," I said. I took out my phone. "Because actually I usually just go to Starbucks."

"Ha," said Stella.

"Ha-ha," I said as I directed her to Greenleaf. "There are three of these in the world. Will that still work for you?"

"Three? Hmm." Samantha thrust her head between the front seats, panting. "Yes. Three is the cutoff," she said. "Three."

Samantha stayed in the car, which Stella had parked just outside the café. We took a seat by the plate glass window, and it was almost like we were all there together. Almost but not really.

"They have great hot chocolate here," I said. "You want one?" I stood up and patted my jacket pockets, looking for the little pouch I put money and dog treats in.

"Really? Sure. I thought you'd never been here."

"That's what the phone told me," I said, making my way

to order, orange streamers and witches' masks and cutouts of beheaded heads dangling from the counter.

After refusing the invitation to "pumpkinify" my drink with that relentless autumn flavor I have always despised, I came back with two normal hot chocolates, regulared, swirled high with whipped cream.

"I despise Halloween," I said as I handed Stella hers.

"Is it Halloween?"

"Thursday," I said. "Cannot wait."

"I'm in costume all year long," Stella said. "This day is no different, right?"

"Hmm."

"So."

"So tell me about Jared."

"Oh, what for? I need a life. I've got, like, no friends because of that guy. It's kind of nice to just sit here in fucking Greenleaves or wherever we are with someone my own age."

"I think you're older."

"Roughly," she said.

I nodded into my hot drink. "My sister's age."

"Anyway, your plan. Why don't you stay with me!" she said.

"That's a nice offer, but I'm not really staying with anyone," I said, blowing on my hot chocolate. "I mean, I guess I'll be staying with Connor." The thought exhilarated and panicked me.

"Well," she said. "Just as like a base camp. Whatever you decide."

I took a sip and a huge swipe of the cream. "He wants to meet in Annapolis," I said. "So weird. He's coming from New *Hampshire*."

"Huh. Is he really into crab cakes?"

"I have no idea," I said.

"So how are you getting there?"

"Hadn't thought about it yet," I said, though my first thought had been Tim. He would have done it. But then I would have had to tell him why.

"I'm thinking out loud here. I mean, why Annapolis? How on earth does a person get to Annapolis?" Stella asked.

"It's not that far. But it is, umm, an unusual destination."

"Yeah. I know a couple of people who got fake IDs in Annapolis. But that's kind of it."

"So you," I said. "Are you going to get back with the Philly boy? With Jared?"

Stella went dark. Like the lights went *out.* "Doubt it," she said.

"Okay then," I said.

At first I thought it was the heat of the chocolate, making its way, like, through my body as I went to ask her more about this development, but I soon realized that was not in fact what I was feeling. "Oh my God," I said.

"It's not a big deal. I just don't want to talk about him now." Stella clearly had not heard me. She took a massive gulp of her drink.

It was still happening. A warm rush down my leg. I don't know why, but I couldn't move. I didn't know which would be worse. To get up and run to the bathroom, leaving a trail of who knows what behind me, or to sit there and just, I don't know, die.

"Stella," I said quietly.

"I'll totally take you." She nodded at me like it was a pact no one could break. "Like I said, I just really dig driving. Listening to music on my own."

"Hey," I said again.

"What's wrong?"

I can't say what my face revealed in that moment. If it appeared as stricken with horror as I was, or if it looked as sad, or as in disbelief, as I also was. I can't say anything about that moment other than I hope I never have one like it again.

"Lizzie, what's wrong?" I heard the swoosh of her jacket as she reached across the table to touch my arm.

"It came undone."

Stella looked around the room. "What?" she said. And then I saw her look of recognition.

I nodded.

"It's okay." She stood up. "It's not a big deal at all."

"I don't know what to do," I said.

"It's okay. Let's just go to the bathroom. Take my coat and wrap it around your waist."

"It's not my back that's the problem. I didn't get my fucking period. It's my front." I was back in the land of illness and weakness and not knowing. Just back like I had never again been anything other than this.

"I'll walk in front of you then, and you'll follow me to the bathroom."

"Okay."

Stella stood in front of me and grabbed one of my hands from behind, and I stood and followed behind her. I can't say if there was any evidence of this undoing, as I just looked ahead and went to the bathroom behind Stella B.

I ran into the stall and locked it sort of violently and sure enough, the clasp had come unclasped. I must not have secured it properly. I closed it now, grateful that I had emptied it before Petiquette so it was not the mess it could have been. I tried to clean myself up.

"What do you need?"

"Paper towels," I said.

And just as soon as I'd said so, a huge brown wad of them appeared at the top of the stall door. "Here," she said. "Take."

And then another batch. "Wet with soap and just wet," she said. "Pick your poison."

I could work with both and I did and after several minutes of cleaning and then trying to gather myself up, get myself gathered, I opened the door.

"Hi," Stella said.

"Hey." I looked down and went to the sinks. I washed my hands for a long time.

Stella put her hand on my shoulder. "It's okay," she said. "This is nothing."

I shrugged her hand off.

"Hey." She placed her hand back on my shoulder. "This is nothing."

I looked at Stella then. This new friend, a new person who had been on the moon with me, even if it was just for a brief visit. Connor was not the only one. Perhaps there could be others. "This is not nothing," I said. "So not nothing. It should come with a trigger warning."

"I hear you," Stella said.

"I can't go back to that. That feeling. Being sick again." I tore some paper towels from the dispenser and then wiped my hands and stood up straight and looked in the mirror. It was my actual face now. No steroid hair and freakish round face. My regular Birdy hair. Me. I bent in. I wiped my red eyes with the harsh paper towel. "I'm okay," I said now, backing up from the mirror and again facing Stella.

"You're more than okay. You're a survivor," she said. "This is just a little reminder of that fact."

I nodded. "Thank you," I said.

"No need. A survivor. Don't you forget that."

"Okay." I threw out the towels.

"And now, we're friends."

I smiled a pathetic little smile. "Poor Samantha," I said.

"Yeah, let's get out of here."

I followed Stella out of the bathroom and toward the door. I looked back with a pang of guilt for not having cleared our table: two hot chocolates still covered in cream, barely sipped at. Two girls whose outsides were so different from their insides. All girls. All kinds of scars. All kinds of ways to keep our secrets safe. My secret was safe. Safe, with Stella B.

Slayer

My parents didn't end up going anywhere with Zoe because Zoe decided she didn't need to see any more schools in Virginia and that, after she took the new round of SATs, which would surely put her at near to perfect, she was not going to want to stay in Virginia anyway.

"That is so snotty," I said. To everyone. I was momentarily panicked. It was 8:30 a.m. and I had a plan to carry out. I needed to get myself to Annapolis. I needed to pack whatever a person takes to this kind of thing. All of a sudden I realized this plan, like the last one Connor had hatched, was fraught with the possibility of mishap.

My father was the one who spoke. "There are amazing schools here, Zoe. And publicly funded, which is nothing to sneeze at. College is very expensive!"

Zoe crossed her arms. "I have not worked my ass off for four years to end up staying here. I mean, if I have to go, if I get in nowhere, if you guys won't send me anywhere else, then I have no choice anyway, and so why even look?"

"William and Mary and UVA are not *here*. They are fantastic schools, and I was looking forward to the trip," my mother said, all dejected.

I looked hard at Zoe, eyes wide, and even though she didn't know my plan, she could have seen my cry for help and acted on it. If she saw me, she made no effort.

"Tim and I have plans."

"Oh yeah?" my mother said. "Plans to do what?"

"Well, to study, for one."

"Yes," my mom said. "And . . ."

"And he's making me dinner, okay? He's been reading up on all this cooking stuff and he's making paella! He even bought fresh octopus!"

I tried to stifle my laughter. And then: paella. From Spain. That was supposed to be mine.

My father exhaled. "My God, Zoe. It's one day! Fine." He held his hands up in an *I'm unarmed, don't shoot* gesture. "I give up."

My mother shook her head and went into the den. "You think you might have told us ahead of time, Zoe?" she screamed out. "I made time to do this."

"He just got the octopus yesterday," Zoe said softly. She looked at my dad. "I really don't want to go to a local school."

"Oh for Christ's sake, Zoe. Enough's enough. Your mother is right. Have some consideration for others."

"I am," she said. "I'm not making you go."

My dad shook his head. The disappointed head shake.

My mom came out of the den. "Let me ask you something," she said. "Where is Tim going to school?"

"He's waiting to hear early decision," she said. Which meant he'd been studying with her for hours upon hours and he didn't even need to *take the SATs again*! "Columbia."

"And where are you applying? Your first choice," my mom asked.

"Yes. There. As I've mentioned, it's important for me to be in a city."

"Zoe," my mother started. "You know what? Forget it. I just really hope you remember: life is long. We'll just have to see how this all pans out, won't we?"

Wasn't life, in fact, short? This was another Nanaism. Live now, life is short, right? It can't be both.

"Well I'm going to Stella's." I realized just then that this didn't have to affect me negatively, per se. "For the night."

Everyone turned to me.

"That's wonderful!" my parents said at the same time.

"Wait a minute." He ran his hands through his hair. My poor dad. He was trying so hard to keep up. "Who's Stella?"

When Stella pulled up in her white Ford Fiesta at 9:30 a.m. I had everything ready to go. Well, what was everything exactly? What would I ever take for an overnight with my . . . *boyfriend*? It was extra bags and non-itch creams, some bonus clasps because, dear God, I was not going to let that bag come undone again, but if it did, I was going to be ready. And it was also, *pajamas*. And face cream. Where were we even going to be . . . sleeping? Would we be sleeping? I had no idea what was about to happen. It was like everything before. Wait for the answer. Wait and see.

"Bye, honey!" My parents stood at the front door waving, like I was bravely going off to war. In a way, it had been a war. There had certainly been carnage.

I ducked my head like I was blinded by the sun. Or their love. "Bye." I waved and hopped into Stella's car.

Bob, bob, went the dog head. Hula, hula, went the girl's straw skirt. "You are the most honorable soldier, superhero, pretty as a cat," another unfamiliar voice in Stella's phone in its dock sang.

"Okay." I put my palms on both knees. "Here we go. Who's this?"

"Kate Nash!"

"Okay," I said.

"Kate Nash!" she said again.

"I heard you!" When would the music shaming cease? It was getting tiring.

She gripped the wheel and pitched herself over it, like an old lady looking for an address in the dark.

"Are you stressed out?"

"I don't know. I feel all this *pressure*," I said. We were headed toward the highway.

"What are you guys even going to *do*?"

I giggled. "I have no idea."

"Are you, like, prepared?" She was on the ramp now.

"Stop it. You sound like my mother. Or like my mother would sound if she knew what was happening right now."

"I'm just saying. When I first did it with Jared, it was bad. It got better. But the first time was not a lot of fun."

"I don't even know if that is happening!" I said. "Like, I honestly don't think it will. Remember the thing that keeps me from people? That thing that came undone. That could happen. Can you imagine?"

"Jesus. That's an extra layer of fear. But also? That thing brought us closer," she said. "It made us friends."

I leaned back. She was not wrong.

"Here we go," Stella said, merging onto the highway.

And there we were, on our way.

I can't say I was 100 percent excited. I guess I was . . . trepidatious. Is that a word? I know it's a feeling, and also there was the fearful feeling, and I felt them both when Stella B turned into the marina in Annapolis. It was a marina, by the way. I'd seen a lot of water when I'd mapped it, but for some reason it still surprised me. And yet here we were, boats moored and rocking in the near distance, a bunch of piers, pools, a white napkin place to eat. The place was *posh*.

"Will you look at this place?"

"I know. Crazy," I said, opening the car door. I felt like it was this massive effort to get out. Like I had to pitch myself onto the pavement.

"I'll wait here," she said. "Just here, in this car. Waiting."

"Don't," I said. "It's fine. You've wasted so much time on me already." I was out of the car with my bag and leaning in her open window. "I'm okay!"

"I'm going to wait."

"Okay," I said, a little relieved. I have never felt like I fit in somewhere less. Truly.

When I turned around, I saw him. Connor.

He took my breath away. There he was. On a sailboat. Standing between two sails. At the end of the pier. Waving to me.

Stella craned her neck to look through my window. "Holy hell, is that him?" she said.

I waved back at him.

"For real?" she said. "Is your life real? You are such a fun friend to have! The dramz."

I turned to Stella. "I know."

"You are so finished," she said.

"I know," I said again. I gathered up my strength. To go to Connor on his boat.

"That boy will slay you! With his bow and arrow he will slay."

Campers, put down your bows and arrows. That's what I thought: how before that moment arrived, my life was headed somewhere so different. "Thank you, Stella," I said. "Really. For everything."

For a moment I wondered if I was leaving forever. I turned from her car and walked slowly, heart pounding, but somehow without falling over, toward the pier.

There he was. Strawberry-blond shock of hair swept to the side. Cinnamon spray of freckles. Bluest eyes, squinting, hairline fractures at the corners already. Dark jeans. Gray Vans. Frayed blue oxford. Down vest. Hello, Connor Bryant. Smiling—no, beaming—at me.

"Hi," he said.

"Hi, Connor," I said. I didn't recognize my shy voice.

"It's a pretty perfect day for a sail." He reached out his hand to me.

"What is it with you and boats?" I said. I turned to wave good-bye to Stella, a signal that she could go.

Then I took Connor's hand and carefully stepped in.

Moorings

The boat. Picture a sailboat: it looked like that. *Sea Fever* was painted across the side in indigo-blue script. Two sails, crisp white triangles, the jib and the mainsail, white, white. Remember: I went to camp! I knew when the boom was heading my way. I knew there was a rudder and a till and a hull and a bow and a stern and standard and port side, and once I'd sailed a Sunfish on the lake, all alone. But my experience ended there. This was a big boat! And Connor was on it. On the *bow*.

After he helped me in, I stood there sort of dumbly for a moment. What were we supposed to do? We hugged *very* awkwardly. And then the awkwardness melted away and we hugged for real. We had never done that before. I had always been so breakable. There were a million firsts already.

We broke apart. "First of all, this is yours, right?" I said, sitting down on a cushioned bench, port side. Connor seemed completely different at every turn. Nana had a prism on a string that sat on this table in her hallway, and in the late afternoon it would catch all this hazy light. You picked it up and the light jumped off the glass top of the table and hit the walls and the ceiling. You spun it and the light shot to another wall, another part of the ceiling. That was Connor, a prism catching light. Where would he be refracted today? Might he have stolen a sailboat? I didn't *think* so, but he kept surprising me, and not always in a great way.

"Well my family's, yes."

"And how did you get here? Are you allowed to even be here?" I imagined he was in some kind of lockdown facility. But maybe it was really just a school with a retro sound system.

"It's the weekend," Connor said. "We can leave on the weekend. I drove down last night."

I was dubious. I had several friends from camp at regular boarding schools. There was not a lot of freedom involved in their weekends at all. "Oh. So you have a car at school?" I was starting to not want to have this conversation, but somehow I still felt compelled to bring it up. Everything around me was blue. On the outside. Blue sky, blue water, Connor in his sky-blue shirt, his blue eyes. "*That* car?"

He laughed. "Yup. The one thing that my mother didn't get rid of." He was undoing the rope tethering us to shore. What was that? A *lanyard*? A *halyard*? "Are you cold?"

I can't imagine having kept that car. Every time I got in it, I'd think about the accident. But wouldn't I think about it every time I got in any car? "A little." I rubbed my arms. I had on a flannel shirt over a T-shirt, a light cargo jacket over those. How did I know I was going to be *sailing*?

Connor went down below and came up holding a sweater. "Wear this." He threw a fisherman's wool sweater, big and soft and stretched out at the waist. I took off my jacket and pulled it over my head. You know how you can buy boyfriend sweaters? Well, this was an *actual* boyfriend sweater. This was the inspiration for an entire *line of clothing*. I was already thinking how to get it home with me so I could wear it every day for the rest of my life.

"Suits you," he said.

I looked down at it as if I couldn't believe it was real.

Then there was a lot of checking of the sails, the devices along the dash. I tried to let myself just . . . be. It was hard to let not knowing what was about to happen be a good thing. But I tried it out. Being in the moment. Not in the past or in the future. In this moment now.

"Connor Bryant, you never cease to blow my mind." I shook my head in mock disbelief.

He looked up. "I aim to please," he said, winding the line and placing it on deck. "You. I aim to please you."

"Your work is done here," I said. "This is just insane."

And then we were off.

And then we were at sea.

Stars and Stars

So what can I say? We sailed—no, *Connor sailed us*—across the Chesapeake Bay, where once I had gone on a field trip to learn about estuaries.

This is what he did: He walked around. He lowered the boom. He manned the sails. He tied and untied knots. He caught the wind. He told me to watch my head. He let me steer. He checked compasses. We looked out at the water, our hair blowing wildly in the wind.

He sent me down into the galley for grapes and crackers and cheese, all on a platter in the little fridge, and Diet Cokes.

It was a little house down there. A lounge area with cushioned couches built in. And behind that was the bedroom, which came to a point just above the headboard. I leaned in the threshold and wondered how many people had slept there. And who they'd been. And who they'd slept with . . .

It actually made me a little seasick, and after spotting the bathroom, I walked back up with this tray of food and set it on the table, which was nailed down between the two sets of benches lined with pillows, life preservers stored inside.

I watched Connor at the wheel. He was every memory I'd

ever had of him at once, all the good, all the times he came in to see me when I was sick and didn't know what was happening to me. Once in a while I slipped: as he looked out at the water and away from me, I couldn't help but think of him in that car, at the wheel in the Beamer, hand on some girl's knee, stoned.

"Hey," I said, picking grapes off the stem and popping them in my mouth. "Does anyone know you're here?" For my part, no one knew I was even gone. For the first time in a long time, I wasn't where anyone would expect to find me. Off the leash: exciting and terrifying.

He nodded. "Sure."

"No one knows I'm here," I said.

He grinned at me and looked back out to the water.

I looked at Connor looking out to sea. "Look!" He pointed out, just beyond our boat.

I shielded my eyes with my hand and looked out. Three gray bodies arced in the sunlight, and I could see the flash of gray fins dipping in and out of the water, three faces shaped like smiles. Dolphins. They dove and swam beside us for several moments before they were gone, far out to sea.

"This is just amazing." I turned to Connor. "Isn't this just amazing?"

"I know. Sometimes they play by the boat. I like to think it's always the same ones."

I was disappointed for a moment that Connor had seen these dolphins—had seen *this*—before, but I shook it off. "Wow," I said.

"Incredible," he said. "A good omen, I think."

I nodded. I turned to face him. "It is!" I said.

He smiled.

"Okay," I said. "Where are we going, anyway?"

We ended the trip at a marina—no! a port of call—on Kent Island. We got off the sailboat and onto a dock and walked up this grassy hill to what turned out to be *Connor's house*, which was large and white with blue shutters, little anchors cut out of them, and set against the trees, the leaves turning these spectacular colors. When we got closer, I could tell the house was, I don't know, falling down a little? Eaten and beaten down by weather, maybe. There was a wraparound front porch with worn wicker chairs, some frayed reeds sticking out from the legs and arms, and two wooden bench swings you could imagine drinking cold lemonade on if it was summer. But it wasn't summer anymore, and when Connor opened the screen door and walked us across the porch and then into the living room (did I mention the seahorse door knocker?), the house felt old and drafty.

"Is anyone here?" I asked Connor.

"Just us," he said.

"Does anyone know we're here?"

"Yes? My parents were like, go ahead, bring your girlfriend to our house on the bay and stay the weekend! No, stay the week!"

"I see." He said *girlfriend*. Which went great with my boyfriend sweater. Which was better than my name after a sentence. "So, no."

"No one knows where you are," he said, making his hands into wolf paws. "Grrrr," he said.

"Stop!" I was happy to finally be alone with Connor, but that he was playing with me creeped me out a little.

We stood in this large room with huge windows and Persian rugs in all colors of brown and beige and gold thrown about. Old stuffed couches were strewn with tapestry-covered pillows. It smelled a little like hay in there, and it looked just effortless and like all the couches, pillows, rugs, curtains, framed photos, and vases just somehow ended up there.

I placed my bag on the floor and looked out the window facing the water at the dock where the boat was moored.

"So this is it." He reached his arm out to encompass the room.

"Yeah. Amazing." I watched the boat rock gently in the water. "What's *Sea Fever*?" I asked.

"A poem. My father likes these sea poems."

"I like it," I said. I had seen some awful boat names. *Master Baiter. Buoy, Oh Buoy. Dock-a-Dent.* This is what happens when you live near water.

I followed Connor into the kitchen, all yellow and open to the light, shelves stacked with multicolored ceramic bowls and plates, a long wooden table with uneven planks of wood. Beneath the window seat that faced the bay window, looking out to the backyard, were baskets overflowing with board games and candles and old blankets.

"This was my grandparents' place," he said. "Great-grandparents? I can't remember, to be honest. But it's been in the family. Old-time Maryland. That's us!"

"How cool," I said.

Another shrug. "Well, it is cool for my parents, because it's a pretty short drive from DC. So they can come and go easily."

It was all so beyond my realm. Last year we spent two weeks in Cape Hatteras. We ate hush puppies and crawfish more times than I could count. So there was that.

"Once it was all so grand," Connor said. "This life."

"Seems pretty grand now," I said. I felt teeny and lost, but Connor didn't fill up the space much either. The grandness didn't seem to have much to do with him.

"But once"—he looked up at the chandelier, covered in dust—"once this was all brand-new."

The being-alone and no-one-can-reach-me part turned out to be sort of great. We sat swinging on the porch bench and watched the sunset, holding hands beneath a horse blanket Connor pulled out from under the window seat in the kitchen.

And then, when the sun went down and it got very cold and we got hungry, Connor found some oatmeal in the cupboard. He made that and added brown sugar and raisins and maple syrup, and it might have been the most delicious dinner I'd ever eaten ever.

Soon it got very dark and there were stars everywhere. We went out on the lawn, blanket around our shoulders, and looked up at them. Big Dipper, Little Dipper, Cassiopeia; it was like a planetarium out there. We walked down to the rickety dock and watched the dangling moon, like it was suspended by an invisible string.

"Hey," Connor said, bringing me close. It was warm beneath the blanket, and I felt him all around me.

"Hi," I said. I let go. I was in the moment.

The blanket dropped and he pushed some hair out of my face. "Birdie," he said. He traced my eyebrow—one and then the other—with the side of his thumb. "Bird."

I hugged him tighter.

"I love you," he said. He kissed the top of my head.

The shivering. From the cold, from that kind of kiss. I was silent.

"Do you? Still?"

"Still," I said.

"I'll take it," Connor said. "Hey, you're shivering."

"It's cold!"

"Let's go in," he said. And then, turning, he held my hand as we walked up the lopsided stairs. "So. Want to see my room?"

I giggled. "Yes," I said, and followed close behind.

Well, being in the moment was swiftly behind me. Because now I was going into his room and I had to contend with what would happen in that room. I do not see how people stay in the moment. People who say they do this—what, *Buddhists?*—they have to be liars. All of them.

Also? I was always following Connor. In the hospital hallways, out to the rowboat at Fletcher's, up those stairs.

"Bathroom?" I said, opening a door, stacks of neatly folded white towels, the smell of insects and dust. "I need the bathroom."

"Linen closet," he said. "Here's a bathroom. If you need it. Whenever. This can be just yours. I'm the last door on the left." He pointed down a long hallway.

I went in and shut the door, waited for his footsteps to recede down the hallway. I was trembling. Trembling from fear and hope and worry and happiness but mostly from fear.

I checked to make sure everything was okay and that I would not humiliate myself in a terribly obvious way, and I tried not to think about what it would be like for someone else—for Connor—to see it. Did he have to? Was there a way around it? Maybe we would only talk, I thought, as I left the bathroom and padded down the hall, my arms out, fingertips brushing the cool walls. Who knew what I wanted or what would happen, I thought, as I stopped, unsteady, at the last door on the left. Connor's room.

Then I went inside.

Moon Inside

It was dark when I entered; it smelled dusty and salty and open to the sea, the sky, the sprawling lawn, if that could be a smell. Connor was a blue shadow on his bed, grasping his shins in the dark. I could hear the lapping of the bay from the open window behind him.

"Hi, Lizzie," he said. He placed his head on his knees. He looked girl-like and fragile, and I put my hands on the bed and then my knees and I crawled up next to him, drew my hands around my shins as well.

"Hi."

Connor lifted his head and I could see his face shining in the dark, ghostlike, his lashes blinking, so ethereal they could have been sprinkling fairy dust as they opened and closed and opened again. He kissed me, and it was different from any of the other kisses—his or anyone's before. It was serious and sort of hard, but not in a bad way. It was like he meant it.

We kissed for a while and then we were lying down, side by side, and I couldn't help myself; I froze. I didn't want to, but then I felt the gentle pull of the bag as gravity shifted it. I broke away from him, breathless.

"Hey," he said. "Come back." He wrapped his arm around my back, his fingers pressing at my waist. It was a sure, swift movement that also made it seem like he had done that move many times before.

I peeled his hand away.

Connor shifted and then propped his head on his elbow. "What?" he said, smirking at me. It was kind of sweet and kind of awful. He touched my nose with the finger of his free hand. "Tell me."

I sat up and placed the pillow in my lap, clutching it to me. "Okay, so this is just normal stuff, nothing about anything, just normal moving forward two people talking."

"Okay . . . ," he said slowly.

"Okay, so." I could feel myself sounding like I was about twelve. I couldn't help it, though. "You've had sex before, I'm assuming."

He sat up. Crossed his legs. "Yes," he said solemnly.

I let out my breath.

"Is that a problem for you?"

"It's not a *problem*," I said. "It's just that, well, obviously I haven't. And I don't know. It feels strange. That you have before and I haven't."

"I think it's nice," he said.

"Well, you're always the one in charge!" It just slipped out.

"I don't feel in charge," Connor said. "I feel very un-in-charge, actually. I feel like everything is new and slightly scary."

"Scary? Why? I'm scaring you?"

"No." He ran his hand softly along the inside of my calves,

beneath my jeans. "I just am very aware of what you've been through. Your body."

Oh my God, please don't let him say the word "bag." It will ruin this for me. It will, I thought. I swallowed so loudly I'm sure they could hear it across the bay in Annapolis, which, by the way, I could see through the eerie fog that lingered now on the water.

"So a lot of times."

"A few. Yeah. A bunch, I guess."

I didn't want to bring up the girl Tim's friend knew. I just didn't want to go down the path of everything that was before, and yet, here I was, heading there. I couldn't help but wonder if he was including her in that group. If he'd had sex with this girl and then not spoken to her again. Like Zoe had said.

But more than all that was bodies. All those perfect bodies of the girls Connor had to have touched. I could picture their smooth and unscarred stomachs.

You think the worst is behind you, but it's never behind you. In fact, saying something is the worst does not leave room for all the bad stuff that can follow it. You say the pain is nine, but you mean ten. You leave room.

"I want to say this is so different, but that sounds stupid and cliché."

"Yeah," I said. "It does."

"But it's true. It's just so different. It's about everything with us."

I nodded.

"You know what would help me?"

"Are we here to help you? I had no idea. I thought this

situation"—I brought my shaking hand out to show the dark room—"was more to help me."

"Really? To help you?"

"That sounded selfish," I said. "It's not to help me. It's to help us?"

He laughed and kissed me. Sweetly, peck-like, a question, and then a longer, better kiss that I guess sort of answered it. "Maybe we don't need help," he said.

"Maybe."

"Can I see it?" he asked me.

I gasped. I remember the sound I made very well.

"No!" I clutched the pillow harder.

He tried to ease the pillow out of my lap.

I held tighter.

"It just needs to happen."

"Why?"

"Because then it will just be normal and everything will be normal and the only slightly awkward thing will be that you have never done it before and that I have never done it with you before."

I let go of the pillow and lay back on the bed, crossed my arms. A wooden plank was probably less stiff than I was in that moment.

Connor laughed at me. "You totally don't have to," he said. "It was just a thought."

"You really want to see it?" I said.

"No, Liz," he said. "I really want you to show it to me."

I felt my body relax. What would be the worst thing? There

were so many worst things, but really, there only can be one.

"Okay!" I said. "Okay," I said again, softer. I unzipped my jeans and kicked them off. There was still my underwear to contend with, but taking that off seemed like a lot to deal with at once. So I just left them on, the bag tucked in.

I was thankful he didn't ask for the light.

He stayed propped on his elbow. He ran his fingers along the left side of my stomach, which was not the bag side. I held my breath. I felt my power, the power that had gotten me there and let me be in this house, eating Connor's oatmeal and looking at his corner of stars, the power that had let me live a while now without experiencing that crippling shame. But now I could see I would never save Connor. And it would always be him who had the power not to love me.

We were silent. The moon was practically inside the room with its ghost-white light.

"So. There you have it."

Silence.

"Aren't you going to say, I think you're beautiful? Or something else sort of fake?"

"Well, I was going to say that, I'm not going to lie. But you sort of took the wind out of those sails."

"We could drop the sailing references," I said, looking at the row of sailing trophies that glinted on his shelf. "Just for the night."

"Okay."

"So what will you say then?" I was reaching for my jeans.

He paused and looked hard at what I could only call the

contraption. "Looks like you lost that catfight," he said.

It made me laugh. It made me feel like he was telling the truth.

"Can I put on my jeans now?"

"Yes," he said. "But really you do look beautiful." He was looking now at my face. "It's been said a million times before, but I haven't said it to you a million times yet."

He saw me. I could feel it, like, in my cells. And that power returned. My secret—evil kryptonite—was no longer a secret. Connor had seen it. My self could no longer be used against myself. Now there was nothing left to hide.

"You're like a superhero," he said, sitting up.

"Hardly." But I wondered if he was saying something not so different than Stella had been saying.

"So much strength."

I was silent as we lay there, clothed, bathed in moonlight on Connor's bed. I could feel everything. The fleecy downy hair of his arm on my neck. The salt thick in the air. The soft comforter. The creaky shifting of the old house. The bay moving against the shore. Once I had thought no boy would ever love me because of my illness and this body I now lived in, and here was Connor, who sailed me across the water to here, and who didn't just love me despite it, but a little bit because of it.

I felt so open to him, and connected. And then I did another thing I never would have expected: I brought my legs around him. I placed his hands on my waist and I brought my hands to his face and I kissed him. The biggest, most romantic kiss I have ever had.

He unbuttoned my flannel shirt so slowly I thought I'd die.

And then he pulled off my tank top beneath it and held me very close to him. He undid my bra. Somehow we got our pants off in an un-clumsy way and somehow Connor got a condom out of the night table drawer and somehow it happened in the exact way it was supposed to happen, which was easily and like we'd known each other and been together this way before. Familiar even though it was utterly strange. And somehow when Connor was on top of me, his chest to mine, his stomach to mine, his legs and mine intertwined, somehow I forgot about the bag. It was just Connor and me and everything that was ahead of us.

He crawled off me, and I quickly put on his T-shirt to cover up. White V-neck, Connor's sea-boy smell.

He sighed deeply. And held out his arm for me to crawl into the crook of it. "Hi there," he said.

"Hi."

The moon, the bay, the boat creaking, bats swooping.

"Hey," I said, leaning on his bare chest, perfect, not sunken but also not overworked and muscly. Perfect for me. "Hi."

We Were There

I lay under the comforter with Connor, so warm, like it was us two huddled up against the world, against the coming winter, my lips on his shoulder and his chest and his arms full around me, the heat of the place where his hair met his neck. I did get up several times for the bathroom, but it was okay and soon it was morning, the gray light shining through that window, the sun's fall heat making its way into our room. I remember getting up with Connor—his wild red hair, bloodshot blue eyes, crooked smile—and then, before leaving his room, looking back at the messy bed, the down comforter pulled back, pillows indented where our heads once were, this place where we had slept, evidence that we had been there.

We ate more oatmeal (it must be said that there hadn't been a lot of complexity or variety to our meals), and I remember thinking how strange that no one had tried to call me to make me come home. But it hadn't even been twenty-four hours; no one even knew I was missing. As we got on the boat and Connor unwound us from our moorings, I wondered if this would—or could—ever happen again.

———

Back in the parking lot there was Stella leaning on that ridiculous white car, Samantha panting in the backseat, when, after what seemed like a pretty complicated backing into the slip, we got off the boat.

"Hey." She nodded her head at Connor. "How goes it?"

"Good," he said, pulling me aside by my elbow.

I hugged him, hard.

"I'm going to finish up stuff on the boat, okay?"

"Oh, sure." I was so stupid thinking you just tie it up and head for your car. "Do you want me to stay? Can I help? Stella will wait. When I texted her from your house, I told her it could be a while."

"Help?" he asked. "Like all the times you helped on the boat? Or with the . . . oatmeal? Those kinds of helping?"

"No. This kind!" I kissed him again.

"I'm good," he said when we'd parted. "Have to make sure everything's okay on the deck, and bring in all the lines, tie up the fenders and so on. And I've got to get back to school today. Before I turn into a pumpkin."

"So you're driving up there tonight then?" Pumpkinhood. I remembered.

"Mm-hmm," he said.

I didn't see an overnight bag. Had he just driven down with a wallet and the keys to the magic house on the hill by the bay? "When will I see you?" I asked him. I was skeptical.

"Next vacation is Thanksgiving, right?"

"Right!"

"So then," he said.

"Meanwhile," I said. But what was meanwhile? "Can you take another weekend?"

Connor seemed to think it over. "Just one," he said. "The more you stick around, the more brownie points you get."

"Okay," I said. "But please, don't get lost again, okay?"

"Why do I know you'll always find me?" said Connor before he kissed me. And then he turned back to the boat.

I watched him walk along the dock, someone I would once never have known. He ducked onto his boat and began to take unfurl the jib. *Jib.*

"Are you just completely ruined now?"

I jumped and turned to see Stella stomping behind me in her scuffed-up black Docs. "Hi," I said. "Ruined?" Was I?

"For everything else. Ruined."

I rubbed the outside of my arms. "Totally." I leaned into her and she guided us back to her car. I opened the door and pitched myself inside.

"Just destroyed," I said.

"I want to hear everything," she said as I clicked in my seat belt and readied myself for home.

My mother was reading the paper and my father was out back planting bulbs when I walked in the front door. It was barely 3:00 p.m.

"Hey!" I said. How many times could I arrive here a totally different person? How many more times? How many more arrivals?

My mother turned down a corner of her paper and looked at me over her reading glasses perched on her nose. "Liz?"

"No, Mom, it's Jesus Christ."

"Charming," she said. "I thought it was Zoe! I don't know why I thought you were coming back later." She went back to reading her paper.

I went upstairs to check on Frog and change and put on my own cutoff sweatpants, ones I wore at camp before any of this. I pulled the drawstring tight.

I miss you I miss you I miss you, my phone said.

Who is this? I wrote back.

This is your mother, he wrote. *I know what you did last night.*

It gave me shivers to think of it. The whole night, the whole day, the whole . . . *event.*

Thank you.

Thank YOU.

Who ARE you?

I'm that guy? From the hospital? With the cute dog?

I know, I typed. *I remember him.*

My mother was still reading, glasses back up on her nose, her paper upright before her, when I came back downstairs.

Through the plate glass window behind her, I could see my father leaning over in his yellow Crocs, planting. I had a secret. I had this big, beautiful secret now. Something for myself. Something private. That no one could examine, open up, take out.

I watched my father stand and place his hands, still gripping his shears, on his hips as he surveyed his little patch of garden. I hugged myself. And I wondered what flowers would be coming up this spring.

After

Before I knew that Connor would get lost again, which he became, terribly so, I went back to my regular life. I continued training Mabel and doing my homework (we'd moved onto *Antigone* now . . .), and, bizarrely, I hung out a lot with Michael L, who, surprise, surprise, had a girlfriend now, so in a way it was like things used to be when I had pined and pined for him. Only that was gone now. How nice was it not to yearn and ache and want and want? But how is it that one second you will die for someone to only brush by you, and then the next, just nothing?

But it was great to be friends. He tried to get me out and about more. The week I got back from my adventure with Connor, he convinced me to go to a field hockey game.

"Don't think so," I said initially. What would going to a hockey game possible do for me? Aside from make me sad.

But he insisted. "You gotta support your girls, Lizzie! You're strong enough."

I wasn't sure, but it seemed wrong not to go. And it involved too much explanation.

From the bleachers I watched. The sidelines: big yellow plastic barrels of Gatorade and water. The gleaming bench. The pile of extra hockey sticks; the land of lost toys. And Mr. Crayton cupping his hands over his mouth from the sidelines, screaming. And yes, my old team on the field, *moving*. Lydia. Dribbling out front. Her plaid skirt. Her shin guards. Her ponytail. On the field Lydia was still herself. She was quick and nimble and beautiful. How I missed her as I watched her do what we had once done together so often.

I missed all of it. The grass, the scorekeeper, that *smell*, the pep talk before, the talking-to we got during, the losing, and winning.

No going back for me. Elbows on my knees, head in my hands, Pumas on the bleachers in front of me. I missed being teeny. I was smaller than I'd been before the hospital, but tininess was behind me. I turned to Michael, who was crouched over. "I'm going to be sick," I said.

"Fuck," he said. "What do you need?"

I looked out at the field. "No, no, just watching this. I just can't. I'm leaving, okay?"

He moved to stand. "You sure? It's kind of lame to just leave."

"Oh well."

"Okay, I'll come then!"

"Nah, I'm good!" Whodathunkit: Michael L would turn out to be the nicest guy of all. "I'm going to walk home." I stood up and looked down at him. In any other life I would have chosen him. In any other moment in my life I would have stayed and waited for him anywhere. "Thank you, though," I said. *Such* a prince. Who knew.

I felt him watching me as I made my way down the bleachers,

one for each step, the sound of feet stomping on metal. And then I was out the exit the nonathletes use to leave the field.

When I was out and crossing through the school parking lot, I could hear the crowd cheering behind me.

There's a shortcut through this apartment complex by the train tracks that I used to take when I walked to school, back before my mother started dropping me off and picking me up each day. *Before* before. After leaving the hockey game, I went down that little path and sat on the train tracks. I laid down a penny, like Zoe and I did when we were kids, waiting for the trains to come, watching the penny tremble and then running, coming back for it, all flattened.

I sat on the cold metal tracks and dialed Connor. Straight to voice mail. It was the drill, our drill, I knew. I didn't leave a message. Also part of the drill. Maybe he had his phone; maybe he didn't. It was so hard to know. But if he did have his phone, he knew it was me. He knew my number.

Then I called Nora, because I missed my obnoxious, selfish, *criminal* friend.

"Dahlink!" Nora said when she heard my voice.

I picked at the sticks along the tracks and decided to tell her about Connor. "Hey, hunny!" I said. "I miss you!"

"Likewise, Bun-bun," she said. We had just taken to these odd forms of endearment. Bizarre but sweet. "I'm so glad you rang. I wanted to tell you about this party I went to this past week-*end*. Just cracking, I tell you. Crack-ing."

I sighed. There was no talking to Nora. Or more, I didn't want to talk to her. Our relationship was just me listening. "Cracking?

How is everything over there?"

"Smashing, my good friend. Sma-shing. Three kegs. Dancing on tables. That was me, of course. Did you have to ask?"

"I thought your parents were keeping you home, Rapunzel-style."

"That's all over," she said in her regular Nora voice. "They couldn't bear me. Shall I tell you about the game of Truth or Dare that went *très* far afield?"

"Lovely," I said. I toed the dirt. There were smashed beer cans and burnt sticks scattered across the tracks.

"Et vous?"

"Tu," I said.

"Tutu!" said Nora. "I need one. Lots of tulle and sequins. Hot, hot pink."

"A good look for you," I said.

"Bien sûr."

"Anyway, same ol', same ol'," I told her. "Living the dream over here."

I heard her sigh, air out of a tire. "Actually," Nora said, "actually it's all shiit here. Really, doll, school is shiit, the party was shiit. There was no dancing. Not on tables, not on chairs, not even on the hideous wall-to-wall carpet. Truth or Dare was a snooze. I had to be home by ten p.m. Honestly, I just can't wait for camp."

The tracks rumbled beneath me. That meant at least three minutes before it arrived.

"That's the only time it's any real fun. Angelo or no Angelo. That will be aces, my dear. Aces. Not so far away, really. In some ways."

"I'm not going back to camp," I said.

"Of course you are! You'll be all done with being hanged, drawn, and quartered. And we'll be counselors! After all these years. It's finally going to be *our* turn. Our time," she said. Her accent was just regular now. She was only herself.

I hadn't thought it over really, but just then I knew. "I'm not going back. I'm going to be volunteering with Mabel. In hospitals and old-age homes. I'm training her now."

"That sounds perfectly dreadful," Nora said.

"And maybe I want to try and work at a vet's. Maybe Mabel's vet even."

"Dear God," Nora said, British once again. "Is this for college applications? No one cares if you like *animals*. That's not going to get you into *college*. Sign up for Model UN or *debate* and call it a day."

"True," I said. "About the apps."

The train was getting closer. "Well, there you have it anyway," I said. "I gotta go. I'm about to lose service," I said, holding the phone up to the oncoming train.

"Talk soon, luv," she said.

"Talk soon, Nora," I said.

I imagined watching sick dogs come into the office, and I imagined them leaving healthy.

I hopped off the rails, slipped my phone in my back pocket, watched the train speed by. *Chugga chugga chugga.* Everything was different now. I held my face up to the wind. Where was Connor? Was he okay? When would he come back to me? Why wasn't I worried? For some reason I wasn't worried.

I imagined holding kittens and snakes and birds with broken wings.

I watched the train recede in the distance, and I went to get my penny. It was flat and smooth and as warm as a stone on the beach.

What can I say? I just felt so happy.

How Lost

I expected not to hear from Connor, but I didn't expect it would be for so long. It took about a week and then, suddenly I got nervous. Very nervous. Was he all right? Did he ever even get back to school? He was lost again. With Connor that could mean just so many things. How lost? How deep into the fairy-tale forest did he go? Would he find his own way out? How long would it take? Would I have to grab the nearest woodsman and my own ax to find him?

Why had I just assumed that he was fine and I was fine and we were fine? What kind of moron was I? Why had I not been nervous? Because the longer Connor didn't contact me, the longer I realized that I was still the girl in the hospital, waiting for the sound of a boy and his dog to come walking down the hall.

And beneath all that was also that Connor had revealed himself to be someone else. He was a little sad and also broken. What do broken people do? Many different things.

I was broken but I was healing.

"Connor," I said into his voice mail. "Connor! Please call me."

"Hello? Hello. It's Lizzie. Please, tell me you're okay."

I called always. Like, thirty times. I called at least thirty times by the time the letter arrived.

Letter 3

This is how I feel: that I will never be good enough for you now. That you are this pure angelic fixed person and that while you think I helped you, I didn't because I used you to help me and now you're better and I'm still the same and you need to go be better with someone better.

This is how I feel: that you got better, you were cured, but that I will never be cured, because there's no Thing to cut out or draw blood about. No IV.

This is how I feel: oatmeal.

This is how I feel: that you are so special. That you don't see it at all. How smart and funny and unique and pretty you are. It's not for me to tell you: look at yourself. But you must know, Lizzie, that you are moving through the universe with power, and that night on the shore, even the trees noticed it.

This is how I feel: at sea will never mean anything bad again.

This is how I feel: that I don't care that I don't know about the future. The immediate one. Like where I'll go. I got kicked out of Stone Mountain. I really wasn't allowed to leave on the weekends. It's pretty much lockdown there. I snuck out and took the bus home and took my car. And it was worth it. That moment when I saw you see me on the boat. That was worth everything.

This is how I feel: that even though I'm back in DC (!!!) and even if my parents are keeping me away, I don't need to see you because I can feel you. I feel you everywhere. But I want to let you go. I have to.

This is how I feel: wherever they send me next, you will always be with me. Verlaine too.

This is how I feel: horse blanket. Swing. Cassiopeia. Open window. Raisins. Moonlight.

Yours always,
Connor

Making Contact

You're in DC? Seriously?

Connor. Please pick up the phone. Hello!

Connor. I got your letter. Can you please talk to me?

Connor. This is Lizzie. Come on! How long have you been here?

Hello? Are you ever going to call me back?

Fuck you, Connor. I'm not going to call you again.

How many messages do I have to leave here?

Fuck you, Connor.

Hello?

And then, finally, there was a voice.

"Yes?" the voice, the woman's voice, said.

I was so shocked to hear a human that it took me a long moment to respond. "Oh, hi! This is Lizzie Stoller." I paused again. I was pretty sure who I was talking to, but I wasn't positive. "Is Connor there, please? I'm sorry, I thought I was calling his cell phone."

"It is his cell. This is his mother," the female human said.

"Oh!" What a great way to meet Connor's mom! I thought. But then I thought, something terrible has happened or is about to happen. "Hello, Mrs. Bryant. Sorry to leave so many messages, I just haven't heard from Connor in a while." Like forever, I thought. It has been seven centuries since I have heard your son's voice.

She sighed.

I was silent, a kind that was waiting for someone else to break it.

"I'm very sorry, Elizabeth, but Connor can't talk to you or see you," Connor's mother said.

The last adult to call me Elizabeth was my great-aunt Leonora from Buffalo, and that was at her husband's funeral. But of course that was not the important part, and the important part just then began to register. My heart beat in my ears.

"I know you're a lovely person," she continued, "but Connor has exercised a lot of poor judgment around you."

"Around me?" I said. Because what was I supposed to say? Again I found myself out of the land of age appropriateness. I was shaking.

"Well, poor judgment in general, but now, with you. He can't see you anymore. I know it's painful for both of you. I'm sorry about that. I really am."

I began to cry, as softly as I could.

"I'm sorry, dear. I'm just trying to protect my son. He needs to find his own way right now. This has been hard on everyone."

I was still crying.

"I hope you can understand," she said. It was a little bit of a question but not one that was asking for an answer.

"Yes," I said. "Can you please tell him that I called?" I wondered if he had gotten any of my messages.

"Of course I will."

"Can you please tell him that I"—I stammered because I didn't know how much to say—"that I miss him?" is what I decided on.

"I will certainly tell him that. And I can tell you that he misses you too. Let's just try this for a while and see. Let things cool down. I don't have to tell you that leaving school and taking out the boat and bringing you to the beach house was not responsible or acceptable," she said.

"No. I know."

"I know you've been through a lot. Both of you really have. Not what most teenagers deal with. But let me tell you because I'm older and I know. That is not enough. It feels like it is, but it isn't."

I was sniffling but I didn't try to cover it up. I couldn't tell Connor's mom that it was enough. That what we'd been through was everything. Because she was a lawyer, and I'm sure there was some statute that proved me wrong. And because she was Connor's mother and she was holding him hostage.

"I will tell Connor I spoke to you, Elizabeth."

"Thank you," I said.

"Good-bye then," she said.

"Good-bye, Mrs. Bryant," I said before I threw my phone across the room and threw myself on my bed. Good-bye Connor Good-bye Connor Good-bye Connor: those were the only words I could hear or see until Zoe knocked on my door and called me down for dinner.

Finally, Listening

"Not cool," Stella said when I called and told her about the letter and the conversation with Connor's mom. "So he just never went back to school? After we saw him at the marina? He totally lied to you. So not cool."

Again, I thought, but I did not say this. "But did you hear what I said about the letter?" I asked her. "It was so sweet and also he seemed so . . . *pained*."

"Read it to me," she said.

I was on my bed, picking at my blue comforter. I hated blue now. Everything about it. "No, Stella, that would be a betrayal."

"You're kidding, right? You have got to be kidding."

"No! I'm surprised you are asking me. You're so, I don't know, *moral*."

"The guy has sex with you and doesn't call you. He says he's doing one thing and he does another. He's a liar. I think morality is sort of out the door now."

I was silent. "I just don't think it's like that. Or only like that."

"Your call."

"Stella," I said.

"What?"

"Come on. Don't be mad." Just then Frog jumped from her rock into her water. *Plop.*

"Sure," she said. "Not mad. The guy's an asshole."

"I need to tell you," I said. "What happened."

"There's more?" she asked me.

"So much more."

"How could there possibly be more?"

"Not sure you'll think he's less of an asshole, but here goes. . . ."

So. I told Stella the story. About the Thing. Everything about it. It felt so good, this . . . unburdening. And I realized then that I really wanted to see how she saw it, from what slant of refracted Stella prism light.

When I was done with the story, the story of Connor, Stella was silent. "Wow. Well, it explains a lot," she said. "Here I thought he was just this sort of angel taking care of you and showing up for you and doing all the right things until he started doing the wrong ones."

"Well. He was that. He is that."

"Yes and no."

"Yes."

"Hey," said Stella. "Thank you for telling me all this."

"I haven't told anyone. Not even my sister. No one. Do not repeat, okay?"

"Of course not. Of course not. I'm just trying to process everything. Explains a lot but doesn't make it all better, does it? All it does is make it more complicated."

"Yes," I said. "That is what I'm saying. That has been the problem, all along."

"So complicated."

"I mean," I said, "do you think Connor is a bad person?"

"I don't even know what that means. What does being a bad person actually entail? I don't know him. It definitely seems like he did a bad thing. That is not really up for debate."

"No," I said. "It isn't."

"Do good people do bad things? All the time," Stella said.

"Anyway, with all this"—I shrugged, like I was shaking off the conversation—"can you please tell *me* something now? Something important? So I don't feel like the asshole always talking, never listening." So I don't feel like Nora, I thought. Please don't let me be a version of Nora, the one without the Brit vocab and fake accent.

"It's okay," she said. "I'm good at listening."

"No, I need you to tell me something. Something important. So we can be a little equal."

"How to choose," Stella said.

"Choose," I said.

"Okay."

I was silent.

"Okay, here goes. So Jared?"

"Yes! Jared!"

"He's a senior at Penn," she said. I wished I could have seen Stella's face right then. Like if she was proud or ashamed of this fact.

"Wow. Old man." I laughed.

"Well, I knew him from DC. When I was a freshman, I used to go see shows a lot. Downtown."

"Really. That's insane." Just so cool. When I was a freshman, I was still making Shrinky Dinks with my mother.

"Well. I was just so angry. My parents were getting divorced. No one noticed me and I would sneak out, and the music, that kind of screaming and stuff, it helped me," she said. "I never drank or did drugs or anything like that. It was really the music for me. Like I needed it."

"You are amazing," I said. "How you know yourself. And how you do what you need to."

"Jared hung out there too. 9:30. Velvet Lounge. U Street. He went to Wilson."

"Teen dream," I said. I guess it was kind of mean. But it was so calculated cool. So.

"Not exactly. We started going out when I was fourteen. And he was eighteen."

"And you stayed together for so long. That's kind of amazing, Stella." I picked up David B's God's eye. I held it up to the light. A talisman.

"Actually, it was statutory rape."

"Wow. I was not expecting that." I put down the God's eye and went to my bed. "Did he *rape* you?"

"Well, legally, right? Look, I'm not saying I felt raped. I was totally into him and into it and complicit, but legally, that's what it is. And it's illegal for a reason. I mean, what did I know when I was fourteen? I was like some weird fucking child bride."

"Totally. I totally see what you mean."

"We went out my whole high school career. And I kept it this secret. From my parents, from friends. You went off for a night. I would go for whole weekends. I lied all the time. I never did anything in high school. No football game or school play or mock trial or science club. I was always with Jared, wherever he wanted me to be," she said. "And when he wasn't around, I was just studying and reading and playing guitar and writing in my diary about my parents' hateful divorce. That's why my grades are so awesome."

"That's crazy! I mean, I just had no idea," I said.

"How could you? You never know what's up with anyone, do you? I mean, how would you know? I would have to tell you. And you would have to tell me."

"Are you going to press charges?" I asked. Was that even the way you said it, the way you asked?

"No."

I had thought Stella would. She's just that way. As in justice pursuer.

"I probably should, but I think it would only be out of spite. I think if he was dating a fourteen-year-old now, I would. To protect her. But he's dating just a regular twenty-year-old. Just another regular girl. Who isn't me."

"Are you crying?" I asked.

"Me? No. Why would I be crying? It's done. It made me *me*. Here I am. Me. And I'm free now. Hello."

"Hello, Stella B." Stella. Another person I would never know if my life had just stayed on its regular course. If I was just me before, Stella would have never had a word to say to me.

"Hello, Elizabeth S. Now we know everything."

For some bizarre reason, I pictured those paper towels at the top of the bathroom stall door, crumpled up in Stella's hand. Here, she'd said.

"Everything," I agreed. And I was also thinking: What could I possibly offer Stella? What could she ever possibly want from me?

"Take," she'd said.

I wanted to give. I was just so ready to give.

Zoe had started coming to Petiquette with Greta—my mother had had it—and she and Stella and I would hang out afterward. They were both in the same grade with those same about-to-be-going concerns. But I was the link between them in their differentness and sameness. Their humanness. My sister. She was all perfect on the outside, nails pink, lip gloss, hair in a ponytail, good clogs. And I've already said what Stella was and was not.

Even though the only person I told about the accident, the Thing—ever—was Stella, I told Zoe everything else. It was one night when we all went to the park at Cabin John and sat out in the cold watching the dogs let out all their energy from having to sit and stay and shake everyone's hand. All the stars. They really are the same everywhere. Just wherever you are looking up at the sky.

"And now I can't even talk to him," I said.

"Give it time," Zoe said.

"I hate that expression," I said.

"Well? Can you imagine? Connor's parents are probably just recovering from everything," Stella said.

"Recovering from what?" Zoe said. "I think my sister is the one who's recovering."

I shot Stella a warning look. Would her ethics make her speak or be quiet? I now knew her well enough to be pretty sure it was the second option.

"Don't panic," Stella said to me, and I didn't know if we were talking about telling my sister the story or about Connor. "He has always come and gone. I'm not sure that's okay in general, but it makes sense for now. Right?"

"Okay," I said, totally panicked. I knew where he was now, that he was okay, if okay was exactly what you'd call it, but would I ever see him or hear his voice again? And forget about touching or holding.

I might not ever see him again. And in the back of my mind, I could not stop considering Mrs. Bryant's last few words to me: how maybe everything that had happened to us was what brought us together. That it was the only thing we had.

But how do you know? Who's to say? What makes anyone connect, *click click*, and what makes that connection stick? I want to know who is to say. Mrs. Bryant? Is there some kind of law or *statute* for that? She could be right. That there might one day be other things that brought us together with someone. Separately.

I was crying again.

Zoe had been silent. "I had no idea you were even dating him," she said.

"Dating? I mean really, Zo."

"Well, seeing him. I mean, I told you about what he did to Tim's friend. Is he even, like, a good guy?"

"He is," I said.

"But did you ask him about her?"

I had in my own way asked about her. And he had answered. He had said, once he hadn't been very nice. "Did you not hear me about everything else?" I asked her. "Like all the wonderful stuff I just told you? And my subsequent despair?"

"She loves him," Stella said. "You know what that's like, right?"

Zoe grimaced. "I don't know," she said. "This just sounds like a mess."

"True," said Stella.

"Hello? Right here. I am my own person, you guys. Can we just stick with what's at hand? He exists. It is not, should he exist or is it a good idea he exists, but he does and now I need to get back to him."

Zoe turned to me. "Who are you?" she asked.

"Me. I'm me."

"I think you're awesome," Stella said.

Zoe gave Stella a sideways look.

"Thanks," I said.

"We have to trust you," Stella said.

"She's *my* sister!" Zoe told her.

"So trust her then," Stella said. "You have a better idea?"

"Trust," I repeated.

Oh, how I wish I could have.

We sat that way awhile, our legs crossed in front of us, the dogs these eerie silhouettes jumping and twisting against the sky, until the deep, deep cold of the grass chilled us all over. We stood and brushed ourselves off and let the dogs into the cars and then climbed in ourselves. Zoe turned the heat up as high as it would go. I felt the heat on my face. I waved bye to Stella B and then I looked at my sister. Zoe. We were so separate now.

"Tim got into Columbia." She looked down at the wheel.

I didn't know if I was supposed to cheer or boo.

She rubbed her hands together and then put both hands on the wheel. "I have no desire to go to Columbia," she said.

"Really?"

She shook her head.

"Well, why are you applying, Zoe? There are a million places. You could practically go anywhere."

She shook her head again. "I'm not."

I squinted.

"I said I am but I'm not. I don't want to be in a city. I don't want to be scared all the time. And I want to be on my own."

"That's great, Zoe. That you know that about yourself, I mean."

"I love Tim," she said. "But it's not a forever love."

I didn't say anything. How did she *know* that? How could anyone, even Zoe, possibly know that?

"Was he ever? I mean, did you ever feel that?"

She shook her head. "No."

For me? Connor? Yes, yes, yes. Forever and ever and ever love.

"Then why?"

"He was like my best friend. He was what I needed but not really what I wanted."

I looked at Zoe.

She was crying as she put the car in drive. "When did everything get so serious?" she asked. But she wasn't just talking to me.

"I know." I swallowed. I thought of Tim loading up my iPod. How he jumped up to help me as soon as I needed it. I was going to miss him. A lot.

My sister took a deep breath and let it out, moved the car gently out of the parking lot. "So sad and so serious," she said, and then we were on the highway, heading home.

Canine Good Citizen

This is what Mabel could do: Sit politely for petting. Kindly greet a stranger. Come when she was called. Walk on a loose lead. Get taken, briefly, away from me. Sit and stay. Be polite to other dogs. Walk through a noisy crowd. Be examined. In my opinion, this made Mabel better than most people, but what it also did was get her that Canine Good Citizen certificate.

We had this stupid little ceremony after our final session at Petiquette, and we all clapped as each dog went up with his or her person to get her certificate. Samantha was first, and I watched her prance across the floor, so feminine in this bulky dog body, her fur gray and velvety, something I'd like as the material for a cape, if I ever wore a cape. And then there was Stella next to her, all sharp corners and quick movements. She was more cat than dog, on the outside anyway.

When it was Mabel's turn, we went up together and when Esther, split ends on high alert, bent to give me the piece of paper, I burst into tears.

I tell you, I am one thousand years old now. I am like Nana. I cry when I see anything that might have made a person struggle. An old lady crossing the street. A little kid pressing super hard on her crayons. A man with one leg. A movie with a star-crossed love . . . pretty much anything.

My parents were there. They were both madly clapping as if I were, I don't know . . . on the field. Scoring a goal, say. There they were, cheering for us.

And when Greta and Zoe came out from so-not-getting-a-certificate-probably-never-would, the whole girl band plus the dad celebrated by stopping off for ice cream on the way home. Have you seen a dog eat an ice cream cone? It's pretty hilarious and wonderful.

"Strawberry," I ordered.

"Ecch," said Stella. "So girly."

Connor. He was everywhere, in everything about me. Like in the *DNA,* as Mr. Hallibrand used to say. DNA. I licked my strawberry cone, felt my bag stir a little. One day soon, it would be gone. This was just a holding pattern until I was healthy enough that they could hook everything up inside. Connor was right. I'd be scarred, but this would all be gone. I would still have scars and *complications,* I was told, but it would almost be as if it had never happened.

So where were Connor's scars? Where do they go when they're not, as Stella says, making the body more interesting?

We were there. Together. I know that we were. But when would the golden boy with this golden dog be back?

I just had no idea.

Butterfly

In the end, I stuck with the sick children idea. I wanted to be able to sit down and have Mabel sit next to me, and I wanted to hold some bald little boy's teeny hand and say, *No matter what, it's going to be all right.* It would be a lie and it would not be a lie.

And so I did. Just before the holidays, I went back there. With Mabel.

"While I can't say I'm enjoying reliving pulling up to this place for the thirty thousandth time, I am enjoying that you are going in there as a healthy person and coming out in an hour," my dad said when he dropped us off.

Full circle, as they say.

"Me too," is what I said out loud, and I think my voice wobbled a bit.

"I'll be around the corner. In the café that is *not* the hospital cafeteria," he said. "That coffee was so shitty."

"Yeah, well, the morphine was pretty subpar as well."

"Touché," he said as I went into the back and clicked on Mabel's leash.

"Ready?" I asked her. "See you soon, Dad."

"Yes." He looked down at his hands or at the keys in his hands. "Soon."

Mabel jumped out and then we were in the lobby, where I showed our documents, and then we were on the elevator headed up to the twelfth floor.

The elevator dinged and Mabel and I stepped out. Those same orange chairs where Connor had told me about the girl he'd watched be killed. Back when that story was the story of someone else.

I looked out the window. The scaffolding from the construction was down, and the piles of dirt were just little anthills now. How long before you can actually tell what a building will be? Because I still had no idea what was being built here.

I walked to the nurses' station, strung with paper candy canes and Santa's hats, and blinking red and green lights. Everything was both cheerful and dark, the way Christmastime always seems to me. Mabel's nails clicked along the hallway. It reminded me a little of going back to camp as a counselor. Like I could see everything I used to do and love: the gum tree, the archery targets fastened to bales of hay, the plaques in the auditorium with all our names. I was there to tell the campers what those things were and how to see them and use them now.

Really, all those things were far behind me and so were these bright fluorescent lights, the old people slumped in wheelchairs, the empty gurneys, the doors slightly ajar, where I could see people crying and holding hands.

Click click went Mabel's nails. It was hard not to remember

Verlaine's footsteps, headed toward my room.

"Look at you!" It was Alexis, who had been there when they'd put in my central line. "Lizzie!"

My hand fluttered up to my chest. It happened practically automatically. I thought I was just another patient to her. One of so many. But maybe she remembered everyone. Maybe they all did. We were their campers.

"And who's this?"

"This is Mabel," I said. I was being talked to as if I were twelve. Ah, well, I suppose I would always be sick to these nurses. I couldn't really blame them.

"Hello, Mabel!" She came out from the nurses' station and bent down. She held out her hand for her paw, and Mabel gave it to her.

"She just got her certificate!"

"How great," Alexis said.

"We're just here to say hi. My job—our job—is at the children's hospital."

By now some of the nurses had gathered around, some I recognized, some I didn't.

"That's really great!"

"Doesn't start for a few weeks, though," I said. "After the holidays."

"Hi, Lizzie." Collette. She was shuffling around the counters and emptied a few cups filled with paper clips and pens and other office stuff.

Collette.

"You look great. How are you feeling?" She came out from

behind the nurses' station and squatted. But more to talk to me.

She held out her hand. On her palm was a plastic barrette. It was purple. It was shaped as a butterfly.

"I found this in your room when you were gone. I don't know why, but I saved it. It was so sweet and it reminded me of you. And it made me think of you flying away from here. Maybe I just knew you'd be back. Or that Connor would be."

Just the name made everyone freeze a moment, but I didn't say anything.

I shook my head. "That's not mine."

"No?" she said.

I shook my head. I remembered those barrettes. Red and yellow and purple, all over that little girl's head. "That's Thelma's daughter's," I said.

She nodded, looking down. "Well, I guess I saved it for you for some reason. Would you like it?"

"Yes," I said. I remembered her peering around the curtain. Thelma's daughter who was now only her father's daughter.

Collette pressed the barrette into my palm, and we both stood up.

There was an old lady struggling to walk along the hallway. She waved slowly at us as she passed.

I put it in my pocket.

The butterfly.

"Thank you!" I told the nurses as I waved good-bye and heading back to the elevators with Mabel. I couldn't breathe. I had thought I would visit with everyone and bring Mabel to see some of the patients, but I couldn't stay another moment. And as I headed down from twelve, dinging past each floor, I fingered the barrette in my pocket. I'll keep it for you, Thelma, I thought. It was a dumb thought, but it was the one I was having. Then there was a slight jolt in the elevator, as if Thelma was answering me. Or, I thought more realistically, it was some random malfunction that was going to trap me there in that hospital forever, but then—open sesame—we were in the lobby and then we were out the door fast, I don't remember my feet even touching ground, and then we were around the corner at the café with the decent coffee. There was my father hunched over the newspaper, eating a scone, crumbs on his cable-knit sweater. He looked up at me and I felt in my pocket for the hard plastic and the raised little bumps along the bow-like wings. I have it, Thelma, I thought as I waved to my dad that we were done and ready to go home.

Out of the Blue

I think, when I look back, this is a story about two people who never thought they could be loved back. And this is the story of those two people loving each other back and back and back.

It's a miracle, actually, that Connor showed up in the hospital just when I happened to be there, needing him. I can't speak for Connor anymore. I think I know what he'd say about all this, but you just never know what's going on with people, even the ones close up next to you. This is my superpower. That I understand all that now. Able to leap tall buildings with all my . . . empathy.

The butterfly stayed in my pocket, everywhere. It was there when I went grocery shopping with my mother and when I went to school and when I was alone in my room doing homework on that dumb study buddy. I could feel it always and it was there too when Michael L and his new girlfriend *Genevieve* (eye roll: of course she's French) and I went for flowers to take to Dee-Dee on her opening night, just before school ended for the holidays. I felt for it in my pocket and through the whole show. And can I just say? Dee-Dee was amazing. Over-the-top fantastic. Who cares she spent four months in character? Pretending. Who doesn't? Really. Tell me someone who doesn't pretend.

I hugged her crazily backstage. *Deedeedeedeeee*. I said. *Dee*. I was so proud to be her friend. She'd been busy and I'd been sick and maybe we'd meet back at the beginning again. Or maybe it would just be this. I'm still not sure. But Michael L and Genevieve and Lydia and I leaned against the bike racks anyway, lingering until Dee and Kenickie came out the side entrance like movie stars after the show. Her parents were there waiting, but we just wanted to wave to them and blow them kisses. Dee-Dee had her arms full of roses. Who knew which ones were even ours?

Stella B got in early to Princeton. *Princeton*. I couldn't imagine her going away. I bought her tiger ears and a tiger tail and also, I made her a CD.

My music. Sad and pretty.

I lay on my bed and watched Frog and listened. I drew a crescent moon. I pasted on two magazine hands. *People help the people*, I wrote. I cut out and then pasted on the teeniest yellow bird.

My people. Angus and Julia Stone: "Good-bye to my Santa Monica dream . . . You will tell me stories of the sea, and the ones you left behind." Birdy: "People help the people, and if you're homesick, give me your hand and I'll hold it." The Beatles: "There are places I remember . . . "

All these words saying, softly, everything I want to say. To Stella, to Connor, wherever he was out there, whatever he was doing. To the world. To Dee and Lydia, to Zoe. Tim. "And you laugh like you've never been lonely." That's what Ben Howard sings. "'Cause it's just the bones you're made of."

All the music. To anyone in the world who has ever held my hand.

Stella was wearing her tiger tail and ears when we went hiking together at Great Falls with the dogs. It was one of those freakishly beautiful and mild January days, the kind you only get one or two of but you can rely on arriving every year. My butterfly was in my pocket then, too. Butterfly in pocket and Stella in front, her little tail twitching as she climbed, sun shining down in those crazy rays of light.

And that's when Connor finally called.

"Oh my God," I said to Stella. "It's Connor." I sort of lamely held out my hand with the ringing phone.

"Did you think he'd disappear forever? Are you going to answer?"

"Hi." I said, answering.

I barely had service and I stopped along the rocks, looking out onto the crashing water. Someone was actually kayaking in there. In a wet suit, with a helmet, navigating the insane waves all alone.

"Can we meet?" Connor said.

We hadn't spoken for what? *Two months.* "I'm sorry," I said. "Who's this?" Below the crash and spray of the water. The man—I think it was a man—with his double paddle held high. Connor couldn't be serious. Not even a *hello*. Not even an *I'm sorry*. Nothing.

"Seriously."

"I'm not home now." I was angry now and I watched Stella

stop and turn, her black fleece covered in gray hair. (The fleece was Stella's only concession to hiking; her Docs were her only hiking boots.) Her stupid ears that pressed down her spiky hair made her smudged eyes look sort of perfect silhouetted against the extra-sharp winter sun.

"Can we meet at Fletcher's?"

"No! You can't just call out of the blue, Connor. I was so worried!"

"Why not? Why can't I? I haven't exactly been on spring break here, Liz."

"Not even a letter! I've been so worried. And so sad." I paused. "And so pissed! We had this amazing night and then you totally ditched."

"I'm sorry."

I was silent.

"It wasn't like that at all. I didn't ditch. I didn't."

"Anyway, I'm with Stella, like, on this mountain right now."

"This is not a mountain!" screamed Stella.

"Okay, on some cliff. Anyway, I'm not home!" Inside? I wanted to meet him. I wanted to do whatever he said. But that was no way to be. I couldn't keep . . . unlocking my turtle shell. One day it just wouldn't fasten on again, and I'd be stuck full-on without my . . . *exoskeleton*.

"Where are you guys?"

"Great Falls," I said. It was actually not at all far from Fletcher's Cove, but I didn't say this.

"Lizzie," he said. It was only my name, but in it was all these different emotions at once. A prism in a word.

"I'll try," I said. "I'm trying. Give me an hour."

"I'll be there in less than twenty minutes, waiting," he told me, and then he clicked off.

And then he was gone again. I looked out at the crashing water, but I didn't move to leave. I wanted to see him and I wanted to never see him again. What would happen if I just didn't go? How long would he actually wait for me?

"Well?" Stella said.

"B," I said, as if this was a name I had always called her. "I'm so sorry. But I think we have one more stop."

Stella, hands in her pocket, turned around in the sun. *Twitch twitch* went the tiger tail. "It's okay," she said. "I can do one more. I've got one more in me."

"I want to be there for you too," I said. I meant it.

"I know that," she said. "But you are the one in it right now. So where to?" she asked as we followed the dogs back to the parking lot.

Bones

"I guess I'll wait here with the dogs," Stella said as we pulled into the lot. Hula, hula went the girl. Bob, bob went the dog. "And then I guess you owe me a million dollars."

"I'm so sorry," I said.

"I'll just listen to your supersweet, super-girly music and mellow out. I look at it as my contribution to finding a cure for ulcerative colitis." She crossed her arms and leaned back, shut her eyes.

"Ha. I'm sorry. But I can't drive on my own yet! I mean, I still only have my learner's." Getting my license hadn't been first and foremost on my mind.

"I realize," she said. "It's no big deal."

"I guess," I said. "Thank you, Stella. Really." I turned toward the boathouse.

The last time I was here I could barely walk. I was skinny and breakable, and I had leaned on Connor the whole way down. Now, he was separate from me. I saw him from where I stood, alone, far away. His feet dangled over the rickety peer and Verlaine sat next to him, tail wagging along the splintery wood.

Oh my God, it was like some crazy ad for perfect boy clothes or something. Tousled Connor, green down vest, old sneaks, sad eyes, golden retriever. When would my heart stop skipping, just at the sight of him?

Question: Who do you go to first? The boy you love or the boy you love's dog?

"Verlaine!" I said, running toward them.

Verlaine is so elegant and . . . trained. He wagged his tail some more and sat and smiled at me. When I patted my chest, he brought his front paws up and dog-hugged me.

"Hi," I said through his scruff. And then: "Hi." I looked through the scruff to Connor.

He stood up and we hugged. This is what it was like: like all the parts of me that had been exposed, all my nerves and cells and synapses, were finally again connected. *Click.* Connor.

I could feel him crying. Or maybe that was me.

The last time we were here, we'd gone out in that little boat and he'd had to carry me out of it. I had thought I might die then. Of illness, of shame, of sadness. But I lived and I'm not that sick person anymore.

I wondered if he could even lift me now.

"What brings *you* here?" I asked him, weaving my fingers through his. It was amazing to touch him again. I had thought maybe I would never touch him again.

He looked down. He squeezed my hand, hard. "I have to leave," he said.

"Why are you even telling me this? I haven't seen you anyway. I mean, what's the difference?"

"Well, there's a difference to me. My parents have been trying to get me into this place in California, and they finally made space for me."

"California!"

"Yes! That's what I'm saying. Even if I haven't seen you, I know you've been near."

I nodded, swallowing.

"After I got kicked out of Stone Mountain, this was where they wanted me to go."

"Got the Stone Mountain memos. I feel bad about that."

He nodded. "It was my fault."

To that, I said nothing.

"It wasn't unpleasant. Precisely the opposite. It was so worth it."

"But you lied! Again! And you've been here, just a town away from me." Just to say it enraged me. I was angry that we had lost all that time and I was mad that Connor had lost it for us. "Again!"

"So I could see you," he said. "Greater good."

I was silent.

"How are you, by the way?"

"By the way? I'm fine. I'm going in for surgery next month. All fine!" I said, falsely bright.

"I want to be there for that. When you wake up." Connor gripped my hand harder. I felt his bones.

"I don't see how that will happen, do you? I'm a long way from California." I imagined waking up from the anesthesia and seeing Connor's freckled, sunny face. "But I want you to be there too."

"I've got to go really soon. My dad is waiting at the restaurant down the road. I'm just going to text him when we're done here."

"Done?"

"Just with this particular good-bye."

I looked at him. "Okay. Slow down. Give me a minute. I'm always trying to catch up with you."

"This place has, like, four kids to a classroom. Everyone gets their own horse to take care of. That's what my parents were so into. They want to help me. You don't see me. When I'm alone. I have to say I fell back on some bad habits."

My mind went there. Right there. The girl. The one who he never spoke to again. And how many others? "What kind of habits?" I asked him. I was shaking.

"Nothing that involved me leaving the house. Or being with another person. Nothing like that."

I breathed out.

"It's not like that. It can just get really bleak where I live."

"I'm so sorry," I said. "I wish you could have told me. That you could tell me."

"I know. I know."

"You could have."

"Anyway, so the horses. You get to take care of something that needs you so much. But also gives a lot back," Connor said.

"Yes. I get that. That's what you do." I shivered.

"DC. My parents think it's a shitty place for me. All the people I smoked with. The scene of the accident. They're not totally wrong. I want to be better."

"And me."

"No," Connor said. "Not you. Never you."

I smiled. Just a little smile.

Suddenly, Connor snapped Verlaine's red leash on his collar. "Can you take him?" he asked, holding the leash out to me.

"Sure," I said, taking the leash. "Hello, Verlaine! Want to go for a spin?"

"No." Connor looked at me so seriously. "*Take* him take him."

I didn't stun easily by then—what could be more shocking than what had already happened?—but here I was, stunned.

"Connor."

"Please, Lizzie. He loves you. He's always alone at my house. He's already changed," Connor said. "He chews things up. He barks a lot. He's used to companionship."

I knew he was also talking about himself. My new superpower told me so. I wonder what it was like for Connor, when he was invisible in his room.

"If I'm all the way in California and know he's all alone, I won't be able to . . . concentrate on getting better."

I imagined my parents. Voilà, I'd say. Please give a warm welcome to Dog Number Three!

"Okay." What else could I say?

"And that you two will be together makes me so happy." He seemed suddenly lighter. The old Connor, as bright as if he'd borrowed the sun. "And Frog. I bet she's huge now."

No kidding. Frog was growing bigger by the second, already the size of my palm. Zoe said we should have a ceremony and let her go in the backyard, but that isn't true about turtles, that they want to be let go. They can die that way, trolling the suburbs, looking for home. "Okay," I said again, resolved, and trying to quiet the noise of dealing with my parents in my head.

"I want to be there when you go in for the surgery. But it will be hard to maneuver."

"Don't," I said. "That's how you got into this mess, remember? At least part of the mess anyway."

"I'll be back for summer, though," he said. "For sure."

There were a few boats out on the water, some rowers, and a father and son in a canoe farther out. The sun was so bright on all of them.

Connor hugged me, tightly. So, so tightly. "I won't check out again. I won't," he said. "I promise."

I hugged him back with everything I had. All my strength and love and openness. There was no shell to me anymore at all.

I felt the hard plastic when I placed my hand in my pocket. "I went back," I said. "With Mabel. To the hospital. And Collette gave me this." I brought it out and opened my palm. "It was Thelma's daughter's," I said. "This butterfly." I placed the barrette in his hand, and he curled his fingers around it. "I don't know, I know we didn't know Thelma or anything, or really talk to her that much, but I just feel like it's some kind of talisman, I think. From the past to the future." Had the God's eye brought me luck? I think that it had.

Connor's phone buzzed. "I know that's my dad," he said. "We have to go. All my stuff's in the car. Catching a plane in a few hours."

I swallowed.

"Well, bye then," I said. "Again."

"Bye."

But we didn't move. We just looked at each other.

Abruptly Connor squatted down and hugged Verlaine. I couldn't watch. It was too awful.

He stood up and faced me. "I love you," he said.

"Me too," I said. "Love." Would I ever hear the word from Connor and not feel fluttery and light?

He kissed my nose. Then my lips. Just lightly. So lightly and sweetly. "I'll be back," he said.

"I know you will. I have your dog."

"No, but *I'll* be back. I just know it."

I nodded. Good-bye again.

And then I turned to leave with Verlaine, who kept looking back to see if his person was coming too.

But his person wasn't coming, not then anyway.

I turned around and waved to Connor, my Connor. The golden boy.

I watched him put this butterfly in his pocket. Proof that we had all been there.

Why would I put Frog in the backyard like that? I thought as I headed back to Stella and the dogs I knew were waiting with the heat and the music on. It was a random thought, but that was what I was thinking then. I couldn't look back at Connor. I thought how I would just get a bigger tank. And then a bigger one and then a bigger one.

I looked down at Verlaine, who was walking with me tentatively. Stella's car was just around a patch of trees. I will hold on to Frog forever, I thought. We will grow up together. Together, we will grow strong.

I startled Stella, who was zoning out to Angus and Julia Stone. "I don't know how you stay awake listening to this shit," she said, sitting up. "It is peaceful, though."

I held out Verlaine's leash. "Parting gift," I said. I opened the door for Verlaine and he hopped in. I climbed in the back with him.

"A real beauty," she said as she looked in the rearview.

I nodded. "I know." I hugged Verlaine. "He's a keeper," I said.

When I went away to camp six months ago, I left behind one dog and a life of regularness. And then I was counting losses. I lost so much about my life, I'd thought. But when I walked back toward my house that day Connor and I said good-bye again, I had: everything. Three dogs, a turtle, a true friend, a new job, someone I loved so much it hurt my heart to think of it. What was missing? Nothing was missing anymore.

Almost everyone was here.

After Stella dropped us off, I struggled up the front steps, stumbling over the three dogs I held by their collars. She honked her horn and sped off. Her horn? It played "Johnny B. Goode." I heard it all the way down my street.

They pulled every which way, straining against my grip. I looked up at my house. That white front door. My mother's newspaper. My father's garden. My sister's textbooks. I leaned down. For a brief moment, the dogs were still. And then, I let go.

Acknowledgments

Apparently, it takes a village of Jens: Thank you to Jen Loja, who got me started on this and cheered me to the finish. Thank you to Jenn Joel, for her invaluable help and insight. And thank you to Jen Klonsky, for believing in this project early and seeing it through with me. I'm also grateful to and for many others: Thank you to Elissa Schappell, who has been such a stunning reader for me over the years without exception and to Meg Wolitzer, for her support, her candidness, and her friendship. Thank you to Emily Chenoweth, Joanna Hershon, and Madeleine Osborn. And to 61 Local in Brooklyn, for that way-back table. Thank you to Pedro, my best critic. And to Julian. Thank you, Julian.

Turn the page for a peek at

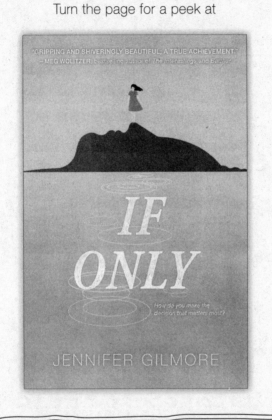

"GRIPPING AND SHIVERINGLY BEAUTIFUL, A TRUE ACHIEVEMENT."
—MEG WOLITZER, bestselling author of *The Interestings* and *Belzhar*

IF
ONLY

How do you make the
decision that matters most?

JENNIFER GILMORE

BRIDGET

March 2000

Will the sweetness swallow all the bitter? Is that a way to start a letter? I knock the pen against the side of my head like I'm taking a cartoon test and I'm cartoon-thinking. What would I say? If I were to write a letter, I mean. My pen—pretty, peach-colored. It says *Be Brave* along the side.

"Really?" I had said to Dahlia when she gave it to me. I'd held it out to her, like I wanted to give it back.

"Really," she'd said. "My mother gave it to me when I started getting into coloring books again."

I'm wondering this—sweet bitter—while I'm waiting for Dahlia now at the café. I have no idea. I mean I'm sixteen, but I am not a total mess. I have done things I'm not proud of, I've made some bad choices, true, but I am not on drugs and I'm not about to start now. My family will help. I can do this, I am thinking, but I am also thinking that I can't. Do this. Not even for her.

I know it's a her.

She is.

"Bridge," Dahlia says. "Hi, honey," she says, shaking off rain.

She takes off her hat. There's that smell of rain, too. I know you know it.

"Thanks for meeting," I say.

This is our winter place now, but we're inching toward spring. We like the table in the nook that hangs over the creek. It's out of the way here, an extra ten-minute walk, but we do it and when we do we know it's serious.

"Of course. What's up? Why so crazy urgent?"

"You want hot chocolate or something? Cider?" Also they have amazing hot chocolate.

"What's up?" Dahlia asks me again. "Your hair looks good by the way." She reaches out and pulls the chunk of pink I dyed last night. My private celebration I think. Because last night I'd decided.

But anything changes my mind. All kinds of thoughts. People. A photo in a magazine. A girl with headphones alone on the street. A woman holding a wobbly toddler's hand.

"I want to keep it," I say.

She looks up. "That's insane. You can't. You and your mom already decided. *We* decided. Are you insane?"

"When I think about it I can't stop crying. I can't."

"Let's look at some more profiles from the agency. You will find the right people. They will be the right parents."

"Will they be, though?"

"My mom's adopted," Dahlia says. "Remember?"

"Gorgeous Lulu! I always forget that part about her."

"Closed. All the paperwork. She's got no idea who her birth parents are. Could be anyone. She looked for a long time. This is so different. The baby will know who you are. She will hear you laughing. My mom always says mine was the first laugh that she recognized."

But what if I never laugh again? My heart, I think, is breaking. Dahlia's mom. I can't help but think of her dad, Raymond, too, all messed up from the Vietnam War like so many of the fathers in this town. Mine, too. They got drafted—no choices at all. Go there. Kill people. Come home. What kind of a choice is that?

Our mothers aren't friends anymore.

Their mothers were best friends, too. Valerie and Lulu. Both their boyfriends went away and came back, changed. That's when my mom got religion but Lulu stayed the same, I think, stayed long hair and Joni Mitchell and Janis Joplin and peace signs, long as I've known her.

This kind of breaking heart, though, mine, it is different than when Baylor and I broke up. That was an all-over-my-skin-hurts, I-can't-move thing. Even my teeth. Like I had the flu or something. Like I needed my mother but I didn't need my mother I needed Baylor. Just to hear his name, still. All kinds of feelings. All the songs are true: the heart breaks. Because what if you can only do it once? Love. Once. Like that's all the universe lets you have. To protect you.

But turns out this is worse. I wonder now, watching Dahlia, who doesn't have to think of any of this, which makes me hate her for one second, will my heart just be breaking forever? Over and over and over again?

"I can raise this little person," I say. It doesn't come out strong at all. I don't sound like anyone's mother.

"There is more for this baby out there," Dahlia says. "If you love your baby, you have to be able to see that. Give it a future."

"Her," I say, smiling. "Not it."

"I know." Dahlia grins back at me. "You can choose it for *her*. And *she* can know who you are."

And what's so great about that, I'm thinking. Who am I?

I want time to tell me what to do. The more time I don't decide, things get decided for me. Like having an abortion. It's too late. So that's not a choice now either. It's been too long. And even if that was not the choice for me, I am not judging anyone now. We are all just trying to live through this without breaking, you know? We are all doing the best we can and I understand every one of us. I love us all. Will anyone else? Love us, I mean. Love me. Ever again. Who could?

So which one am I? The one who keeps her or the one who lets her go?

It becomes less confusing to me the more I say it, the more Dahlia says it. It is so hard to think of the future. When I saw those pink lines—the ones I jumped over into positive—I wish I could explain it. I had thought pink meant it was a girl. (Yes, seriously.) And then I have to think about what's in front of me. Baylor and I were already broken up, and I knew I could get him back with this, *this*—he is not a mean person or anything, but he so doesn't love me. And now, this growing thing. Every morning I woke up crying. I still wake up crying as soon as I remember that nothing has changed.

I need to decide.

Next to us, at the table by the window that looks out onto all the evergreens, a lady is crying. It's almost like she's doing it for both of us. She's weeping. There's a painting of bluebirds in a nest that hangs above her head and another lady reaches out and takes her hand and it feels so sweet to me I want to go over and hug them. Actually I want them to come over here and hug me. Like take me up and just make all this all go away in a way my mom isn't doing. At all.

My mom thinks what I did was wrong. It's hard for her to understand me. Believe me that goes both ways. I mean, if I had a kid, which I almost do, I would be more understanding. Baylor says he'll break up with Rosaria and marry me. He is a good guy and that is the right thing to say but that's the wrong thing to do and the reason is wrong. I know all this, but part of me—most of me—would still really like Baylor back. I would like him away from Rosaria that is for sure. My parents have money, I mean not piles of it or anything, we're not rich at all, but we're okay. We have a house and a car and growing up I had a dollhouse and a bike with a pink banana seat and roller skates with their own key. I could do this, I think. But then I think, this is no life for any of us. Least of all, you. I look down at my belly like it can hear my thoughts. Like you can. You you you. Who are you? Who will you be?

I am growing in every way I can. Someone needs to tell me the answer and it is not Baylor and please don't let it be my mother.

Dahlia is snapping her fingers at me. "Bridget!" she says in between clicks. Her nails are painted dark green and I can see the colors of them moving through space. They match the evergreens on the outside. "Let's look at more of the profiles. Maybe you haven't found the right people yet."

Do I look at her blankly?

"To give the baby to."

Give? How could I. I know Dahlia's right and I can see the answer there, waiting, delivered. One day soon I will put her in someone else's arms. I will answer someone's prayers. I will be wanting for the rest of my life. That is true love and even I know I might never get it again. Even I can see that.

"How's the letter?" Dahlia says.

I roll my eyes.

"Just say, well, whatever you want to say. About how much you love her. Because you do love her. That's why you have to let her go."

I feel the tears streaming down my face again, salt salt salt. I lick them when they reach me. Potato chip tears.

"Who told you that?"

Dahlia cocks her head. "I don't know," she says. "That's what my mother says about her first mom. You're showing a little, by the way."

I am half-disgusted; half-thrilled but I can't say it. "Now?"

"What is it? Three months?"

I nod. "And a half."

"You could start?" says Dahlia. "The letter. It could be kinda fun."

Fun? Nothing is fun anymore. I grimace.

She urges me with her head. "Writing. You could start."

I want to say: Be Brave. To both of us. Write it on this lined paper, on my skin, over my broken heart. But it's already on this stupid pen and that makes it impossible. That's what I feel, though. Be brave. Am I talking to her or to myself? Be a warrior, I want to say.

Meet me on the other side.

"Maybe you want, like, one beautiful letter that says everything," Dahlia says.

I look over at her. She is so pretty, Dahlia, like her mom. She wears makeup—really dark eyes sometimes, or even purple, which somehow works on her, I don't know how—but she also is pretty just in her Hello Kitty onesie, reading magazines next to me on the couch. I reach out to touch one of her long curls. Boing. "Boing," I say.

I crumple the blank sheet into a tight ball.

"Wait!"

"It's wrong," I say. "It's all wrong." I throw it at her.

"You can really tell now," she says softly, looking at my belly.

"Heard you the first time," I say. I am willing that part away.

My father can't look at me. At the dinner table his eyes are just fixed straight ahead. Chews his food, holds his fork in folded hands beneath his chin. Up and down, up and down. What would he even be like with her? Will he hate her or love her? I do think sometimes with boys—men, I guess—you just can't tell. Girls, we are always just on the side of love. We are. Everyone is a bird with a broken wing. Here is my wing. It is broken. It has always been broken.

Mom thinks that's because I don't go to church regularly. And that drove me to Baylor.

"I know," is what I say out loud. How can I say it? Every little thing is about this decision. One thing sways me one way, one the other. Those pink strips. I am tiptoeing along it, tightrope-walking. I can still see that moment when my life changed to this. "I can't believe I have to do this in summer."

"Baby doll dresses."

"But at least no school. I mean, no one noticed."

Dahlia gives me a side look, the one that goes with the smirk. "What?"

"People know," she says quietly. "Come on."

I don't say anything. Of course they know. I know that. I just was pretending. I was pretending that when this goes away it will never have existed at all. It won't even be gone by the time school starts.

I look down. It's still cool enough for boots—Docs—and I can still see the tips of my toes. I wriggle them in my hot boots. My feet are swollen. I feel myself becoming someone else. I am growing and growing. I want to stop it; it's too fast for me. I want to kneel down and pray; I want the answer there, on some altar, our altar, where once I used to stand and sing, where once a pastor touched my forehead with water. There it is, my answer, maybe the Lord is telling me, maybe I can see it there, my answer.

Maybe I was born a sinner and maybe this little person was sent to save me.

From what?

"Baby doll dresses and long sweaters," Dahlia says and already I am dreaming.

If only, I'm thinking. But if only what? If only what. That is what I want to know.

IVY

This is what she gave me: a quilt stitched with roses, the fabric stiff as cardboard, never washed, packed away. A pink dollhouse, new and shining; inside it there are so many rooms. And inside those rooms is wooden furniture: chair, couch, bed, television, bookshelf, sink. How many times did I rearrange all this? Slide the beds to the living room, TV in the library. Bathtub in the bedroom. But it's all the same because it's so easy and light to move pretend stuff around. And the rooms aren't real anyway.

A photograph that I have pasted into a silver locket. I keep it on a string in a jewelry box and I wear it around my neck when I am angry. I have a letter, that came with me. Proof of purchase, I guess. I have all the things that say: You were not abandoned, you were not left, you are special, you got chosen.

Your parents are the parents who raised you from the moment she left you.

When she was sixteen. I am sixteen now. Patrick's band, the Farewells, played last fall in the backyard beneath a striped yellow tent, in case of rain. It rained. It always rains here. "We are the Farewells," the lead singer, Alex, said into the mic at the beginning of the set. So serious but no one was listening.

Deviled eggs and cheese fondue. Buckets of lemonade. The Farewells and their flasks of whiskey, their earnest punk pop. Claire with a bottle of Coke in each patch pocket of her dress.

Sweet sixteen. My moms came out and danced like it was the wedding they never had. Our dogs ran in circles and sneaked table scraps until they passed out beneath the food carts.

I am grateful for my life. I wouldn't want it another way, to be someone else. But you wonder, about everything. Who else could I be? Anyone, really. It could have gone any other kind of way, which is a weirdness I can't get over.

Sometimes I admit I want the her of her; on the bad days it doesn't just sit there, it becomes me, the way I want to know. All the possibilities. Those days the words sting more: the ones you don't know about. Like when I overhear the lead singer of Patrick's band, Alex, refer to his little brother as an idiot and then, he says, he's so got to be adopted. There is no way that kid is related to me.

I mean, I'm right here. Alex? I think those kinds of words matter.

People: Don't say "gay" to describe something dumb. And don't say "adopted" to say someone's dumb either. All of us, we can hear you.

We are right here.

The photo, an *actual* photo you can hold: my moms and my birth mom and me, this little package with a red face wrapped up in a blanket with the faintest pink and blue stripes. There I am at the center. I am the prize. I have never not felt that way. Like the most-ever-wanted prize. The photo hangs on the wall by the stairwell, along with photos of my moms and my grandparents, and everyone as a child. The grandparent children photos are most remarkable to me because they're, like, colored in. There is one of Gram up there, and she's got this mass of black hair and she's only a year old. And her huge blue eyes are shaded actual blue. And then this colored-in pink lipstick. It's bizarre. That and the photo of my grandpa Harry, who I never met, playing tennis at Columbia University in a V-neck sweater—those are my favorites.

In the photo with my birth mom you can just see the side of her face—you can't really see her so well but it looks as if she's been through some kind of a war. Her hair is all over the place, like she'd woken up from thrashing to nightmares. There's a streak of purple in it. The eye that you can see in the picture is swollen, or maybe that's just how her eyes are. I never knew her, after. She wears a hospital gown. There's a plastic bracelet around her right wrist. It might say her name or it might say my name. How would I know the difference? Is there a difference anymore?

But you can't tell who she is from the picture. Like, what would she be wearing on the outside? Little tight skirt, overalls, maxi dress. You can't tell what she'd put on to become herself. What kind of a girl she is. She's just *young*. Insanely. To be a mom, I mean. The age I just became.

We have the same mouth, though. I can see even from half of it what her whole smile might look like.

My moms are dressed like my moms. Mom looks so pretty. Her hair is all black then and cut blunt, straight as a razor blade slashed across her chin. She has the loveliest hair, shiny and straight. Not like mine. I only look like me, though no one would ever notice it. I move my hands like they do now. I smile when they smile. We laugh at a lot of the same things.

But not everything. And I laugh totally different. I have never heard anyone with my laugh. Patrick, I say, tell me what I sound like.

"You," he says.

"Well, I want to sound like someone," I say, and he doesn't get it.

Where do I get these eyes, then? Gray blue. I think they look empty. Moms have dark eyes, both of them.

So I have the rough quilt and the dollhouse, but sometimes I think the only thing I got from her really was that mouth, these features. The me of me but not the I.

This is what I look like: dark hair, just a little wavy. White skin, porcelain doll–style on good pretty days, but bad in the sun on all the days. The eyes. They're a little too far apart if you ask me, but on the flip side, I have cheekbones people like to comment on. As in: cheekbones higher than the Alps, which is what my New York City gram always tells me. My Atlanta grandmother has never mentioned them at all.

In the photo Mom is wearing a sleeveless collared shirt and her arms are thin and lovely. She's looking at me like I might have hung the moon. Mo is behind her, and her light hair is cut close to her scalp. It's not gray yet. So many freckles splashed across Mo's face. Mom's more serious. Always.

No one is looking at my birth mom. Not even me.

Me! Teeny as a loaf of bread everyone looks like they want to devour. A loaf they know they can't slice up to share.

All the photos.

So some days it's okay that I have never heard my laugh on someone else, or that she disappeared before I was even a year old. Totally disappeared—no more contact at all. Look, I know things are hard for all of us. I mean, my friends are sad and angry and some don't know who they are, really, on the inside. Claire is none of those things. She, like, came out fully formed. She does what she wants. Or that's what it seems like to me, as I'm never as sure of myself. How do you *know* you want to go to sleep now, for instance? How do you know you want a long bath and not a quick hot shower? I just don't know. Patrick, I think, is more like me. He's got these hippie parents who accept everything he does. They float about him. There is a lot of amaranth and patchouli around.

For me, there's also this extra added part. Of not knowing. Of all the maybes. Could have beens. The feeling I might have been erased and drawn back into life by someone who doesn't know my face.

The story is not that complicated. It is either I was wanted or unwanted. My story is I was left behind or I was stayed with. I mean, I know, as in, I've been told, that my birth mother loved me so much she let me go. She chose them and they chose her and they chose me and we all had this choosing thing that made us us.

So what would have happened if she'd kept me? I would be a different girl. What would she be? Who? It is the strangest thing. To know this. To wonder about this world that almost was. The almost of me, the I that never was. And then: the me I became.

Why did she hand me over in the end? What did I do that was so bad? Was it when I was inside her or when I came out?

That is what it feels like on bad days. On good, normal days it's just: she was a mess. She was a kid. I would have returned me, too. I can't even keep a goldfish alive. That is a horrible story, my goldfish story, for another time. But can you imagine? When I think like that, yeah, it makes tons of sense. Find the people who are you but a million times better.

Anyway, that's not how the story ended. It ended with the three of us. Me, Mom, and Mo. There are ten million photos now. All digital. Girl triangle. The beach. Hiking. Me graduating from nursery school, kindergarten, middle school. High school will be in two years. One, two, three, four candles, all blown out. There's one photograph with her, too. Maybe I'm a year old, standing, wintertime, hat and gloves and big puffed coat. She is kneeling down and holding my hands. But still, I can't see her face.

All the photos, so many years of us, a better, bigger life. Pets and parties and school and tutors and piano lessons and ballet and ice skating and sometimes theater and restaurants and vacations on the beach, in the mountains, and pretty dresses. I am lucky; I am special. In a way it's more and in a way it's less but no matter what, I am always holding on to these two things at once, these two stories, these two ways of seeing things, and I can't say I'll ever really know if I was lost or if I was found.

So there is a quilt, a dollhouse, a few photographs, and, also, there is a letter.

Here. In my journal, pressed tight as a flower. I bring it out more since my birthday, run my hands along the careful bubble script. A child's letter. To another child. Only sometimes, just to touch it and wonder.

You, she calls me. *You.*

Now I run my hands across the letter. She pressed down hard; the paper still rises up around the ink. It feels like she meant it.

But does anyone know? Were you lost or were you found? Tell me.

Exactly.

Funny, poignant, and heartbreaking, don't miss these novels from JENNIFER GILMORE!

JOIN THE

Epic Reads

COMMUNITY

THE ULTIMATE YA DESTINATION

◀ DISCOVER ▶
your next favorite read

◀ MEET ▶
new authors to love

◀ WIN ▶
free books

◀ SHARE ▶
infographics, playlists, quizzes, and more

◀ WATCH ▶
the latest videos

www.epicreads.com